# SINS OF OMISSION

## RACISM, POLITICS, CONSPIRACY, AND JUSTICE IN FLORIDA

## JAMES H LEWIS

JAMES H LEWIS

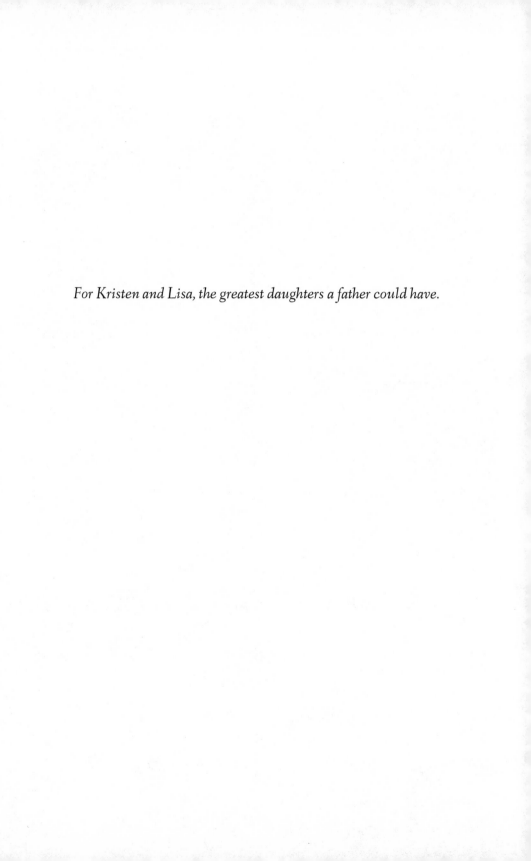

*For Kristen and Lisa, the greatest daughters a father could have.*

# PREFACE

## *August 29, 1955*

Alonzo Taylor crept past the Jacksonville Naval Air Station on US 17, adhering to the speed limit. The sun turned a fiery red as it settled over the Florida peninsula, but with the temperature hovering at eighty-five degrees, he kept the window rolled down to provide ventilation.

Taylor avoided driving after dark, but this was an exception. He had intended to leave the AME church earlier, but when the planning meeting concluded, the ladies' circle offered dinner to the project coordinators. The women had spent all afternoon frying chicken, baking cornbread, and steaming carrots, zucchini, and okra as the window fans roared in a futile attempt to push the heat out of the kitchen. They had put themselves out, and Taylor didn't have the heart to walk away.

Bishop Faraday then asked him and his fellow pastors to spend another half hour discussing church district matters. Knowing Taylor had a long drive ahead, the bishop had offered him his spare bedroom, but Taylor declined. He was a weekend pastor, unpaid, serving for the glory of God. He had to open his print shop early

Monday morning. Besides, he never left his wife and children on their own overnight.

Dusk descended. The four-lane highway narrowed to two. As the median vanished, a line of cars clogged the opposite lane, heading north toward Jacksonville. In his rearview mirror, Taylor saw a passenger vehicle approach at high speed. The driver flashed his beams and honked at him to speed up. Taylor maintained his speed. When northbound traffic cleared, the car sped around him. The driver glared as he passed, shook his fist, leaned on his horn, hurled an unheard epithet, then swerved back into the southbound lane, almost clipping Taylor's front bumper.

He didn't let the anger get to him. He was accustomed to it. A white man could drive five, even ten miles above the speed limit without fear of being stopped. Let Taylor change lanes without signaling, drive with a broken taillight, or exceed the posted limit by even two miles per hour and he risked being pulled over. Once the officer realized Taylor was "one of those agitators," he would spend his night in a cell.

So here he was, out on the open road as darkness enveloped him, creeping down the highway toward home, and singing "Ride the Chariot" at the top of his lungs. For a moment, he pushed his apprehension aside and reveled in a rare moment of privacy. He was alone and free behind the wheel of his prized '52 Studebaker Starlight whose design was the object of good-natured ribbing from his parishioners. "Are you coming or going in that thing, Brother Taylor?" one asked at least once a month. "I can't tell the front from the back."

"My brother helped build this car on an assembly line up in South Bend," he responded. "I'll drive nothing else."

He noticed the truck's headlights as soon as he turned off the highway onto Raven Road. He didn't know how long it had been behind him. Though Taylor kept to the speed limit—neither too fast nor too slow—the driver did not try to overtake him, remaining a city block behind. Taylor sped up; the truck matched his speed. He slowed down again; the driver backed off.

His chest constricted in panic for a moment until he forced himself to calm down. The driver wasn't trying to overtake him. Perhaps he just meant to frighten him. Taylor recognized intimidation. You didn't register black voters in Hampton County without the midnight call, the anonymous note, the scrawled threat on your windshield. Still, he wished it were any other night but Sunday so he could pull into McHugh's Service Station and stay until he felt safe.

Passing the shuttered gas station, he turned on his high beams and drove through the corridor of slash pines, shifting his gaze from the road ahead to the truck behind and then to the speedometer. Aside from the feeble light provided by the crescent moon, only the two pairs of headlights pierced the darkness.

The road snaked back and forth as it paralleled Gale Creek, but straightened out once he'd crossed the narrow metal bridge. Here things changed. The truck raced to close the gap between them.

A dozen thoughts flashed through his mind as he tried to reassure himself. He wants to get by. He waited until he passed the curves. Taylor held his speed. The truck pulled within inches of his bumper. He sped up to increase the distance, but the truck closed again, blinding him with its brights. Perspiration beaded his forehead and rolled into his eyes, stinging them. He wiped it away and returned to white-knuckling the steering wheel.

There was nothing here. This was paper mill land, trees on both sides but no houses, no outbuildings. How he wished he'd pulled into McHugh's.

Taylor recalled a side road up ahead, dirt or gravel, perhaps a logging road. He hunched over the steering wheel to block out the reflected headlights, his hands gripping it until they were bloodless. He rolled up the window, a defensive impulse that his rational mind told him was futile.

There. A hundred feet ahead. He cut his wheel to the right, swerving toward the side road as the truck rammed his back bumper. His car careened off the road, jerking to a halt in a thicket of palmetto. Taylor's chest struck the wheel, his head cracked the windshield, and he collapsed against the side door as the car came to rest at an angle.

Alonzo Taylor lay stunned. Blood trickled down his forehead and into his right eye. The engine crackled as it cooled, and he heard fluid draining from beneath the car. Oil? Radiator fluid? Gasoline?

The truck's reverse gear howled as it backed up the road. Its tires slid across the asphalt as it braked to a stop. Then near silence, broken only by the mating call of a barred owl: "Who cooks for you? Who cooks for you all?"

Taylor began to pray. The Lord is my shepherd...

Then panic. I have to get out, have to hide somewhere. Dear God, protect me. He pushed at the car door, but it struck something soft, unyielding, and gave only a few inches. Bracing his feet against the floor, he reached for the latch on the passenger door and pushed, aware for the first time of a throbbing pain in his left shoulder. His foot slid across the opening at the base of the passenger door and lodged, his calf now wedged between the seat and the door. Oh, sweet Jesus! He cried out in pain, but suppressed it as approaching boots sucked at the mud. Two furtive voices, so low they were almost whispers. He didn't make out their words, but recognized one of the two.

He couldn't escape. He was trapped in the vehicle. Alonzo tried to curl up on the floor, twisting his leg as he stretched. He bit his lip to stifle a cry, felt the blood pumping through his temple, tried to suppress his rapid breathing. Everywhere was the smell of pine tar and muck and his own blood.

He heard them ease through the thicket, felt the car give as someone leaned against it. "Is he dead?"

"There's only one way to make sure. Here, you take care of him. It's time you grew up."

A moment of hesitation, of uncertainty, a muttered protest he couldn't make out. Then the double pump of a shotgun. Alonzo Taylor heard nothing else.

# PART ONE

## NOVEMBER–DECEMBER, 2017

# FIRST THEY CAME FOR THE MUSIC CRITICS, AND I WAS NOT A MUSIC CRITIC, SO I DID NOT PROTEST

Alan Rudberg tossed the newspaper onto his desk in disgust. He hung his sports coat on the back of the door, swallowed the last of his coffee, put on his glasses, and scowled as he picked up the paper again. Sixteen pages, only four devoted to news stories, of which three were local. That was all there was to the Tuesday edition of Oregon's largest newspaper, known to its many critics as *MacPaper*.

For the moment, Rudberg was less concerned about what was in those stories than what was not. Missing was the surprise decision by Oregon's governor, Brenda Kuhn, not to seek reelection. Public radio had reported it only an hour before, airing a live interview with her during a segment of *Morning Edition*. It was likely to be the biggest political news story of the week. Public radio had it, the state's largest newspaper did not, and, as political "producer" and columnist of the *Oregon Examiner*, this was his responsibility.

While no one ever described Rudberg as happy-go-lucky, the station's scoop left him in a particularly foul mood this morning. Gray had invaded his sandy hair, and the lines around his eyes and mouth had begun to deepen. Slender, but conscious of five pounds that had found their way onto his six-foot frame, he had taken to standing at his desk except when taking notes, pacing back and forth across the narrow confines of his office. That's what he did now as he dialed Art Seymour, the governor's press secretary. "I'd like to get fifteen minutes with her today. I'm doing a column for tomorrow's paper."

"Sorry, Alan, but she said her piece on the radio this morning. I assume you heard it."

*How else would I know?* Rudberg ignored the barb. "She talked mostly about what she feels she's achieved. I want to dig deeper, get a more personal take—her reasons for leaving office, her plans for the future, that sort of thing."

"I don't think you'd care for answers. 'Well, gee, Alan, could it be that the *Examiner* has ridiculed every move I've made to deal with Portland's homeless crisis?'" he said in a pitch-perfect imitation of her whine. "'Attacked every effort to attract business through tax incentives and every proposal to reduce gun violence? I put forward a solution, your paper bats it down. Who needs it?' You think the *Examiner* would print that?"

"Is that why she's stepping down?" Rudberg asked, challenging him by matching his ridicule.

"No, but that's what she'd tell you."

Rudberg tried a few more ploys but got nowhere. He hung up knowing Seymour was right. The *Examiner* had backed her opponent in the last election, and his defeat—and their own—still chafed. Its editorial page subjected her to a torrent of negativity unparalleled in its coverage of local politicians, save for the handful who'd been caught sleeping with aides and pawing interns.

The paper would not print such a column. He would spend his day playing catch-up, interviewing the governor's friends, associates, and members of the legislature, trying to piece together a column that suggested he knew what was in her mind. He would not have a good time.

The flashing light on his phone announced a voicemail message, but before he could listen, the figure of Madge Hazen loomed in the doorway. "Frank wants to see you as soon as possible." No *please*. Just a peremptory command. He followed her through the newsroom to the office of the vice president for content, which in an early day had been called the managing editor.

"You missed a big story today." Frank Sherman did not invite him to sit down, but Rudberg did so anyway.

"Yes, I'm in touch with Art Seymour. She's not granting us an audience, so I'm going around her."

Sherman stared at him over his glasses. "How did you miss this?" *You*, not *we*.

"She's sulking over our editorial positions," Rudberg said. "She doesn't feel she owes us anything. She's getting out of politics, at least for the moment, so she doesn't need us."

"You're the political producer," Sherman said. "This is your beat." Rudberg made no response. His cell phone chimed. He glanced at it. His sister would have to wait.

Someone knocked at the door and entered without awaiting an invitation. Rudberg turned as Tisha Gregory took the chair alongside his, pulling it to the left and turning it to face him. Rudberg took a deep breath and felt his chest muscles contract. Gregory was the HR director.

Sherman tented his hands, leaned back in his swivel chair, and looked past Rudberg. "I'm afraid it's time we went our separate ways."

Rudberg recoiled as though struck. "What are you saying? It's one story." He shook his head, spread out both hands as though to stop an onrushing vehicle.

"You're not on the team. You haven't adapted to the changes. You're not posting stories during the day. You're not tweeting, blogging, meeting your click targets." He circled the air with his right hand to indicate there were many more things Rudberg was guilty of failing to do. "Most days your stories don't show up on the monitor." The bloody monitor that, godlike, ranked the popularity of stories based on online clicks.

"The kind of journalism I do—"

"Is not the kind of journalism we need these days. We've been over this, Alan. One story a day is a luxury we can no longer afford, and you average half that. We're lean here. Lower revenue means fewer reporters. We must fill the void with greater productivity."

"I've spent my working life with this newspaper," Rudberg said, "nearly thirty years."

"We know that," Tisha said, "and we appreciate your long service. That's why we're providing three months severance plus accrued vacation."

"Three months? You offered twice that during the buyouts."

"You didn't take a buyout," she said. "We booked those costs two years ago as part of our reorganization. This is different. It's a termination."

Sherman leaned forward, stacking papers before him in a gesture of dismissal. Gregory outlined additional terms, health insurance through his severance period, a contribution to his IRA. But she was firm. He was to clean out his desk immediately while a security guard hovered to make certain he didn't steal his desk or pick up his computer monitor and hurl it through a window.

As Rudberg struggled to his feet, Sherman added, "You'll do all right. Think about it. You've built up hundreds of contacts over the years—politicians, bureaucrats. You could become chief of staff to one of them—or communications director. Maybe run for office yourself."

Rudberg turned at the doorway. "I'm a reporter."

***

His cell phone chimed as he stumbled to his office in turmoil. "I've been trying to call you," his sister said. "I left a message at your house, your office, and on your cell."

He struggled to focus. "I was about to call you back. I've been in a meeting. I just lost—" He stopped himself, unwilling to share his humiliation. "What's the problem?" Cheryl's calls always represented problems, usually concerning their mother.

"Aunt Bess called this morning. Dad died yesterday."

Rudberg collapsed into his chair. "How? What happened?"

"I gather he drowned. A neighbor found him floating in the river."

"The river? What river?"

"She says he sold his house a few months back and bought a place in Hampton County along the St. Johns."

"Why on earth did he do that? He's lived in Jacksonville all his life." Hearing no answer, he said, "Have you told Mom?"

"I called her as soon as I found out. She didn't react, at least from what I could tell on the phone. You might call her once in a while. You need to visit her."

"I know. I'll do it." *Now that I have time.*

"I visit her every Wednesday night for the prayer meeting. I take her out to church every Sunday. Tom and I have her over for dinner. I could use some support."

"Cheryl, I live in Portland. You live in Austin. When we agreed she couldn't live on her own anymore, I offered to bring her here. You wouldn't hear of it."

"She'd be miserable with all that rain." *Second verse, same as the first.*

"What are the funeral arrangements?" he asked, turning the subject back to their father.

"There are none. That's why they need us. We're the next of kin."

"I knew we'd play a role in his life if we waited long enough. Who do I call?"

"They need us there, Alan—not on the phone, there. I'm flying to Jacksonville tomorrow morning. You need to come, too."

He argued, hedged, dodged, but she was adamant, and there was no reason he couldn't go. With a long sigh conveying his sense of martyrdom, he took down the details and agreed to join her.

"Don't do me any favors," she said. "He was your father as well as mine."

"And what a father he was," Alan said, "walking out on his wife and two small kids. Now we're supposed to drop everything. Pardon me if I don't mourn."

———

He called his wife, but she didn't answer. Stephanie seldom took his calls when she was working, so he left a message. He made reservations on a redeye flight that, with luck, would put him on the ground half an hour before Cheryl landed. He packed his books and awards in a half dozen cardboard boxes. A security guard watched as he loaded them onto a cart, then followed him down the walk of shame through the newsroom and toward the elevator. His colleagues kept their eyes focused on their screens as he passed. Nobody wished him well. They ignored him not out of embarrassment, but fear. *Next time, it could be me.*

At home, he stacked the boxes in a corner of the garage. He'd figure out where to put them later. He called Stephanie and again failed to reach her. He packed a carry-on bag, figuring he wouldn't be in Florida more than a few days, and charged his notebook computer, though he couldn't imagine why he would need it with nothing to write and no one to write for.

By midafternoon, he'd performed every senseless task he could think of. It was a pleasant day for mid-November, the clouds having retreated to reveal expanses of blue sky and the temperature nearing sixty. He walked up Park Place into the Japanese Garden, his personal preserve. Bypassing the tourists taking photographs of Heavenly Falls, Rudberg found a covered bench at the base of a curving stone walkway. A brook burbled within the cover of vegetation. An Oregon junco made a clicking chirp as it flitted about.

The tranquility clashed with his inner turmoil. He was fifty-eight years old and faced starting over. He had spent the last few years hanging on as out-of-town owners, who had no sense of the community and saw the *Examiner* only as a profit center, took over. They cut the staff, established an editorial policy that clashed with the views of most subscribers, reduced home delivery to four days a week, and wondered why circulation continued to drop.

Rudberg wasn't surprised to be sacked. He'd watched as dozens of talented colleagues were forced aside over the past several years—journalists who spent many days, including hours of their own time, digging out details of stories that changed public discourse and, occasionally, public policy. In their place came youngsters content to work for less and skilled at generating "clickbait"—superficial stories that drew eyes to the paper's website and kept them there.

And there was the Allston affair, a libel suit that had cost the *Examiner*—more properly its insurance company—$250,000 and sent the paper's coverage rates soaring faster than the cost of newsprint. Rudberg still believed that State Senator Brill Allston from Eastern Oregon was on the take, but once county commissioners made it clear that future government business depended on loyalty, the contractors who had handed out kickbacks circled their wagons, changed their stories, and altered their paperwork. The commissioners fired the whistle-blower who'd turned over purchasing records to Rudberg and declared they were forgeries. Rudberg had written articles critical of the senator in the past, so his attorneys claimed malice. Rudberg was hung out to dry.

Newspapers didn't lose many libel suits, and almost never to public officials. The verdict had sent fear into every newsroom in the country.

As the peacefulness of the garden enveloped him, Rudberg realized he wasn't unhappy to leave the *Examiner*. His enthusiasm had begun to wane when the staff was pulled from its old building that trembled with the roar of the printing presses and whose halls carried the perfume of printer's ink. While the clattering of typewriters and chattering of teletype machines had been silenced years before, the new, smaller newsroom that overlooked the Willamette River was as quiet as the accounting office it now resembled. Stories of prison conditions and of neighborhood associations fighting gentrification were gone, replaced by news of shootings, traffic snarls, and the latest celebrity to visit the Rose City. The front page now mimicked the mantra of TV newscasts: "If it bleeds, it leads."

Now Rudberg was gone. What next? He would not become a politician's flack. He would not sit at a computer hammering out news releases for one of Portland's apparel companies. He would not become "Mr. Stephanie Brayman," basking in the shadow of his wife's business achievements.

---

She arrived home shortly after 6 P.M., looking as though she'd stepped out of a beauty parlor. "Why are those boxes in my garage?"

"They're—"

"We don't have room for them."

"—books, files, my AP awards—"

"What are they doing there?"

"Steph"—he stretched out his palms to halt the onrush—"I was ordered to clean out my desk this morning."

"What?"

"That's why I've been trying to reach you."

"They fired you?"

"Fired, dismissed, terminated, let go, made redundant. I have three months' severance and healthcare through the end of February. That's it."

"Why? What did you do?"

*What did you do? Thank you for your support.* "Probably what I didn't do. I missed Brenda Kuhn's decision to—"

"Why is she leaving?"

"She says she's returning to private practice, but who knows? Maybe she has something lined up in DC. The point is, I missed it, but that's just a pretext." The radio story had run at 6:45, and

Sherman had made all the financial arrangements by 8:30 before the accounting office was open. "He must have been planning this for—"

"What will you do?"

"There's more. Cheryl called from Austin this morning. Mathew's passed away. I'm flying to Jacksonville tonight to help her make arrangements."

"Why? What's he to you?"

"He was my father, for better or worse, and there's no one else to take care of things. It's not something I want to do, but just because he was irresponsible doesn't mean I am."

He prepared a salad and linguine with clam sauce while she changed. She poked at it and declared the clams "chewy." Between interruptions, he recounted the conversation with Sherman. "He's serious?" she said. "He thinks you should run for office?"

"Or become a flack for a state official or major domo. No, he wasn't serious. It was his way of easing me out the door without a shouting match. Give the guy a little hope, since jobs in journalism aren't exactly hanging on trees, and send him on his way."

"Well, what *are* you going to do?"

"I'll fly to Jacksonville, bury Dad, close his estate, and come home. Then I'll start looking."

"I can check with our communications division."

"No, thanks. I won't become a shoe salesman."

"You'll have to do something. It may not be what you want to do."

"I'm good at that. I've been doing what I don't want to do for some time."

"Do you think that might be part of the problem?" she said. "You've been unhappy for years, griping about the new owners, the reduced size of the paper, the loss of staff. Your attitude may have communicated itself."

"We missed the governor's decision because we're missing a state-house reporter. You can't run a big city newspaper that way."

"You've just made my point."

They sat in silence for a few minutes. "How did Cheryl find

out?" she asked.

"About Mathew? His sister called and told her."

"I didn't know he had a sister."

"Bess," he said. "I'd almost forgotten her. It was so long ago."

"So how is it they're in contact?"

Rudberg shrugged.

"Didn't you ask?"

"No. It does seem odd, doesn't it? I last saw her when I was eight. Cheryl would have been six. I'm surprised she even remembered her."

"And you didn't ask," she repeated. "Some reporter you are."

He let it hang there. "What difference does it make? He's dead, and there's no one else to bury him. End of story."

---

Alongside stories on the Senate's tax bill, the hospitalization of a Supreme Court justice, and an overnight shooting, the front page of the Jacksonville newspaper carried the headline, "Veteran Floridian Editor Apparent Drowning Victim" and a photo of his father that appeared to be of recent vintage. Rudberg turned to the article on page A2.

> Mathew Rudberg, the former managing editor of *The Floridian*, was found dead Sunday at his home near Palatine, an apparent drowning victim. Rudberg was 81 years of age. He joined *The Floridian* in 1958 and served as a city hall reporter and city editor before becoming managing editor in 1986. He retired in 2001, having won numerous awards for journalistic excellence.
>
> Hampton County Chief Deputy Floyd Timmons said a neighbor found Rudberg floating in the St. Johns River. The neighbor believes Rudberg was repairing a dock damaged during Hurricane Irma, fell into the river, and was trapped in the debris. Deputy Timmons said there is no suspicion of foul play.

The story described major news stories on which his father had reported and the growth of the newspaper over his career, but not a word, Rudberg noted, about the stories he hadn't reported. It listed accolades from Jacksonville's mayor, Florida's governor, a local civil rights leader, and others. There was no mention of family. "Funeral arrangements," it concluded, "are pending."

He met his sister at the baggage carousel. She had awakened at 3:30 A.M. to catch a flight to Atlanta, while Rudberg had spent the four hours between Portland and Charlotte nestled between an obese husband and wife, both of whom snored. Despite their exhaustion, Rudberg and his sister agreed to visit the Hampton County sheriff's office before finding a hotel.

"How did Aunt Bess find you?"

"I've talked to her a few times over the past couple years. I've been researching the family tree."

"With all its broken branches and scattered twigs," Rudberg said.

"The sheriff's office notified her, and she called me. She's not easy to deal with," she added. "Pretty resentful."

"Of you? Of us?"

"She says we abandoned him, that we made him a lonely old man."

Rudberg snorted but said nothing. They drove in silence until they passed over the Fuller Warren Bridge. The St. Johns River reflected the tall, modern buildings lining Jacksonville's waterfront in shimmering ripples.

"I'm surprised you never reconnected with him," she said. "Boys gravitate toward their fathers, and since you were both in the newspaper business..."

"Purely by accident, and Dad's career was not a model of journalistic excellence. I didn't seek him out because I had nothing to learn from him. Besides, if I'd tried, Mom would have taken it as a personal affront." He pictured his mother in high dudgeon, quaking with resentment and ladling out recriminations.

Forty-five minutes later they left I-95, headed west on State Road

A13, crossing the Thomas Coupland Bridge over the St. Johns into Palatine. The town seemed lost in the fifties, its downtown streets still paved in brick to match the facades of storefronts. Plumes of steam and smoke from a paper mill upriver marred an otherwise cloudless sky. An odor composed of sawdust, pine tar, and chemicals permeated the air.

"Why did he come here?" he asked. "Why leave a place where you've spent your whole life for a tired little town like this?"

"I have no idea. He was retired. Perhaps he just wanted to watch the sunset."

---

"We figure he went wading in the water for something and slipped. He either couldn't get up or got trapped." Chief Deputy Timmons, a man in his midfifties whose ruddy features had been eroded by too many hours spent in the Florida sun, sat at his desk, a legal-sized file folder unopened before him.

"Trapped?" Rudberg said.

"When Irma came through in September, she backed water up the St. Johns from Jacksonville down to Astor in Central Florida. She ripped out docks and picked up anything near the shoreline. Before folks could start to rebuild, a nor'easter tore through and washed away whatever was left. It's two months since the first storm hit, and the river's just started to empty."

Timmons reclined in his swivel chair and spread his arms wide.

"You see folks on both banks wading around trying to salvage what they can—chairs, benches, fishing rods, water coolers, rowboats, sinks from fish cleaning stands, crab traps with live crabs in 'em—you can't believe the junk that's sitting out there. We've had all sorts of accidents. Some guy stepped on an outboard motor prop last week and sliced off three toes." Cheryl groaned.

"Your dad was either on what remains of his dock or wading around it when he slipped and went in. You fall in moving water at that age and it can be hard to get up again, 'specially if you've washed up under a piling." He leaned sideways in his chair to illustrate the point.

"Who found him?" Rudberg asked.

"His next-door neighbor, a fellow named"—he opened the file folder for the first time—"Henry Parker. Your dad was supposed to come over to his place to watch the Jaguars play the Chargers. When he didn't show by the end of the first half, Parker got curious. He found the house open, but no one inside, so he checked the river."

"How long had he been in the water?"

"The medical examiner thinks he went in Saturday evening. Parker saw him at five, so it was sometime after that. He wouldn't have been poking around out there after dark."

"And his body was still there Sunday? He hadn't drifted downstream?"

"He was tangled in a net that had snagged on a section of dock."

Rudberg turned to his sister to see if she had any questions. "So what happens now?" he asked.

"We need one of you to identify the body. The neighbor identified him at the scene, but we need a formal identification by next of kin. Then we release the body, and you can have a funeral home do the rest."

He paused for a moment. "We had a hell of a time figuring out who his next of kin was," he said.

"We are not a close family," Rudberg said.

"He left us when we were kids," his sister added. "We saw him a few times after the breakup, but that was years ago."

"Well," Timmons said, "I'm sorry for your loss." Neither of them knew how to respond.

———

They drove up US 17 to Orange Park, booked rooms at a hotel near the I-295 interchange, had dinner, and collapsed. The formal identification had been awkward since neither of them had seen Mathew in years. Even so, Rudberg remembered his features, and the man lying on the gurney was a more peaceful version of the photo in *The Floridian*.

Over breakfast the following morning, they discussed their next moves. They needed to make funeral arrangements but had no idea what their father's wishes were. Did he wish to be buried or cremated? Was there a family gravesite? Did he want a church service? Had he preplanned his own funeral?

His move to Hampton County added a further complication. Presumably, most of his friends were still in Jacksonville, so whatever service they held should be there. They were trapped in their ignorance of the man.

"I was thinking about him last night," Cheryl said. "His death leaves me feeling alone—like I'm an orphan now. When Mother dies..." She left the thought unfinished.

"I've always felt alone," Rudberg said.

Cheryl agreed to pose their questions to Mathew's sister, while Rudberg assigned himself to discover if his father had been close to anyone at the newspaper. He started with the managing editor, Mike Flynn, who said he was new to the paper and hadn't known his father well. Rudberg was sent down the chain of command to the city editor, then back up the line to the publisher. After spending a half hour on the phone, he reached the publisher emeritus, himself retired.

Bryce Osgood was only too glad to talk, regaling Rudberg with stories from Jacksonville's past and the role his father had played in covering them. "He kept active, you know. He wrote a weekly column, 'Jacksonville, Then and Now,' until sometime this summer. He wasn't paid much, but he didn't write it for money. He just wanted to stay busy. It was popular, though. People talked about it. They'll remember him."

Osgood was less helpful about personal matters. "Your father was a private man. I'm surprised how little I knew about him, now that I think about it. He used to be different before your mother left him."

"It was the other way around. He left her."

"Really? Everyone has his own truth. I've learned that much. Maybe that's why he shut down after the breakup. Mathew was all business. Some people work to live; others live to work. Your dad lived *at* work." He chuckled at his joke.

"I'll tell you one thing, though. He was respected. Wherever you hold your service, a crowd will show up. Politicians to plumbers, everyone knew your dad."

Cheryl fared no better. "Bess hasn't seen him since she moved into a retirement home in Daytona three years ago. She used to attend a Presbyterian church in Southside and says he would come at Christmas and Easter, but she doesn't think he had any deep ties there. There's no family plot. She's arranged to be cremated after she passes on, but has no idea what he wanted."

"Surely he made a will," Rudberg said. "He was an intelligent guy. He wouldn't have left something like that to chance." He thought for a moment. "We need to get into his house."

---

Two hours later, following Chief Deputy Timmons's instructions and twice getting lost, they stood before a two-story structure on the east bank of the St. Johns River. The home was built with the expectation of the occasional flood. Its bottom level was open, save for a utility room and an earlier model Honda CR-V parked on the concrete slab. Stairs at the front and back led to the living area itself.

Rudberg tried the front door, found it locked, and walked around the surrounding deck to the back entrance where he had no better luck. "We should have asked the deputy for a key," his sister said.

"There was none among his effects. All he had on him were his clothes."

They maneuvered through mud and debris to the river. Though

the temperature had risen to a comfortable seventy-two degrees, the air was heavy with humidity, and Rudberg welcomed the breeze flowing off the water. A wooden ramp jutted out from the riverbank, then disappeared beneath the surface, its broken planks ebbing and flowing with the current. Twenty yards out, a dock and boat lift paralleled the bank, no longer linked to the shore save for water and electrical lines sagging into the river. Rudberg peered into the water at the end of the collapsed stretch of the ramp and tried to imagine what their father had been working on and how he had fallen under.

"He wouldn't have walked onto the ramp," he said. "It's twisted at such an angle there's no place to stand. And as for wading in—even a man in his twenties couldn't repair that on his own." They discussed a few scenarios, but none made sense.

"Why don't we break into the house?" Cheryl said. "Don't we own it now?"

"Let's check with the neighbor first," Rudberg said. "Wait here a minute." He walked north along the concrete retaining wall, past a stand of live oak and palm trees whose bases were matted with debris, and into the yard next door. He climbed the back stairs of the adjoining home and knocked at the screen door.

The man who answered weighed close to three hundred pounds. He wore Bermuda shorts, a torn T-shirt that sported the logo of a St. Augustine seafood shack and didn't quite cover his belly, and white socks with flip-flops. "Mr. Parker?" Rudberg said. He introduced himself.

"Call me Hank. Come on in. Care for a beer?"

"No, thanks. My sister's waiting next door. Do you know how we might get into Mathew's house?"

"Sure do. He left a key with me in case he ever locked himself out. C'mon, and I'll let you in."

Rudberg followed the man along the retaining wall, marveling at how easily he maintained his balance despite his tonnage. "Terrible thing," he said over his shoulder. "He just moved in last July. Didn't have six weeks to enjoy himself before Irma hit. And then this," he said, waving his arm at the surrounding destruction.

"A lot of folks around here don't have flood insurance. I was a boy during Dora. You remember that?" Rudberg nodded, acknowledging the 1964 hurricane that had caused similar flooding along the St. Johns. "So I knew. These folks," he said, panning his arm up and down the coast, "they're waiting for the Feds to come rescue them."

He greeted Cheryl with the same bonhomie. "I wasn't aware he had kids," he continued, unable to stem his chatter any more than the retaining wall had stopped the river. Neither Rudberg nor his sister responded, already tired of explaining the family dynamic.

The living room spanned the back of the structure, affording a wide view of the river. It held a sofa, two armchairs, and a coffee table, none of which were new and looked too formal for this rustic setting, and a flat-screen TV. A small dining room table with four chairs stood at the north end, beyond which was a small kitchen. At the front of the home, two bedrooms flanked the main entrance. One contained a double bed and chest of drawers, the other a single bed, a desk and chair, and a multifunction printer resting on a two-drawer file cabinet. A key ring hung from a hook next to the front door. One of the keys appeared to be to the Honda; the other unlocked the front door. Rudberg pocketed the ring.

Parker kept up a running dialogue throughout their search, telling them when the house had been built, the identity of the previous owner, and how much destruction the flood had caused. "I really liked your dad," he said. "He kept quiet, minded his own business, but he liked to come over to watch football Sunday afternoon and Monday night. He was a generous guy, always brought the beer."

When neither of them responded, he said, "Do you want the key back?"

"Why don't you hold on to it?" Rudberg said. "I'm not sure how long we can stay, and we may need you to let a real estate agent or workman in after we've left, if that's not too much trouble."

"Not at all. Glad to help."

"I see the boat lift out on the dock. Did he own a boat?"

"No. The people he bought it from did a lot of bass fishing. That's the big thing around here. But your dad wasn't into that. I never saw him out on the water."

"Then what was he doing here? He didn't seem to have much connection to Hampton County."

"He wouldn't say. I asked him once. He said he was working on something, but didn't say what. He'd leave some mornings and not get back until evening. Lights were on late into the night. I wasn't snooping or anything," he added. "I just saw that they were on."

"Of course," Rudberg said. He glanced at his sister, but she seemed not to have noticed.

"I wish he'd waited," the man said.

"For...?"

"He had a crew coming out this week to repair the dock. It takes time, you know. There's miles of damage and too few workers. He had no business being out there. I can't think what he was doing."

Rudberg thanked him and got him to leave without insulting him. He returned to the second bedroom and opened the file drawer. He opened his phone and began tapping on it. "What are you doing?" his sister asked.

He turned the modem over and entered a series of letters and digits into his phone. After a few seconds, he held it up. "It's live," he said. "He had internet coming into the house."

Still, she didn't get it. "What do you see here? There's a desk, a printer, and a live internet connection, but no computer. There's a file cabinet, but no files."

She was with him now. He dialed the sheriff's office and asked to speak to Timmons. "No," the chief deputy answered, "we didn't remove anything. We didn't spend much time inside."

Rudberg thanked him and hung up. "Something's wrong," he said. "We need an autopsy."

# A MINISTER WHO DOESN'T
# BELIEVE IN GOD

C hief Deputy Timmons leaned back in his swivel chair, peering at them through narrowed eyes. "How do you know he had a computer?"

Rudberg laid out his rationale—a new printer, the live internet connection, and WiFi. "We haven't even found a phone."

"Maybe it fell into the river," Timmons said.

"What about the file cabinet? It's empty, not even a scrap of paper."

"You don't know anything was even in it." Timmons leaned forward again, drumming a pen on the edge of his desk. He looked over Rudberg's shoulder at the clock on the wall.

"A contractor was scheduled to repair the dock this week." Rudberg raised his voice and leaned forward until he was almost in the man's face. "Why would anyone, let alone a man his age, be horsing around on a broken structure at dusk when someone was coming to fix it?"

Timmons leaned back in his chair and folded his arms across his chest. "You'll have to take it up with Sheriff Potter in the morning. He's gone for the day."

Back at their hotel, Rudberg called his wife's work number. It was three hours earlier in Portland, still the middle of the afternoon, so he got her voice mail. He called her cell and, when she didn't answer, redialed. "I'm in a meeting," she said in a low voice.

"I'll be quick. Mathew's death may not be an—"

"I can't talk right now." She ended the call.

Over a dinner of fried shrimp and oysters concealed in thick batter, Cheryl asked, "What if there's no will?"

"It's called dying *intestate*. In Oregon, the law is straightforward. If there's a living spouse, he or she inherits. If there isn't, the children inherit. It doesn't have to go through probate court. I suspect Florida law is more complex, given all the retirees the state can fleece."

He began to think like a reporter. "We need to see if he had a lawyer I'll look through civil records at the Duval County Courthouse—lawsuits, private property transfers, even going back to the divorce. If he used an attorney, we'll find it."

Back in his room, he looked up the Florida statutes, verifying his suspicion that its inheritance laws were complex. Unless they found a will, Mathew's estate was headed for probate court, which could be expensive and time-consuming.

He puzzled over the strange conversation with Deputy Timmons. Why was he resisting an autopsy? Was he hiding something? He returned to his computer and searched the Florida law on postmortem examinations. Ten minutes later he had a plan.

---

Dr. Amanda Nussbaum, a pathologist at the University of Florida, looked from Rudberg to his sister and back again as they tag teamed the reasons for their suspicions. "They didn't search the house," Rudberg concluded. "They're pushing back on an autopsy. We don't have confidence that we'll get unbiased results from their medical examiner."

"From Sunday evening to Friday morning is a long time," she

said. "We get the best results if we take charge of the body within forty-eight hours. Since he'd been floating in the water for nearly a day... Still, we'll do what we can. You're sure you want to bear this expense?"

"We hope it will come out of the estate," Cheryl said.

"I can't give you legal advice. This will cost four thousand dollars, and toxicology tests may increase that by a thousand or more."

"If the estate doesn't cover it, I will," Rudberg said. He hoped never to have that conversation with Stephanie. "When can you begin?"

"This afternoon. We don't perform examinations on weekends, and every hour that goes by makes it more difficult to get accurate results. Don't expect a report until sometime next week."

"Does this mean we can move ahead with a funeral?" Cheryl asked.

"Again, I can't give you legal advice, but the ME has issued a preliminary death certificate, so I think you can. I'd ask an attorney, though."

Walking back to their car, Cheryl said, "We don't need a funeral. Let's do a memorial service."

"Of course. Why didn't I think of that? And let's do it quickly. Thanksgiving is six days away, so many people will be out of town next weekend."

His sense of urgency was fueled by a late-night conversation with Stephanie, who had commanded his return by Thanksgiving. "David and Roxanne have invited us over for dinner, and Mark and Wendy are coming, too. I need you back."

He'd booked a flight out for Wednesday afternoon—a lousy seat for a premium fare, but a small price to pay for what passed as domestic tranquility.

"I'll call that church he used to attend," Cheryl said. "Maybe they'll let us hold the service there."

"Anything for a price, I'm sure."

Mathew Rudberg, Cheryl learned, had not just attended the Presbyterian church. He'd been a member. The associate pastor recommended that they hold the service Tuesday morning and agreed to officiate. He asked to meet with them Monday afternoon to help prepare his remarks and promised to announce the service from the pulpit Sunday morning. Alan notified *The Floridian* and prevailed on Bryce Osgood to speak at the service. With its former publisher involved, the newspaper would give the service ample publicity.

Cheryl made her own flight arrangements, and over dinner they debated how to spend their weekend. "I'm going back to the house tomorrow," Rudberg said. "I want another look around."

Events soon overtook him. Stephanie called shortly after 9 P.M. and told him a registered letter had arrived from the Duval County Clerk of Court. "An attorney named Franklin Reeves has filed your father's will in probate court." She read through the stilted language. Rudberg was a legatee, she said. He could examine the will at the courthouse any weekday between 8:00 A.M. and 5:00 P.M. There was no other information.

Rudberg checked his watch, though he knew it was after five. "We won't know its contents until Monday," he said. "Cheryl and I have hired a pathologist to perform an independent autopsy. It will cost a few thousand dollars, but the estate—"

"Whatever for?"

"I tried to tell you yesterday. This doesn't look like an accident, and the sheriff's office—"

"What difference does it make, really? You two weren't close. Whatever the cause, he's gone now. I'm not being heartless. It's just not your fight."

"If it were your parents—"

"It would be different because they *are* my parents, they have always *acted* like my parents, and they have been better parents to you than your own father was."

"What's done is done. We've hired her, and by now she's performed the autopsy."

"Just get things wrapped up and be home for Thanksgiving. I wish I could come to support you, but work is brutal right now." *When was it not?*

Cheryl called home and learned that a similar letter was waiting for her. "At least Stephanie let you know," she said. "What was Frank going to do, let it sit unopened?"

Saturday morning, Rudberg called the law offices of Jackson and Reeves. He didn't expect to find anyone there on the weekend and was not disappointed. He searched for the attorney's home telephone number without success. Through working his newfound contacts at *The Floridian*, however, he soon got what he needed.

The attorney was not happy to hear from him. "Under Florida law, I have the responsibility to file your father's will with the probate court. I have done so. You and any member of the public are free to examine it at any time."

"Can you just give me some idea of its major provisions?" Rudberg asked.

"No, I can tell you that you're a legatee and that you're not the only one. That's why you received the notification."

"Did Dad make any funeral provisions? My sister and I are trying to do the right thing, and we're flying blind."

The attorney paused, took a long breath, and Rudberg imagined him debating whether what he knew was a violation of attorney-client privilege. He knew the type and hated it.

"No, he did not," Reeves said, after consulting with whatever precedents came to mind.

"We don't believe his death was accidental." Rudberg outlined what they had discovered at Mathew's house and their subsequent jousting with the sheriff's office. "We ordered a private autopsy and will get the results next week."

The attorney thought for a moment. "He did not have a health care surrogate, so as next of kin, you are within your rights. I trust you to keep me informed."

"Will the estate absorb the cost?" Hearing nothing, he added, "I've just lost my job. I'm not in a position to pay for this myself."

"Let's see what the postmortem reveals. If it was an accidental death, I don't see that the estate should have to bear the expense." He did not offer an 'or else,' but, Rudberg thought, that's why he's an attorney.

"I'm going back to his house today to take another look around. There may be something we've missed."

"No," the attorney said. "You're not to do that."

"I can't go into my father's house?"

"No, not until the estate is settled. You have no right to any of his property until the probate court accepts the will. I am the executor. I am responsible for creating an inventory of all his property and assets, settling any debts, and filing a report with the court. This will take months. Until the court probates the will, only I or my designees may enter that property. Is that clear?"

It was, though Rudberg had no intention of obeying the directive.

---

They rode to a nearby shopping mall where Rudberg bought a change of clothes and a pair of rubber gloves. Cheryl remained behind, having no interest in Rudberg's planned maneuver. He crossed the river and drove south on State Road 13, through little towns like Switzerland and Fruit Cove. It was a leisurely route, but more picturesque than US 17, and he was in no hurry.

He entered the sandy lane leading to his father's house, edging forward until he was concealed from the road by an impenetrable wall of foliage. He donned the gloves, crept toward the house, mounted the front steps after satisfying himself that he was hidden from view both from the river and the road, and unlocked the front door. He was ignoring the attorney's directive, but it was his house now—his and Cheryl's—and he'd do as he pleased.

He started in the kitchen, searching the refrigerator and freezer, opening all the cabinets, standing on a dining room chair to peer into the top shelves, squatting on the floor to peer into the backs of the lower ones. There was little food here, but Mathew had brought a lifetime's collection of pots, pans, dishes, bowls, glasses, cups, mugs, and utensils with him, squeezing them into every cavity and recess he could find.

Rudberg moved to the bedroom, going through clothing, pulling out all the dresser drawers to check behind them, peering under the bed and mattress, probing the back and the top of the closet, and emptying and repacking the nightstand. He gave the same attention to the second bedroom, which his father had used as an office. There was less to inspect here since he'd already examined the desk and file cabinet, and there was little in the closet. He looked beneath the mattress of the single bed and checked the back of the file cabinet, tipping it to the side, and examining the bottom.

He gave the same attention to the great room, peering up at the underside of the dining table and reaching beneath the sofa. Rudberg moved the sofa and rolled up the rug. He finished with the hall closet which, like the kitchen cabinets, served as a repository for everything his father didn't know what to do with. Returning to the second bedroom, he examined the closet again. The closet in the great room was filled to capacity as was that in the first bedroom. This one was nearly empty, more evidence that someone had stripped any work products from the house.

With a last look around, he left the way he had come. On the lower level, he gave the same meticulous examination to the Honda, checking the trunk, the glove compartment, and beneath the front and rear seats.

Turning to the utility room that lay between the front and rear stairways, he found the metal door slightly ajar. Making certain it was unlocked, he pushed to close it, but the lower part struck the frame.

He knelt and examined the door. It was pincushioned as though something had struck it. He saw dents on the inside. Someone had tried to hammer it back into place.

Using the flashlight app on his cell phone, he explored every shelf, hauling down old paint cans, fishing rods and nets, a tool chest, and stacks of paper towels, toilet paper, and canned goods. A stackable washer and dryer that looked almost new sat against one wall. There was nothing more.

Peering around him to make certain Nosy Parker wasn't watching, he walked to the retaining wall and looked out on the pile of twisted wood that had once formed the dock. He stood perplexed for a few moments, retraced his steps, placed the key ring on the hook inside the door, and closed it behind him.

It had been a waste of time, and, despite the mild temperature, he was soaked. How, he wondered, did people stand this humidity?

---

Since there was nothing more they could do in Hampton County, the pair checked out Sunday morning and drove to Jacksonville, booking rooms at a less expensive hotel off I-95 at University Boulevard. Cheryl decided to attend their father's church, so Rudberg took a rideshare downtown to the main library on Laura Street.

A librarian showed him to a terminal and helped him open the archives of *The Floridian*. Entering his father's name in the search field brought up hundreds of listings, all copies of his weekly column, "Jacksonville, Then and Now."

The first was an article on The Florida Theatre, which, on its opening in 1927, was the largest movie theater in the state and one of its most lavish showplaces. A circuit judge had threatened to shut down Elvis Presley's August 1956 concert until The King agreed to girdle his hips rather than gird his loins. The column documented the theater's decline, its closure in 1980, and its eventual restoration as a performing arts center. Mathew had told the story in an engaging, humorous style that Rudberg admired.

The next few dozen were much the same, lighthearted stories recounting the histories of Jacksonville landmarks and notable events, such as Franklin D. Roosevelt's 1934 visit to the city. Rudberg soon stopped reading full articles, browsing the opening paragraphs.

In the second year writing the column, his father had turned to more serious topics. He had written three columns on a deadly fire at The Roosevelt Hotel in 1963 that had killed twenty-one people. The first told the bare facts, the second touched on the lives of several victims, and the third was a detailed profile of the fire chief who had died in the blaze.

A few months later, his father did a similar series on Hurricane Dora, the first major tropical storm in North Florida's recorded history. It had left over a hundred thousand without electricity for days, cut telephone service to a quarter of the town, and flooded neighborhoods near the river. Rudberg remembered Henry Parker comparing it to Hurricane Irma.

Mathew's column turned to even more weighty subjects during the following year. In another multipart series, he detailed events of August 27, 1960, when a group of black youth tried to integrate a whites-only counter at Woolworth's. A gang of whites armed with ax handles attacked them while police stood by watching. The column called the event "Ax Handle Saturday," and subsequent stories featured interviews with survivors, including a student leader who went on to become a city councilman.

Nearly three months passed before Mathew published another column on a substantive subject—one Rudberg vaguely remembered from first and second grade. In 1964, the Southern Association of Colleges and Schools withdrew accreditation from Duval County's entire school system. The stated reason was the county's failure to provide adequate funding. But, the article stated:

...there were more serious, hidden reasons. A decade after the

Supreme Court ordered an end to racial segregation in the nation's public schools, Jacksonville stubbornly held out.

The community effectively had two school systems, one for whites, the other for blacks. White schools got the newer textbooks, though "new" is a relative term here, and black schools got the dog-eared hand-me-downs, many decades old. While an elected superintendent was nominally in charge of all the county's schools, an assistant superintendent supervised the segregated schools for black students. He had little authority and fewer resources.

Disaccreditation sent a powerful message to the community. Graduates of this school system might be at a disadvantage when competing for admission to leading colleges. The Navy, which then as now was Duval County's largest employer, expressed concern over how the finding would affect the morale of base personnel with families.

Not all citizens expressed disappointment at the news. Rutledge Pearson, president of the Florida Chapter of the NAACP and himself a Duval County high school teacher, called it "the best thing that could happen" for African Americans. It would force the hand of segregationist leaders, he said. He organized a boycott of the school system for December of that year.

In the next column, Mathew detailed the decade-long struggle to regain accreditation of the school system and profiled leaders in that struggle.

It was nearly closing time. Rudberg did another search and brought up his father's final column, published in the Sunday edition on June 24, "And Now I Become History." It was a chronicle of Mathew's years at the paper, its tone self-congratulatory. *Let others tout your virtues,* he thought with disgust. Nevertheless, he printed the column and left just as librarians were closing the doors.

Rudberg and his sister met for dinner at a riverfront restaurant in Southside, the first time they'd dined on anything but hotel food in a week. Associate Pastor Tim Mellings had not only announced the memorial service, she reported, but had introduced her to the congregation. "Several members came up after the service to say they knew Dad," she said. "I struggled to hide the fact that I didn't. I dread meeting with the minister tomorrow. He'll ask questions about Dad's life, and we don't know the answers."

Rudberg shrugged. "It's not our doing. We have no reason to apologize."

She'd had a conversation with their mother during the afternoon, sharing what little she'd learned of their father's death. "She wasn't having it. She just doesn't want to hear about him."

"She never has. Why would she start now?" A woman at a nearby table chose that moment to bray like a donkey. Rudberg scowled in her direction. "What caused the breakup, I wonder. Another woman? I never asked her, but you must have had mother-daughter conversations."

"I know only what you do. He left us, provided no financial support, and showed no further interest in the family. Mom had it hard," she said. "She did it all on her own. We owe her a lot —everything."

"Yes."

"Which is why, Alan—"

"I know. I'll get down to see her when we're through here." He studied a passing tour boat. "I need to find work. I've lived on my own salary, not Stephanie's, and I'm not about to change that." He might have added that she wasn't about to let him change it, but didn't. His relationship with Steph was his business.

He told her what he'd learned in studying their father's archives, touching on several of the stories he'd found most interesting. "He was a powerful writer—sarcastic at times, witty, and an astute observer. There's deep passion in some of his columns. It surprised me."

"What did you expect? He was a reporter, just like you. People and events intrigued him."

He scowled again, this time taking in the entire room. "Do they have to play music so loud? One group raises their voices to be heard, and then the next table speaks up to be heard over them..."

He leaned toward her to speak without adding to the din. "During my junior year at UT, I had to do a case study on how a newspaper had covered a groundbreaking story. Most of the class chose either Watergate or the Pentagon Papers. That was fresh. Everyone wanted to be Woodward, Bernstein, or Sheehan." He glanced around him and leaned even closer. To observers, they looked like lovers having an intimate conversation.

"I researched *The Floridian*. Maybe it was like you suggested Wednesday—a lonely boy trying to get to know his father. Maybe I was just curious." He shrugged, then looked at her with intensity. "They were distinguished not by what they reported, but by what they ignored. In the sixties, Jacksonville was one of the most corrupt cities in the country. Elected officials in both city and county government accepted bribes, rigged contracts—anything they could come up with to enrich themselves. The paper didn't uncover that. It was a television station. Everyone at *The Floridian* knew what was going on —but they didn't write a word about it."

"Why would they do that? They're a newspaper."

"It's gone through two owners in recent years, but back then it was part of a local conglomerate that included a chemical company, a paper mill, and several other North Florida industries. The City of Jacksonville and Duval County let them pollute, ignore worker safety, run trains through neighborhoods in the dead of night—it gave them free rein. In return, the paper looked the other way while politicians ran the town like a private barony."

Rudberg lowered his voice. "Mathew was the city hall reporter during much of this, then the city editor. It was going on right in front of him, and he wrote," he said with a hiss, "not a word. Nothing. He was not my kind of reporter."

"Maybe he had no choice," she said.

"We all make choices. A reporter not reporting is like a minister not believing in God."

Rudberg had read his father's final column in his hotel room. There was not a word about those dark days in the newspaper's history.

---

The Duval County Courthouse on West Adams Street was an imposing, white building whose open atrium afforded a view up all seven floors to an interior dome. They passed through the security lines without incident and found Room 1173 in the clerk's suite of offices. Rudberg handed the file number to a worker who produced the document within five minutes. They bent over a small table to read it.

They found their names on the second page:

I give to the persons named below the following specific bequests, if owned by me at the time of my death.

1. To my son, Alan Sawyer Rudberg, I give: A savings account established for his college education held at United Community Bank.

2. To my daughter, Cheryl Rudberg Davis, I give: A savings account established for her college education held at United Community Bank.

Several other bequests followed, then, on the following page:

I give, devise, and bequeath to Grace Mary Stewart and Aisha Stewart Moser, in equal measure, all of the rest, residue, and remainder of my property and estate, real, personal...

"What does this mean?" Cheryl said. "Who are these people?"

Rudberg flipped through the rest of the document, his teeth clenched, grunting as he found something of interest. He said nothing, returned the document to the clerk, and ordered two copies.

"We should challenge it," she said as they returned to the hotel.

"I'm not an attorney, but I recall that heirs have less of a case if they're named in a will than if they're excluded. We don't even know how much he left us."

Over coffee in the hotel's breakfast room, he paged through his copy, ticking off those things he found of interest. "He executed this in July, about the time he sold his house and moved to Hampton County. Was there a prior will? Who were the beneficiaries?" He threw up both hands. "Mathew left his estate to a mother and daughter we know nothing about. He had no contact with either of us, yet set up college funds that he never sent us—"

"Strange," she said.

"Bizarre. The attorney must have answers to this. If only he'll tell us," he added. He called Reeves's office, learned he was in conference, and left a message.

---

"Amanda Nussbaum here." The call came as Rudberg was paging through the dozens of phone listings for people named Stewart and Moser. "I was tempted to call you Friday evening, but I waited to check out something at your father's house this morning."

Rudberg asked her to hold on for a moment and dialed his sister's room on the hotel phone. She was at his door within two minutes. "Cheryl's here," he said. "I've put you on speaker."

"Your father did not die by drowning."

"Then what—?" Cheryl said.

"When a person drowns, they take water into their lungs. They hold their breath as long as they can, but at the last moment they take in water, either by calling for help or just gasping for air. There was no water in your father's lungs.

"Also," she continued, "when a person is drowning, their first instinct is to grasp at whatever is at hand. That's not always possible, but when a person falls in along a dock or stumbles in shallow water, we find abrasions on fingertips and material under fingernails. There was none of that here."

Rudberg flashed back to a time in New Braunfels when he'd fallen off an inner tube going down the famous flume and gotten caught beneath a trailing raft. He shivered, reliving his flailing arms and desperate gripping of the rubberized bottom as he struggled to find a way out, his back scraping the concrete bottom of the channel, the sense of utter helplessness as the rushing water fought against him.

"Your father wasn't in deep water. If he had fallen off the dock or stumbled alongside it, there were many surfaces to reach for. The bottom is shallow, so he could have pushed with his hands and knees to right himself. There's no evidence of either. He was dead when he entered the water."

"So what killed him?" Rudberg asked.

"Blunt force trauma. He sustained a blow to the back of his head. It wasn't apparent, because the blow didn't break the skin and your father had a full head of hair. The blow caused a hemorrhage into the dermis and subcutaneous tissues, resulting in a rupture of blood vessels. In short, he had a brain hemorrhage and either fell into the water or was placed there after his death."

"Was it an accident or a physical attack?"

"He suffered a physical blow of some sort, not a bump on the head as you would get in a fall. Whatever hit him wasn't rigid, like a baseball bat. That would have broken the skin. There is nothing on the dock or visible in the water that would account for it—nothing in the proximity of the dock that would have inflicted that kind of blow —no swinging boom, for instance. I have to conclude that someone struck him."

Cheryl gasped. Rudberg exhaled a mighty whoosh. "What happens now?" he asked.

"We send our written report to you, to the medical examiner, and to the sheriff's department. They will take it from there."

Rudberg and Cheryl had more questions, but the pathologist had nothing to add. They thanked her and hung up. The twin mysteries of their father's life and death had just deepened.

## SOMETIMES I FEEL LIKE A FATHERLESS CHILD

"Those incompetent bastards!" Rudberg slammed a file folder down on the desk, went to the window, and yanked open the curtain, tugging at it with so much force his sister feared he would pull it down.

"You need to calm down," Cheryl said.

"They wasted a week treating Mathew's death as an accident. We need action." He began punching numbers into his cell phone.

"They won't cooperate if you barge in and say I Told You So."

Rudberg knew she was right. He stopped, took a deep breath, then dialed Franklin Reeves. "He represents the estate. He'll wield more clout than a pair of out-of-town relatives." His paralegal said the attorney was in conference, but Rudberg insisted she interrupt him. "Tell him Mathew Rudberg's death was no accident," he said.

After a few minutes Reeves picked up the phone and listened as the two took turns recounting the pathologist's findings "Distressing," the attorney said. "Have you informed the sheriff's office?"

"We thought it should come from you," Rudberg said.

"I agree. I'll speak directly to the sheriff. He has to investigate now. It's good that you insisted on a postmortem," he added. "I'll make certain the estate covers the cost."

"Speaking of cost," Cheryl said, "Mathew set up savings accounts for us. What are they worth?" Rudberg winced at her abrupt shift in focus, but she plunged forward. "When do we get them?"

"I can't distribute the funds until the probate court accepts the filing," he said. "As to the amounts involved, I can get that information for you."

Accepting that they now seemed like vultures circling their prey, Rudberg asked, "Who are Grace Stewart and Aisha Moser? What was their relationship to Mathew?"

"I prefer that you ask them. I represent neither party, just the estate. Your father had reasons for leaving them his property, but it's not for me to say what they were."

"Be sure to tell the sheriff about the will," Cheryl said. "Those two had the most to gain by his death."

"I doubt they had anything to do with it, but I'm sure the sheriff will investigate every angle."

Rudberg was convinced Mathew's death was connected to his mysterious investigation, but there was no stopping Cheryl when she was at her most churlish. "How do we contest this?" she demanded.

Reeves cleared his throat. "I can't advise you on that. You'll have to seek your own counsel if you're determined to pursue that course."

"I don't think I care to contest it," Rudberg said, an elliptical approach to gain the attorney's cooperation without committing himself. "I just want to understand who they are and their relationship to our father. How do I contact them?"

"I'll reach out and see if they're willing to meet with you. I can't promise anything. It's"—he paused as he paged through his mental thesaurus—"it's delicate."

He agreed to meet with them the following afternoon to review their savings accounts. "I have some papers your father left in my care. He assured me they have no value, so they're not part of the estate. I'll turn them over when we meet."

November's total rainfall to date fell on the Tuesday before Thanksgiving. It descended in sheets, saturating the ground, sending rivers of muddy water into drainage ditches, and filling gutters to overflowing. Intersections flooded, small cars stalled, and the wake from trucks hurled torrents of water onto curbs and lawns, where they gathered more mud and washed back into the streets.

"Where's Noah when we need him?" Rudberg said. They had borrowed umbrellas from the hotel, but Rudberg pulled up to the side door of the church to spare his sister the worst of the downpour. He parked the car and made a run for it. Still, his trousers clung to his legs by the time he entered the sanctuary.

"Damn!" he said, shaking himself off. Cheryl glared at him.

"This will cut attendance," she said. As it was, latecomers had to sit in the balcony. Mourners began arriving twenty minutes before the service—people of all ages and, judging by their clothing, many walks of life. A number were black, which surprised Rudberg, given that the church was in an affluent white neighborhood.

Pastor Mellings motioned them into an anteroom and reviewed the order of service. After he welcomed the congregation, three people would speak, he would deliver a eulogy, and anyone who wished to say a few words would have the opportunity. The service would close with "Amazing Grace," which Mellings said was one of their father's favorites.

"Who knew?" Rudberg said under his breath.

Cheryl ignored him. "Thank you for putting us so much at ease," she said. "Our relationship—it's a difficult time. We had a dysfunctional family."

"All families are dysfunctional. You're not alone. I want everyone to feel welcome and leave not with sadness, but with joy."

"Thank you," she said. She sobbed, and Rudberg put his arm around her. He couldn't remember ever having done so, certainly not since they were children.

At 10:00 A.M. the pastor led them to a pew in the front row. The organist played "Be Thou My Vision," which had been Rudberg's favorite hymn in his youth. He hadn't been in a church since—since a venerated US senator had died, now that he thought about it.

"Friends, colleagues, family of Mathew Rudberg, welcome!" The pastor was off and running.

He introduced Bryce Osgood, the former publisher, who walked the congregation through Mathew's career at *The Floridian*. He took most of it from the story the paper had run on Wednesday morning while offering a few off-script reminiscences that were alternately entertaining and self-congratulatory. "He was a journalist's journalist," Osgood concluded, "an outstanding citizen of this community, and a friend to all." Murmured amens enveloped the room.

Next up was J. Morris Searcy—a federal judge of the Northern District of Florida. He was a tall man, hefty without being fat, and mounted the steps with a slight limp. Though he appeared to be about Alan's age, he began, "Mathew and I grew up together in a sense. I came onto the bench about the time that he became city editor of *The Floridian*. While we were separated by age, we were united in mutual respect."

He told the story of a criminal attorney who tried to get him to cite Mathew and a television news reporter for contempt of court over some minor infraction of a gag order Searcy had imposed. "I had them both in my chamber," he said. "The TV reporter was shaking, but Mathew was defiant. I told them I wouldn't arrest them, that the gag order applied to attorneys, not the press, and hinted, without saying so, that the defense attorney was grandstanding. But your father," he continued, looking at Alan and Cheryl, "was obstinate. He tried to school me in the First Amendment. Finally, I said, 'Mathew, do you *want* to go to jail? I don't want to send you, but neither do I want to deny you the satisfaction.' It was the only way I could silence him." The sanctuary erupted with laughter.

The last speaker was Lucius Martin, a black attorney in his midforties who carried himself with studied dignity. Built to impress, Rudberg thought, from his prematurely silver hair to his double-breasted gray suit.

"I knew your father well," he said in a quiet voice that demanded attention. "I liked him, I respected him, I trusted him. I read his obituary on Wednesday with sadness—heartsick not only to lose a friend but to find his greatest legacy ignored. I listened to Brother Osgood a few minutes ago, hoping to hear him speak of Mathew's great gift to this community. That gift," he said, his voice lowered almost to a whisper, "was equity, justice, respect for all." He increased the volume with each word, stunning his listeners with the intensity of the verbal thrust.

"In the 1960s," he said, "Jacksonville had not one newspaper, but two. There was *The Floridian* for white folks. Not a word did it carry about anyone black or brown or tan or yellow or any color but white, unless"—and here he paused, his gaze scanning the room—"unless that off-color individual was the suspected perpetrator of a crime." Alan wished he could turn around to see Bryce Osgood's reaction.

"Bob Hayes," he shouted, "went from football artistry at Matthew Gilbert High School and Florida A&M to sprinter stardom at the Olympics, where he became known as the world's fastest human. Yet *The Floridian* never mentioned his name. Because"—he paused for drama—"he had never been arrested." A chorus of amens echoed through the church.

"And there was another newspaper. On the outside, it looked the same as the white paper, except for a small black circle at the top of the front page. It carried the same stories. It ignored the same people. But inside, was a thin crust of bread—a section called 'News for and About the Colored People of Jacksonville.' They never told what color they had in mind, though it was there in black and white..." Nervous giggles mingled with full-throated guffaws. "And it was only delivered to black neighborhoods."

Martin strode back and forth across the platform, clutching the microphone in his right hand. "Then, along came Mathew Rudberg," he thundered. "Mathew Rudberg saw our school system lose its accreditation. While no one in authority admitted it, he saw that one reason for that day of reckoning was that, just as Jacksonville had two newspapers, it had two school systems—separate and *un*equal. And Mathew Rudberg, newly appointed managing editor of this white newspaper, opened its pages to black voices."

Martin stopped, looked across the sanctuary, waited until the amens died and there was utter silence. He stepped off the dais and stood before the mourners. "For the first time black educators, ministers, attorneys, businessmen, and community organizers could address the public through its daily newspaper. And soon their photos accompanied these stories. And then there was only one newspaper, for white and for black.

"Mathew Rudberg risked his career at this newspaper." The attorney's voice was now a full-throated roar. "He braved the scorn of his friends, his colleagues, and his readers. He changed everything. We owe him much. Goodbye, dear friend."

With that, he sat down. Rudberg remained rooted to his seat. He shuddered, kneaded his hands, and looked down in stunned silence as dozens rose to their feet in an outpouring of praise. How could he have been so blind as to miss this?

———————

More than a hundred mourners gathered in the assembly hall of the church. "Where did the church get all this food?" Alan said.

"I ordered it on Saturday, while you were disobeying instructions."

"I wouldn't have thought of it."

"I know," she said. "And the flower arrangements. You didn't think of that either." He glanced at her, but couldn't tell whether she was criticizing or teasing him.

When Lucius Martin came through the receiving line, Rudberg grasped his hand and said, "Thank you for telling that story. I had no idea."

"It was before my time," the attorney replied, "but I heard the story from others, and your father and I became friends. Look," he said, spreading his arm out to encompass those in the room, about a third of whom were black. "They've come to thank him."

"I'd like to follow up with you, if I may."

"Certainly," he said, reaching in his breast pocket for a business card.

Rudberg endured the rest of the procession as one guest after another muttered condolences. He recalled the apocryphal story of President Franklin Roosevelt greeting each guest in a receiving line with the words, "I murdered my grandmother this morning," and none catching it.

Afterward, he made small talk with the guests who lingered. He met the mayor, city councilors, a former speaker of the Florida House, and many of his father's former colleagues.

He spotted Franklin Reeves and walked toward him, but a statuesque woman in her late forties or early fifties stopped him. "You're a lot like your dad." She had sun-kissed, medium blonde hair, a bright smile, and was almost his height. "Same cockeyed smile, same full head of sandy hair, same aquiline nose, same height."

"I'm losing my hair," he said.

"Not so much, I think. I'm Sonja Lansberg." She took his hand in both of hers and held it. "I was a reporter for *The Floridian* before they cut back. I covered Green Cove Springs, Palatine, Palatka—all the river towns. I helped him with the background for a few columns, and he taught me a lot about journalism. He was a fine reporter and a true gentleman."

She favored him with a wide, glowing smile, which he avoided by looking down. "And you? You're a reporter, too, I hear. We'll have to get together. Are you staying on?" An invitation or an honest inquiry? He wasn't certain.

"No, my sister and I leave tomorrow. We need to return to our families. For Thanksgiving," he added. He winced, embarrassed that he felt the need to justify his plans. Over her shoulder, he saw Cheryl gesturing for him. He mumbled his apologies, relieved at the excuse to break off an awkward encounter. Still, he turned to gaze at her and found her smiling at him. *She knew I'd turn back. She was waiting for it.*

"Alan, you need to hear this. This is Joe—"

"Kazantzakis," he said. "Joe Kazantzakis. Just like Kansas, only with a stutter." He laughed at his well-practiced joke.

"He was saying—" Cheryl lowered her voice. "You tell him."

"They're hypocrites," he said, not bothering to lower his voice. "Osgood, Flynn, the whole bunch. Osgood gets up and gives that fawning tribute, the paper sends a big wreath, they give him a two-column spread. 'Look at how we loved him.' Truth is, they got rid of him."

"Fired him? From what? As managing editor?"

"No, that was years back. Last summer, it was. They ended his column, told him it was no longer 'relevant.' It was one of their most popular columns, but they let it go, and him along with it."

"Any idea why?" Rudberg asked.

"What that attorney said, the race thing."

"But that was years ago."

"Read his columns over the past couple years. He was digging up buried stories, things that didn't make Jacksonville look so great alongside the rosy chamber of commerce picture. He wouldn't stop, wouldn't let it go, so they canned him. Read his last column, the one where he says goodbye. He wrote the first two paragraphs. They cut everything else and inserted a reminiscence. They censored what he wanted to say."

An older woman joined them. She glared at Rudberg, oblivious to the conversation taking place. "Was he angry?" Rudberg asked the man from Kansas.

"More like resigned. I asked him why they had done it, and he just shrugged. 'It's just an off-ramp from the highway,' he said, 'but the journey continues.'"

"I take it you're no longer there." The woman touched his sleeve. Turning to her, he said, "Yes? I'm sorry."

"Mathew Rudberg was a decent man," she said. She was a black woman, only five feet tall with furrowed skin and crinkled silver hair pulled back in a ponytail. "He was a great man," she repeated with ferocity.

"Yes," he said. "I was glad to hear Mr. Martin speak so well of him."

"He deserved better," she persisted.

"He did," Cheryl agreed. The woman turned and stared at her.

A younger woman who looked vaguely familiar stepped in and took the woman's arm. "C'mon, Mom," she said.

"He was broken," her mother said. "You should be ashamed."

"Not now, Mom. Let's go." Rudberg searched her face. What was this about?

The woman consented to be led away but glowered at them over her shoulder. Rudberg stared after them, stunned by her anger, indignant that she had invaded their privacy, and wondering where he had seen her daughter before.

---

"I spoke to Sheriff Vickers," Franklin Reeves said as he closed his office door behind them. "I told him we want a thorough investigation. He promised to give it his personal attention." His pause was almost imperceptible. "We'll see."

"What does that mean, 'We'll see?'"

He considered before he spoke, the lawyer in him assembling his argument. "Hampton County is not the most progressive corner of the state. Both the sheriff's and the police departments have had scandals. The FDLE intervened in at least two instances." Seeing their blank expressions, he added, "Florida Department of Law Enforcement. After they investigated two years ago, the chief of police was removed. The sheriff has been there a long time, and he's old school. So we'll see."

"Given Timmons' obstruction, I wouldn't hold my breath," Rudberg said.

Reeves nodded an acknowledgment. "I have the bank state-ments," he said, relieved to change the subject. "Your father invested a thousand dollars in each of the four years you were in college. He put them in CDs and kept renewing them. For you, Mr. Rudberg, the total as of this morning is $19,449. I'm afraid yours is less, Mrs. Davis, because you're three years younger. As of today, your account holds $16,208."

"Not much," she said, "considering." Rudberg suspected it was more than they deserved but didn't say so. The attorney gave her a bland look, having endured similar meetings before.

"Why didn't he send us the money?" Rudberg asked. The University of Texas charged almost no tuition during his college years, and since he'd been living at home, he'd had few expenses other than books and lab fees. Still, a thousand dollars a year would have helped.

"He tried. He told me he made the offer but received no response."

"What?" They spoke simultaneously. "He never wrote me," Cheryl said.

"He didn't elaborate. He didn't reveal much about his family, and it's too late to ask him. He left letters for both of you." The attorney took two sealed boxes from the credenza behind him and placed them on the desk facing them.

"When did he do this?" Rudberg asked.

"In July, when we prepared his will."

"Did it replace an earlier one?"

"No. I'd been after him for years, but he never took the time."

Rudberg considered the implications for a moment. "I'd like to see his bank records for the past eighteen months—his checking trans-actions and credit card statements."

"I'm sorry. I can't do that. Given the terms of the will, it's not really your business."

"I am not trying to challenge the estate," he began.

"I may," his sister said.

"You'll be on your own," Rudberg replied, keep his eyes on Reeves. "Our father was investigating something. His neighbor says he would leave in the morning, spend all day somewhere, and return in the evening. Someone killed him and removed whatever he was working on. I'm a reporter. I'm going to retrace his steps during the last few months. His records may give me a place to start. You can review them first and delete anything you don't think I should see. I'm not interested in his finances. I'm interested in anything that tells me how he spent his time—where he went and who he saw."

Reeves thought about it. "I'll consider it. I must get permission from—from the beneficiaries of his estate."

"Which brings me to my last point. Who are these women? What was their relationship to Mathew? I want to meet them."

"You already have. I thought you knew. When I saw you and Mrs. Stewart having that animated conversation—"

"You're kidding," Cheryl said. "That angry black woman?"

"Yes, Grace Stewart and her daughter, Aisha."

"I can't believe he left all that money to a couple of..." She left the word unspoken, but Rudberg knew what was coming and wished he could get as far away from her as possible.

---

In his hotel room, he tried to open the sealed box, but it was bound with tape and no amount of tearing at it would make it yield. He took it to the front desk and borrowed a pair of scissors, but the box still proved nearly impregnable. He sliced through the bottom. Envelopes and loose papers spilled out on a lobby desk.

"Jesus!" he shouted as he thumbed through the contents. A woman sitting nearby shushed him. He ignored her.

"Cheryl, bring your box down to the lobby," he shouted into a house phone.

"I don't care what's inside it."

"Bring it down. Now!"

Five minutes later, she threw the box at his feet and turned to leave.

"No, stay here." He sawed and sliced around the top and peeled back the flap. "Look. Just look."

She thumbed through the stack of letters, each bearing her name in flowing, cursive script and three words scrawled with a heavy pen: *Return to Sender.*

"He wrote us. Every week at first, then every month, then"—he pawed through his own stack—"two or three times a year. He got discouraged, but he never gave up. *He did not forget us.*"

The woman at the nearby table gathered her purse and newspaper and left.

"The fact he wrote a few letters doesn't change the facts," she said. "He left the family, left Mother, sent her no money—"

"How do we know that?" She stood before him, arms folded, lips pursed. *"How do we know?* Because Mother told us? That's her handwriting. She returned letters meant for us. He put eight thousand aside for college, a lot of money at the time. He—"

"You need to believe in him. I don't." She got up, leaving the box of unopened envelopes behind.

---

Cheryl wanted to return home immediately, but Rudberg suspected she wouldn't be able to change flight plans on the day before Thanksgiving. He left her alone to sulk. He didn't want her company at the moment. He opened and read his father's letters.

> I do not expect a young man of nine to understand why his father and mother no longer live together. I just want you to know that we both love you and will watch over you. You cannot know how proud I am of the fine person you are becoming. I pray that you will remain honest and kind and will look after your mother and sister. With all my love, Daddy.

He continued reading and soon found one written five years later.

This letter may not reach you, but I have to write. I must try to remain in your life. As you enter high school, you are leaving behind childhood and embracing adulthood. I want to share with you something I have learned the hard way, something I was told in my youth but to which I paid no attention. If my letter or my thoughts somehow reach you, I ask you to remember this and try to live by it. *Life is about choices*. We make them every day, good and bad, large and small. When you reach my age, you will be the sum of the choices you have made, and that will be called your character. It will be your only possession that is of lasting importance. I pray you always choose thoughtfully and wisely. Love, Dad.

Rudberg began counting the envelopes but gave up well past one hundred. The number wasn't the point; the lifetime of effort was. There were birthday cards, cards at Christmas, and occasional cards in between. Most contained checks.

I write again, even though I feel more removed from you and your sister than ever. You should enter college this fall. I hope you do. I have no idea where you will go, what you will study, or what your dreams are for the future. I do not know what you look like, although I imagine you to be a younger version of myself. I hope that you are, for I am serious, dedicated, and tenacious, and I'm comfortable with that. Life is a serious matter. I hope you have learned that.

Every check I've mailed, every gift I've sent has been returned unopened. You've received no Christmas or birthday presents from me, but I hope you know that I have offered them. I have set aside $1,000 to help support the cost of your education. I will contribute this amount for the next three years. There is no point in sending you a check since it will just be returned. I have purchased a CD in your name. The money is yours whenever you request it.

This letter was signed, simply, "Dad." No "Love," just "Dad." Tears rolled down his cheeks and fell onto his shirt. He removed his glasses, buried his heads in his hands, and sobbed—cried so loudly he suspected it could be heard in the hallway, but he didn't care and couldn't stop. He stripped his clothes off and showered. He opened the hotel minibar, removed two miniatures of Scotch, broke a few ice cubes into a glass, and drank.

It was enough to help him get ahold of himself. He read more letters and opened more cards, trying to reconnect to the father who had been denied him, a man he'd always held in contempt, but whose life had meant so much to others. What had Stephanie said? *Some reporter you are.*

Sometime later the hotel telephone rang. He did not answer. His cell phone chimed. He glanced at it, saw that it was his sister calling, and let it ring.

He felt that the alcohol had sharpened his thinking. In June Mathew Rudberg had been fired after writing one or more columns that had angered someone at *The Floridian*. Weeks later he'd sold his house and prepared to move to Hampton County, where he had no discernible connection. He'd written a will and entrusted to his attorney a lifetime of letters to his children. He knew that what he was undertaking could be dangerous.

He had given his life for a cause that had great meaning to him. Rudberg resolved to pursue that cause and complete his father's work. He owed him that much.

He slept intermittently, arising at one point to type up notes of everything he knew. When he awoke a few minutes after 7:00 A.M., he called his sister's room and learned she had checked out.

# OLD TIMES THERE ARE NOT FORGOTTEN

Rudberg canceled his return flight, grousing over the airline's refusal to issue a refund. When he called the front desk to extend his stay, however, he ran into a thornier problem. "I'm sorry, sir, but you told us you were checking out today. We're booked solid through Sunday." The clerk checked their other locations but found no vacancies.

It took two hours of searching the internet and calling hotels to land a suite at a corporate lodging facility on the west side, off I-10. "There's a one-month minimum," the receptionist said. He gulped but took it sight unseen.

He preferred not to use his cell phone while driving, having once rear-ended another vehicle while working on a story, but with half the day gone, he made an exception. Lucius Martin answered his own phone. "I'm staying over for a week or two," Rudberg told him. "Mathew was working on a story, and I want to finish it for him. Do you have time to meet, either this afternoon or Friday?"

Martin took his time before answering. "Where are you spending Thanksgiving?"

"I have no idea. I haven't thought about it."

"Come join us. You and I can talk while I fry the turkey, then we'll feed you. Sound good?"

"Good? It's generous. Are you sure it's not too much trouble?"

"It's for your dad, so it's no trouble. It's our pleasure." Martin gave him an address, which he scrawled in crabbed handwriting as he steered with his left hand.

Rudberg checked into his new home away from home and decided he'd lucked into the perfect solution. Besides a full-size bed, an anteroom held a television and desk, and a kitchenette was equipped with a stove top, microwave, coffeemaker, skillets, pots and pans, plates, and utensils. The Wi-Fi was fast enough for his needs.

It was time to face the dragon. Rudberg called Stephanie's office and reached voice mail. He called her cell phone, got no response, left a message asking her to call back, and followed it up with a text message: "Call me. Change of plans." She was unreachable, he mused, in more ways than one.

He had lunch at a chain restaurant across the street and plotted out his day. He would buy groceries so he could cook simple meals for himself, and he needed more clothes. Tomorrow he would visit with Lucius and clarify his direction for the next few days. Friday he would return to the library and finish reading his father's most recent columns. He brought up the library hours on his cell phone. *Closed Friday*. For the second time that day, his plans went out the window.

An hour later, he entered a branch library on Chafee Road and called up the last year of his father's columns. One of Jacksonville's remaining World War II veterans had died, and Mathew recounted an interview with him from several years before. "The Bridge to Nowhere that Went Somewhere" told of the 1970s controversy over the proposal to build a bridge at Dames Point, downriver from Jacksonville. What had once been the object of derision, his father wrote, was now a vital link in North Florida's transportation network.

A three-part series, "The Road to Disaccreditation," chronicled how the 1967 indictments of city and county officials led to voter approval of a plan to merge the two governments into one county-wide municipality. Entrenched Old South Dixiecrats had led resistance to the change, while one of the leading advocates was a Republican state senator. Rudberg wondered whether party elders would tolerate such a progressive stance today, but reading on, he saw why they'd supported the move. The plan ended the practice of electing the entire city council at-large, which had effectively shut out all but white Dixiecrats. Missing from Mathew's series was any reference to how inaction by *The Floridian* had allowed the prior system to flourish.

Rudberg now detected a rhythm to his father's choice of topics, eight weeks of something lighthearted—historic buildings and events, bygone businesses, eccentric characters—then two weeks of something heavy. Mathew had been like a small child, obeying orders to keep the series light until he thought no one was watching. That recognition allowed Rudberg to breeze past the dross and focus on the meaty columns.

His cell phone interrupted him. "Just a minute," he said. "I'm in the library. I need to go outside."

"In the library?" she shouted. "You're supposed to be at the airport. What do you mean, change of plans?"

"Hold on," he whispered.

"Don't tell me you're not coming home."

By now he was standing outside the building. "I can't leave now, Stephanie. Too much is going on—"

"I've been more than patient, Alan. You've been there more than a week now. I only asked that you come home for Thanksgiving. The Brinsons and Fishers will be there, and I will be all alone. It's humiliating."

"Stephanie, there's so much I need to tell you. Mathew's death was—"

"A week ago, and you've done what you can."

"—suspicious. He was working on something. I don't know what yet. But whatever it was may have led to his death. Everything I thought I knew about him—"

"The father who deserted you is more important than the wife who supports you."

There it was. Her high-powered career. Her house in Arlington Heights. "I pay my way," he said.

"Oh, we're discussing money now."

"No," he said. "We are not discussing money. We don't *discuss* a damned thing." With that, he hung up. He left the library and went for a brisk walk in the damp afternoon air.

When had their marriage deteriorated? How had it withered from one of love and respect to mere tolerance, and now not even that? With the loss of his job, the veneer of respect that had characterized her attitude toward him had peeled away, revealing only contempt. How long had she felt that toward him? How much was his fault?

He returned to the library twenty minutes later, having worked off the immediate anger but not the hurt. It was past five o'clock, little more than half an hour until closing time. A youngster sat at his terminal. Rudberg retrieved his notebook and called up the newspaper's archive on another screen.

He focused on the last three months of his father's writing. The first column to capture his attention carried the headline "Who Killed Harry Moore?" It recounted the 1951 murders of the founder of the Brevard County NAACP and his wife in Mims, Florida, a hundred and thirty miles to the south. Mathew had reported the bare facts about the murders, the many investigations into them, and the fact no one had ever been charged. It was a fascinating, heartbreaking story, but had nothing to do with Jacksonville. Why had Mathew chosen to write about it?

His answer came several issues later under a similar headline, "Who Killed Alonzo Taylor?" His father began that column with the stark words, "Between 1877 and 1950, white Floridians lynched more of their black neighbors than did citizens of any other state. Then they dropped the rope and picked up a gun. It was more efficient." Rudberg recoiled at the fact and at the words. The story described how a black businessman and pastor was gunned down on a deserted stretch of Hampton County road after being driven off the road in 1955. Like the murder of Harry T. Moore four years before, Alonzo Taylor's murder remained unsolved.

This column had appeared the week before *The Floridian* had forced his father out. Rudberg sat in contemplation, tracing the connections: Mathew's sensitivity toward injustice, his angry column about an unsolved slaying, his resulting termination, his move to Hampton County, his own death. He reread the column, printed it, and left the library.

---

Lucius Martin lowered the turkey into a stainless steel pot on his back deck. "Now fill it with water," he said.

"Are you going to boil it?" Rudberg asked.

Martin chortled. "What are you, some kind of Yankee? Fill it 'til I tell you to stop. Keep going. Keep going. Now!" Martin raised the poultry rack out of the water and marked the water line with a piece of chalk. They dumped the water into a sink in the laundry room, then dried the pot. Martin refilled the pot to the chalk line with peanut oil, placed it over a propane cooker, and lit the flame.

"Now, we wait," he said, drying the turkey with wads of paper towels. "So tell me about this autopsy." Rudberg summarized what Dr. Nussbaum had told them. The attorney asked a few questions, and Rudberg opened his mobile phone to share the written report, which had arrived in his inbox the night before.

"Whether accidental or deliberate, this is foul play. I hope," Martin said, "the sheriff's office does its job."

"You're skeptical."

"Hampton County's law enforcement agencies won't win any

awards from the ACLU," he said. "Competence is not one of their strong points. You know how Hampton County got its name, don't you?"

Rudberg did not. "Wade Hampton was a slave owner and Civil War general who recruited an infantry group named 'Hampton's Legions' that he funded himself. He was a hero of the Confederacy. After the war, he came up with the 'Lost Cause' movement that mythologized the 'Great Southern Way of Life'"—the attorney did a perfect imitation of white southern drawl—"and denied that slavery caused the Civil War. 'Oh no, pay no attention to what we said at the time,'" he said, returning to mimicry. "'It was about states' rights and Yankee interference in our Noble Way of Life.'" Martin had them both laughing.

"He became governor of South Carolina, a US senator, and supported a group of armed terrorists called the Red Shirts, whose principal aim was to keep blacks away from the polls. A peach of a guy. That's the Hampton in Hampton County, and his spirit hangs over it to this day. Don't get me started," he said, "or I'll tell you about the Jacksonville high school named for the founder of the Ku Klux Klan. We only got that changed last year."

Throughout this discussion, Martin monitored the oil temperature. Now he submerged the turkey in the hot oil, which bubbled and frothed as the moisture in the skin boiled off. "This will be the best bird you ever sank your teeth into."

"Have you ever heard of a man named Alonzo Taylor?" Rudberg asked.

"A perfect example of what I was talking about. A brilliant young man of thirty-five, a family man with a wife and three kids. He owned a print shop in Palatine and led a church congregation on the side, taking nothing from the offering plate. Someone ran him off the road on a Sunday night after he'd spent the day with voter rights organizers here in Jacksonville. Murdered him by firing a double-barreled shotgun into him at point-blank range. The Hampton County sheriff's department couldn't find a suspect. Two decades later, a prosecutor reopened the case, but they still couldn't solve it. Fancy that. But let some poor black dude cross a lane on a highway without signaling, and three cruisers converge."

Martin's teenaged son, Amos, joined them. The youngster had eyed Rudberg warily on his arrival, but once told that their guest was the son of Mathew Rudberg, he relaxed. Now he eavesdropped, taking in every word while his father draped an arm over the lad's shoulder. Rudberg eyed the pair, aware of how much he and Mathew had lost.

"Mathew wrote a powerful piece on Taylor's murder in late June," Rudberg said. "A few days later, someone at *The Floridian* forced him out, even shelving his final column."

"I remember. I gave him some background. He sat right in that chair and quizzed me. I didn't know much about Taylor's death at the time—it wasn't in schoolbooks, you understand—but I sure could describe the state of law enforcement there."

"A week later, a final column appeared under his byline—his swan song—which made it appear he'd retired. But the truth is they got rid of him. They let him write a farewell column, but spiked it and substituted a contrived history of his career. It's unlike anything he'd written previously. Totally out of character. The next week Mathew put his house on the market. He saw a local attorney, Franklin Reeves—"

"I know him. He does wills, but not well. Don't quote me."

Rudberg chuckled. "He made his first and only will and entrusted Reeves with some personal letters for my sister and me. He was preparing for the worst. He bought a small house across the river from Palatine. A neighbor says he spent long days away and often worked late into the night, but his computer and files are missing, so I don't know what he'd uncovered, if anything."

"So you think he got too close to something, and they killed him."

"I do."

"And that something was—"

"For starters, the identity of Alonzo Taylor's killers. Maybe more.

His column drips with anger over the murder and the lack of action on it. He became obsessed. It's the only explanation for his sudden decision to move there."

"Can't you men talk about anything but work?" Nora Martin joined them on the patio. She stood behind her husband, her hand resting on his shoulder.

"Alan thinks someone murdered Mathew," he said, turning to look up at her. She clasped both hands over her mouth, turned, and walked away, Amos following her.

With that news, a somber mood prevailed as they ate. No one felt thankful. But the turkey was, as Taylor had promised, the best he'd ever eaten, moist, with dark, crispy skin. "How are you going about this?" Martin asked.

"I'm not sure where to start, but I've asked Reeves to get me Mathew's most recent credit card and bank statements. They may hold clues about where he spent his time, who he met, that sort of thing. He's seeking permission from two women who are the principal beneficiaries of Mathew's estate, Grace Stewart and her daughter. Do you know them?"

"I do." Martin locked eyes with his wife as he answered.

"Do you have any idea what their relationship was?"

"You'll have to ask them," came the curt reply. Nora cleared her throat and rose from the table.

Ignoring the apparent sensitivity of the subject, Rudberg said, "I need your help. Please call them and ask them two things. I'd like to see his bank records, and I'd like to visit with them. The mother doesn't like me. She feels we misjudged Mathew, and it appears we did. My sister and I were fed a version of him that was just plain wrong. I know that now. Please tell her."

"I'll see what I can do."

He left with enough turkey and trimmings to get him through the weekend, an unopened bottle of wine, and a warm hug from Nora. He also carried the conviction that Lucius and his wife were hiding something. Still, they seemed willing to help. That was the important thing. And it was the best Thanksgiving he'd had in years.

---

The weather turned cooler and drier the following morning, and Rudberg took a long walk before breakfast. Over pancakes and sausage, he scanned *The Floridian*. Shoppers were expected to flood malls on Black Friday, Supreme Court Justice Bertram Marshall had returned home from the hospital, police had arrested a suspect in the fatal shooting of a Texas state trooper.

Franklin Reeves called shortly after 9:00 A.M. to inform him that the Hampton County medical examiner had reclassified his father's cause of death from *accidental* to *pending*. "That means additional investigation or test results are needed before an exact cause can be determined," he said, interpreting the legal jargon.

Rudberg asked a few more questions about the process and moved on. "Have you decided whether I can see Mathew's financial records?"

"I've asked Mrs. Stewart, but she hasn't decided."

He did not tell the attorney he'd asked Lucius Martin to help arrange a meeting. Reeves was unlikely to appreciate Rudberg going around him.

He next called *The Floridian*'s managing editor. After an exchange of pleasantries, Rudberg told him the ME had changed the cause of death. Further publicity, he reasoned, might shake loose some leads.

"What's changed?" Mike Flynn asked. Rudberg told him about the autopsy and, after they'd discussed it, promised to forward a copy of the report.

"I need something from you," he said. "Why did you let Mathew go?"

"Who told you that? He resigned."

"Maybe so, but when you ask someone to resign, it's tantamount to firing him. So why did you do it?"

"That's a personnel matter."

"It's a *personal* matter to me. I've read his last few columns. He stirred up issues that others wanted left alone."

Flynn paused several seconds before responding. "It's not the first time you've leaped to a conclusion without having all the facts."

Rudberg was stunned at Flynn's injecting the old libel case into their discussion. "I want a copy of his last column."

"It ran in the last Sunday paper in June. It's online."

"Not the ghost-written version. The one Mathew wrote and you killed." If Flynn would make this personal, Rudberg could too.

"We don't turn over our notes. You know that."

Rudberg assumed a conciliatory tone that he did not feel. "I am not trying to create conflict. I'm trying to learn what he was investigating after he retired. I've found clues, but there may be more in that article."

"There's nothing there. It was another tirade, the same thing we'd counseled him about for months."

"I want to see it."

"I can't give it to you even if it still exists, and I'm fairly certain it doesn't."

Rudberg was certain it did. He knew how newspapers operated in the electronic age. Nothing went away. Words and sentences piled up in a mountain of electronic sludge, a ceaseless accretion of the important, mundane, and insignificant.

But he didn't say so.

---

Coupland Paper and Pulp Mill roared at full throttle, three tall stacks disgorging steam and heaven knew what else into the atmosphere. The EPA was probably monitoring the air and water quality these days, but Rudberg remembered from his boyhood that mills like this had fouled the St. Johns and pumped a noxious stench into the air over North Florida.

He drove through the neighborhood surrounding the plant, passing homes that were little more than shacks surrounded by dirt-filled lots. Youngsters, all black, played outside in the warm fall sunshine. Across Highway 17 and farther from the mill, he passed more substantial middle-class homes, all of which appeared to be based on the same architectural plan, an African American Levittown.

Rudberg crossed the Hampton River, a tributary of the St. Johns, and drove through Palatine's town center, exploring neighborhoods south of the business district. Unlike the checkerboard street pattern north of the river, roads here curved through borders of live oaks. Homes here were more substantial, the architecture more varied, and the children uniformly white. Some houses looked to be at least a century old, encircled by wide porches. He suspected that the only words spoken inside were draped in superfluous vowels.

The road wound up a small hill that afforded a sweeping view of the river. Four stately homes that seemed pulled from the pages of a Faulkner novel were set back from the street, surrounded by ornate steel fences, painted a uniform black. Here, he thought, is where Palatine's ruling class lives. The road wound down the southwestern side of the hill and several blocks later rejoined US 17.

He returned to town and parked near the square, bought a tuna salad sandwich from a deli, and sat on a bench in the middle of the park. Ahead of him was a long memorial that bisected the square. Returning half the sandwich to its wrapper, he approached it for a closer view. The wall contained the names of those who had perished in past wars. It was in five sections. The central slab, which appeared to be the oldest, carried a tarnished metal plate, "Memorial to Hampton County Confederate Dead." On either side, slabs of more recent vintage memorialized the dead of World Wars I and II. The outermost wings were the most recent, containing the names of those who'd perished in the Korean, Vietnam, Iraq, and Afghanistan conflicts.

Facing them, and behind the benches where he had been sitting, was a statue of a dignified figure in a double-breasted suit. He read the inscription at its base.

---

This was a town divided by race and united by tradition. The South was so different from Portland. Here, everyone knew everyone else, their successes and failures, forebears and offspring, triumphs and transgressions. At home, few were natives, most were from somewhere else and might be in transit to still another place, semi-anonymous even to their closest friends. Heroes and history draped across Palatine like the Spanish moss across the branches of its live oaks.

---

Rudberg called Stephanie at work, reached her voice mail, backed out to talk to her secretary, and learned she was off for the day. He called their home and received no answer, tried her cell phone and got voicemail.

He left a brief message apologizing. "I know you were counting on me, but I have to follow up on my dad's death and would have had to hop on a plane and come right back. Let's set a time to talk calmly. You need to hear what I've found." He paused for just an instant, weighing what he was about to say. "There's a story here, a big one. It may be marketable. I'm not just indulging myself." Another pause. "I love you."

---

Saturday morning brought a call from Lucius Martin. "I see *The Floridian* has the story on Mathew's autopsy."

"They got it from me. I'm stirring things up. A neighbor may have seen something or someone that seemed inconsequential when everyone thought his death was accidental."

"It puts gentle pressure on the sheriff's office. That can't hurt. I've also talked with Grace and Aisha. They're willing to meet with you on the condition that I attend and that it be on neutral ground."

"That's fine with me. I welcome your help."

"They're wary, Alan. You have a lot of persuading to do." They agreed to meet Sunday afternoon at his home.

Despite a blanket of fog, Rudberg drove down the coast to St. Augustine to reawaken memories of his childhood. He had a basket of fried shrimp and a beer at a restaurant near Ponce de Leon's Fountain of Youth, which he avoided like all the city's tourist traps. He strolled the faux Spanish Colonial architecture of St. George Street, jammed with holiday tourists taking pictures, smoking cigars from the Cuban hand-rolled shop, and dashing in and out of shops that offered "authentic" Chinese gewgaws. At the end of the street and past the Cathedral Basilica, he emerged onto the Plaza de la Constitución, which the local guidebooks did not admit was the old slave market. Here, auctioneers had once sold people like furniture, separating men from their wives and children.

He drove south to Anastasia Island and found a secluded spot in the low-lying dunes from which he could gaze out at the ocean. Wrapped in welcome solitude, Rudberg considered what he would say to put the two women at ease.

---

Rudberg arrived first and tried to banter with Lucius and his wife, but Nora was having none of it. She paced and wrung her hands. She had sent their children to spend the afternoon with their grandparents. "You may hear things that shock your sensibilities," Lucius said. He too was in a somber mood. "Don't react."

They arrived a few minutes late, were led into the living room without looking at him, and accepted Nora's offer of iced tea, which Rudberg knew contained more sugar than tea. Lucius introduced the three to each other. The women did not offer their hands, and Rudberg remained seated.

"As I've explained, I had the chance to visit with Alan on Thanksgiving Day," Lucius began. "I became convinced of his good-will. He asked to meet with you and promised he is not trying to challenge the will. You agreed and asked me to attend as a neutral third party. Let us begin with a prayer."

Rudberg hadn't expected this but dutifully bowed his head. "Dear God, we ask you to bless this meeting and all those here present. We ask you to open our hearts and minds so that we may achieve understanding. We ask you to envelop us in a cloak of kindness and respect. We bless and praise you. Amen."

He nodded to Alan to begin.

"Thank you for meeting with me. I appreciate your openness," Rudberg said. "I didn't know my father. My parents divorced shortly after I turned eight. Neither my sister nor I were ever given a reason for their split. We saw little of my father for the next two-and-a-half years. My mother always told us he didn't care for us."

He gazed at Grace Stewart. "I now know that this was untrue." There was just a flicker of reaction in her eyes.

"When I was ten, my mother moved to Austin. Neither of us ever saw our father again. We didn't hear from him, though I have since learned that he wrote to us, sent cards and presents on holidays, and tried to contribute to our college education."

"And sent child support," Grace added.

"Child support?" Rudberg was incredulous.

"He transferred money into your mother's bank account every month until you and your sister turned eighteen."

Rudberg cross-examined her on the point, but she did not yield. "I knew none of this," he said, looking from mother to daughter and back again, pleading for their acceptance.

"Why didn't you reach out to him during all that time?" They were the first words Aisha Moser had spoken.

"My mother poisoned us," he said. "I don't know why. I'll ask her, but I don't know that she'll answer me. In the years since I've left home —" He paused and thought about what he was about to say, then changed course. "I have no excuse. Had I known the role that he played in this community, I would have welcomed the chance to learn from him. I never made the effort. No excuses. I'm to blame. I want to do whatever I can to right that wrong. He was working on something important to him. I'm working on what it was so I can complete his legacy."

She nodded but did not smile.

"May I ask—how did you come to know him?"

"He hired me," Grace said. "I was a young widow. My husband died in Vietnam. I was raising a son on my own. I had a business college degree and nothing more. I came into the paper looking for a job in the business department. There was nothing open, but he was looking for an assistant in the library—the morgue. I spent my career at *The Floridian* and ended up managing the department." She smiled at the memory, nodding as though that finished the story.

"That's wonderful," he said. "What I don't understand, though, is the personal relationship. He left everything to the two of you. That's a commitment."

Grace looked toward Lucius for help, but he said nothing.

"Tell him, Mother."

Grace stared at her hands folded in her lap but said nothing.

"You were lovers," Rudberg said softly.

"She was a widow," Aisha said. "He was a divorcé. They were lonely. They knew and respected one another. They fell in love and stayed together all their lives."

"But never married?"

"The paper had rules against fraternization," Grace said. "You couldn't enforce that today, but back then was different. One of us would have had to quit, and we both needed our jobs."

Rudberg nodded.

"But an unwritten rule was greater than that. If people had learned that he and I were together, we would have lost our jobs and more. That was the South. So we did what we needed to do."

Rudberg looked at her and smiled. The room was still. Three pairs of eyes bored into his. And he understood. "Ah, yes," he said to Aisha. "You are..."

She nodded. "I'm your sister."

# HOLIER THAN THOU

If you're paying attention, nothing should come as a surprise. Rudberg sensed the three of them take a collective breath. Obeying Lucius's admonition to avoid reacting, he forced a smile. "From the moment we met, you seemed familiar. I see it now. There's a lot of my sister in you."

"Not so much, I think." She laughed.

"I'm serious. It's the way you look to the side without moving your head, the way you frame your hands when you speak—"

"As you're doing now."

"We won't need a DNA test." She and Lucius chuckled, but Grace continued to study him like an amoeba under a microscope.

"I know this is awkward," he said to her, "but tell me about Mathew. I remember him as a tall, rather handsome man who always seemed serious. I don't mean stern. He wasn't that."

She regarded him for a moment. "He was serious. He didn't joke much, though he could tease with sarcasm. He was kind, thoughtful, always concerned about others. He liked people, but he was private, almost secretive.

"Of course," she added, "he had to be, given our relationship. It went beyond that, though. He kept his thoughts to himself. He expressed his feelings only through his writing. Because of that, he often surprised people. Here was this quiet, reclusive man who would burst forth in print with something that had such passion, such energy."

Intensity colored her words now. She wore a slight smile and seemed removed from the room for a moment. "He looked like you."

"Poor man," he said.

"That's what he would have said. Ironic—" She searched for the right word.

"Self-deprecating," her daughter offered, and her mother nodded in agreement.

"After Aisha was born, did he support her?"

"Support? He provided for both of us. He was generous. He made the mortgage payments on my little house until it was paid off, helped with the groceries, paid for dance lessons. We both had incomes. I wasn't living off him like a kept woman. But we were his family, and he supported us as a father should."

"He paid for my college tuition," Aisha said, "and all my living expenses."

As he asked her questions, Grace Stewart became voluble. Mathew Rudberg was her favorite topic, and she'd seldom allowed herself to open up about him. And while they had entered the room expecting him to feel angry, he was intrigued. Here was an entire part of his life about which he knew nothing. "Tell me," he said, "what do you know about the divorce. Why did he leave our family?"

"He didn't!" She leaned forward, almost shouting at him. "She left him. She kicked him out, took out a restraining order—which was all nonsense, by the way, but do you know what that could have done to his career? She cut off all contact with him. Then, after the divorce, when she discovered we were spending time together, she up and left, taking you kids with her."

"Why did she do that? What came between them?"

"Race," she said. "He broke the newspaper's color barrier, put black folks on the front page. Their friends and neighbors turned on them, and she couldn't stand it. I'm not saying it was easy to take. I know how those people were—still are, many of them—but she was his wife, and he was doing his job. She was so vindictive she not only left him and denied him his children, she threatened to ruin him. 'You come near us, and I'll swear you beat me.'"

It was a different portrait of his mother than he'd heard before, but as he recalled the language she had used when referring to his father and her freely expressed attitudes toward blacks, it had the ring of truth.

"Why did he move to Hampton County last summer?"

"He was working on a project," Grace said, "something he'd found down there that intrigued him."

"Any idea what it was?" Rudberg asked.

Both women shook their heads. "As I said, he was secretive about his work, even to me. Maybe he was trying to protect me. If I didn't know what he was doing, I couldn't be accused of leaking the information."

"I think it concerned a murder that took place sixty-two years ago, a man named Alonzo Taylor."

Grace nodded. "He had me search for clippings on that story years ago, back when we were both still working. He was angry that there weren't any. He wrote about that murder last spring."

"As you saw in yesterday's paper, an autopsy shows Mathew didn't drown. We're pressing the sheriff's department to investigate. I'm convinced whatever he was working on led to his death. All his records are missing from his house. His computer is gone..."

"He'd bought it when he left the paper. It was brand new."

Rudberg smiled and nodded. The computer was real; he hadn't imagined it. "I'm trying to figure out what he'd discovered and have nowhere to start. I'd like to examine his bank and credit card records to see where he went, how he spent his money—anything to give me clues. His records belong to you now. May I see them?"

The two women looked at each other but said nothing. "You can review them first. I don't care about how much he spent, just where he spent it. I need to see his expenditures since he left the paper." Again they looked at one another.

"And his phone records," he added. "Who was he in contact with? I need to know that."

"We'll discuss it," Aisha said.

---

It had been a long day of football. Henry Parker had finished his last game, the Steelers defeating the Packers, and his last six-pack of the evening. He stumbled into the bedroom, intending to brush his teeth and fall into bed when he saw the sky ablaze. He pulled the curtain aside and stared intently until he was certain what he was seeing.

Momentarily sobered, he made his way to the kitchen and dialed 9-1-1. "There's a fire in my neighbor's house," he said. "The whole place is going up."

He gave the address and directions since their dirt road was on few maps. "No, there shouldn't be anyone inside. The owner died a couple weeks ago, and no one is living there. But hurry."

It took over half an hour to assemble the volunteer firefighters, some of whom were similarly indisposed, and get the district's two trucks to the scene. By then, they could only train their nozzles on the glowing timbers that had once supported Mathew Rudberg's home.

---

"Mrs. Stewart and Mrs. Moser have agreed to share the past year of your father's financial records with you," Franklin Reeves said.

"That's generous, more than I asked for."

"But you must sign an agreement promising that you will share none of the information with other members of your family."

Rudberg nodded. Their trust didn't extend to Cheryl.

"I advised them against this. I gather you spoke to them."

"I did, and I pledged in front of a witness not to contest the will."

"Well, it's their choice. By the way, your father's house burned to the ground early this morning. I got a call from the sheriff's office about an hour ago. A fire inspector will investigate, but they suspect arson. A pair of teenagers has been setting fires to empty houses since the flood. The sheriff's office hasn't been able to catch them."

No, Rudberg said to himself, this wasn't the work of young vandals. I helped publicize the fact that the medical examiner has changed the cause of death. Someone's covering his tracks. I wanted to stir things up, and I did.

───────────────

"What are you doing?" Stephanie almost screamed into the phone.

"For the past three days, trying to reach you."

"I just went online to check our credit card transactions. You have nearly two thousand dollars in bills. Hotel rooms, meals, car rental, clothing, and now a huge bill to some extended stay outfit."

"It's for the entire month. I can cook my own meals there, so you won't be seeing as many restaurant charges."

"Alan, I don't know what you think you're doing there. You have no job, no income—"

"As I've tried to explain, there is a story here. Mathew's death was no accident, he was trying to solve a murder case more than six decades old. Someone didn't like it, and that someone torched his house last night. I'm not on a lark."

"Is it totally destroyed?"

"The house, you mean? I haven't seen it yet, but I'm told it burned to the ground."

"I hope insurance covered it."

"It doesn't make—" He stopped himself. If he told her he didn't own the house, he would find himself in a verbal box canyon.

"You've been drinking the Kool-Aid, haven't you? You go down to bury a man you hardly know and for whom you have contempt, and he's suddenly this great reporter, investigating an old murder, and doing the Lord's work. And you feel compelled to follow him down the rabbit hole."

"Now that you mention it"—and he thought he'd already tried to explain this—"almost everything I thought I knew about him was wrong. Mother—"

"I knew it. The moment you left, I knew you'd get sucked in. Well, I don't have to put up with it. I'm not financing your little trip down memory lane."

How many clichés could she pack into a three-minute conversation? He picked his way carefully through the next few sentences. "You don't have to. Some of what he left was earmarked for my education. Think of this as furthering my education."

"But you *have no job*."

"There's a significant story here. I've explained this. I may be able to sell it, even leverage it into a new position."

"How about your sister? What does she think?"

"She's gone home and left things to me. There wasn't much she could do here."

"I'll give you until Friday to wrap this up."

"Or else what?" he demanded. "I'm not your damned puppet." He held his phone away from his head and tapped the red button.

---

Not content to sit around waiting for Mathew's bank records, Rudberg spent the afternoon at the library searching for news accounts of Alonzo Taylor's murder. As Grace had found, there was nothing in the online archives of *The Floridian* other than Mathew's column.

Going through microfilm records of old newspapers was a laborious process and produced no results from 1955. Was it possible the paper had not covered the story? He found a 1988 story reporting that the state attorney had reopened the investigation, but a diligent search revealed nothing further. Had the trail run cold after more than three decades?

He had more questions than answers. Aisha called and asked to meet with him, and he invited her to dinner.

He spent the next hour searching the records of other newspapers that served Hampton County. He found nothing on Alonzo Taylor or on any reopening of the case. It was as though the murder had never occurred.

Aisha had picked a soul food restaurant on North Main Street. He arrived early, ordered coffee and sat at an empty booth. He was the only white man in the restaurant, but the other patrons ignored him. He recalled the advice a state representative had given him when he sought her help recruiting black members to the board of a Portland library. "It's easier if you already have an African American on the board. No one feels comfortable being the only person like himself in a room." Now he was that lone person and knew how it felt.

She arrived fifteen minutes late. "Thanks for waiting for me. I wasn't sure you would." Had her tardiness been a test of some sort? He wasn't about to ask.

She ordered chicken drumsticks with macaroni and cheese and collard greens, along with a large glass of cola. He opted for fried shrimp, mac and cheese, and green beans. Both plates arrived with generous helpings of cornbread, which was cloyingly sweet.

"I'm sorry about the house," he said while they ate. "I may have inadvertently caused the fire by tipping *The Floridian* to Mathew's autopsy. Someone rushed to destroy evidence."

"I don't know what we would have done with it," she said. "Insurance should cover the loss, and riverfront property may be worth more than the structure."

Rudberg reviewed his search through newspaper archives. "I would have been more surprised if you'd found something," she said. "Like Mr. Martin said, blacks hit the papers only when they did something wrong. If they did something right or were victims of a white person, it didn't occur."

They ordered dessert, and he took her advice to try the sweet potato pie. "Speaking of libraries," she said, "that's why I asked to meet with you. I'd like to help you put Dad's story together."

"Help how?"

"You don't know what I do for a living? I'm an archivist for the historical society. I dig through papers, historical documents, and old records and decide what to include in our database. I help researchers find what they're looking for. I sift information and find the kernels. I can't spend full time on this, but if you need research, I'm your gal."

Rudberg agreed. He needed the help, and this would be a chance to get to know her.

---

Rudberg reported to Franklin Reeves's office the following morning, signed the nondisclosure agreement, and received a file folder containing photocopies of monthly statements from two accounts. After picking up road maps from AAA and a whiteboard, magnets, and colored highlighters from an office supply store, he returned to his room and began color-coding the entries—green for restaurants, blue for gasoline, pink for household supplies.

He mounted the map on the whiteboard and marked locations where Mathew had made purchases, highlighting those he had visited multiple times. He found two curious entries that were off the map, visits to Waycross, Georgia, where Mathew had not only eaten but spent the night.

He called *The Floridian* and requested a high-resolution file of the photo that had accompanied the story of his father's death. All this took most of the day. He finished the rest of the Thanksgiving meal and spent another hour going over credit card records. A couple of purchases intrigued him, and he resolved to follow up in the morning.

Over breakfast in the lounge, he watched the news. A Senate committee had reported out tax reform legislation, Justice Marshall was back in the hospital, there'd been a shooting death not half a mile from this hotel, but he heard nothing about the investigation into his father's death or about the arson.

Back in his room, Rudberg studied the two entries that had interested him the night before. Mathew had paid a substantial sum to an electronics store in Mandarin, across the river. Rudberg assumed this was where he'd purchased his computer and perhaps the printer as well. He'd paid a hundred dollars to a company called CloudBurst in San Mateo. Searching the name on the internet, Rudberg learned the company provided cloud storage. He dialed their 800 number, made his way through the phone tree, and reached someone named "Dale" for whom English was not a first language. He was helpful, however, and once Rudberg explained the situation, gave instructions on how to reset the account's password. There was only one problem, he realized after the call. The reset process required access to his father's email account, and he had neither the username nor password. Nothing about this would be easy.

*The Floridian* emailed his father's photo. He saved it to his computer and took it downstairs to the business center, where the attendant helped him print ten copies on photo paper.

Rudberg called Aisha and explained the problem with the cloud account. "I have his email address, but have no clue what his password was."

"Try typing *password*."

"I doubt he would be that careless."

Nevertheless, he tried three variations on the word, lowercase, uppercase, and mixed case, but got nowhere. He tried Aisha's name, adding her birthdate, mixing up cases. He was about to give up when he had a blinding flash of the obvious. He dialed a West Coast number. "Hello, Dad. You're up early."

Rudberg apologized to his son for the hour, explaining where he was and what he was doing. "I can't believe you're expending all that energy on your father."

"It's a long story, Eric. I'll tell you everything when we get together, but it's important that I do this, and I've hit a roadblock."

He explained what he needed. Eric said, "We'll just reset the email password."

"That's easy for you to say."

"Give me his email address and yours." Rudberg did. Moments later a six-digit code appeared on his cell phone, and he read off the numbers. "Now give me his mother's maiden name." Rudberg answered this and another security question but was stumped by the name of his father's first pet and his best friend in high school. Eric asked where his father had attended elementary school; Rudberg was chagrined to have to call Aisha for such basic information.

Eric led him through the process of setting up a separate profile on his computer for Mathew's files, then asked him for a password that he would recall. "Something complicated," he said, "something only you would recall." The email problem solved, they unlocked Mathew's cloud account. Files popped up in the folder while the computer downloaded months of his father's undeleted emails.

He thanked his son for all his help, but before he could hang up, Eric said, "Dad? Everything all right between you and Mom?"

He thought hard before responding. "No, but we'll work it out."

"I know she can be—challenging."

"I'll never speak ill of your mother. You know that. She just doesn't like uncertainty. Once I get this business of Mathew's resolved and find work, we'll be fine."

He wondered if he was being truthful—to himself as well as his son.

## And Now I Become History

This is my final column for this newspaper. As Al Gore once said, it's time for me to go. I cannot depart, however, without recounting a chapter in my career of which I am less than proud.

Before I retired to write this weekend column, I served as a reporter, city editor, and managing editor of this newspaper. During the late 1950s, I witnessed small acts of corruption in city and county government that I did not report. In the 1960s, these small acts became major, and still I did not report them.

While I remained silent, theft, rigging of contracts, acceptance of bribes, and other criminal activity grew until it permeated local government. It was left to reporters for other news organizations to lift the curtain and bring it to a halt.

Why did I aid and abet this activity? Because the owners of this newspaper at the time prevented me from doing otherwise. They owned major industries here, and, in a corrupt bargain, the city and county allowed them to break the law in return for this newspaper turning a blind eye to their misdeeds.

They are gone now. The newspaper was sold to other local interests and then, seven years ago, to its current owners, whose sole interest is in producing honest, quality local journalism. I am as proud to work here today as I was ashamed to be associated with its predecessor.

Wait, you say. If you knew what was happening, why did you lend your name to it? Why didn't you leave?

I went along with those who themselves went along because I had a wife and family to support. All I knew was newspaper journalism, and Jacksonville was the only community in which I cared to practice it.

And then I found a cause to which I could devote myself. One of the central causes of Jacksonville's corruption was race.

Both city and county government officials were elected at-large, ensuring that our city's substantial black population was in the minority in every race for city council, county commission, and school board.

By denying African Americans a voice in their government, the white power structure kept schools and neighborhoods segregated, wages low, and power concentrated in the hands of the few.

The effort to marginalize our fellow citizens extended to this newspaper. For many years, pages of *The Floridian* were for whites only. We drew a curtain around neighborhoods to the west of Interstate 95 and north of Union Street, pretending they did not exist.

When our public schools lost accreditation in 1964, I worked to end that practice. Leaders in business and education like Moses Cunningham, Yvonne Jackson, and Luther Hastings demanded to be heard. I handed them a megaphone. If I couldn't work to reverse the corruption in local government, I could chip away at one of its principal support beams.

In this simple act of revolt and reparation, I hope that I helped change this city for the better. I know that I helped to change this newspaper. Along the way, I made many friends.

I leave my little soapbox behind with the hope that whoever documents the history of Jacksonville in future years will record that we listened to one another, respected each other, and built a stronger community together.

Rudberg checked the document's statistics. Mathew had written the column on the Friday before it ran, saving it at 2:58 P.M. He must have submitted it at the last possible moment, trying to prevent his editors from making any changes. The ruse hadn't worked, but Mathew had copied the original to his computer.

---

On the last day of November, Mathew Rudberg's body was cremated. Alan had choreographed the morning with Grace and Aisha, conscious that while he was legally authorized to make final arrangements as next of kin, they were closer to him.

They arrived dressed in black, the same dresses they had worn to the memorial service. He also wore the same suit, shirt, and tie, but he had no choice; he'd brought nothing else. A wheeled gurney supported the closed coffin in a small chapel of the funeral home. Rudberg had rejected the director's offer of canned music. The three sat quietly, waiting for something to happen. Finally, Rudberg spoke.

"Mathew, I wish I'd known you. While I never felt your presence, I always felt your absence. I am thankful that your friends and loved ones have given me a window into your life and work. Wherever you are, I want you to know that you have my respect." He paused, his voice about to break. "Amen," he concluded, aware of how awkward this sounded, coming from a man who didn't know how to pray.

Aisha spoke more eloquently. "Dad, I thank you for raising me to be strong and independent. I thank you for taking me on walks, supporting Mother, providing for my education, and being a loving presence throughout my life. I know that you are in the presence of our Lord and that He has welcomed you with open arms. Farewell, dear father."

Grace was next. She stood over the coffin, her lips moving in a silent prayer. She remained for several minutes while Rudberg shifted, uncomfortable in the face of her grief. She leaned her head on the cloth draping the casket and sobbed. Aisha stepped forward and embraced her, leading her from the room. The funeral director gave a signal, and two attendants wheeled away the box containing the body of Mathew Rudberg.

Alan found the women in a small room containing a desk and two chairs. Grace pulled liberally from a box of tissues on the desk. Unsure what to do with himself, he leaned against a wall near the entrance and waited.

Aisha joined him after a few moments. "That's good for her," she said. "She's been holding it all inside."

"There was no one else in her life?"

"No, Dad was her everything. She loved him with the passion of a newlywed. This must be hard for you to understand."

"Everything is. Not just their relationship, but his life, his work. It's all new to me. These past two weeks have been chaotic."

"Your mother—" she began. She left her question unfinished, which was just as well. Rudberg wouldn't have known the answer.

"I'm curious. Until a few days ago, I'd never heard of you, didn't know of your existence. But you knew about me."

"Of course. He talked about you and your sister often—well, less as the years went by, but he never forgot you. He was bitter toward the end, angry. That probably hurts, but you say you want the truth."

"From what he told you, what did you think of me?"

"Truthfully? I thought you were a selfish, privileged snot."

"And now?"

She looked directly at him, opened her mouth to speak, stopped herself, then said, "I'm trying to decide."

---

*And how do I feel about her?* Though he'd struggled to conceal it, Mathew's secret life had stunned him.

A child of any age is troubled to learn that a parent has a relationship with someone other than his spouse—the last vestige of innocence stripped away. Mathew's relationship had produced a child. This product of a parallel family—like a parallel universe—had walked the earth for nearly half a century. He could have run into Aisha any number of times—in a restaurant, airport lounge, or concert—sat within ten feet of her and never known.

And she was black. Rudberg knew this shouldn't make a difference. The fact of her existence should be more of a shock than her race, but it still penetrated his lily-white shell and forced him to confront his prejudices.

*I am not proud of myself*, he thought as he drove back to the west side. *It should not be entering my mind. I'm better than this.*

Aisha had shed light on a dark corner of his soul, and he recoiled in shame.

*Holier than thou.* That's what he'd been whenever colleagues, friends, or his mother tossed out some racist remark, blithely assuming he felt the same simply because they shared the same skin color.

*Holier than thou. Only I'm not. I'm just the same as they are.*

---

Rudberg called the sheriff's office and asked to speak to Sheriff Vickers. He was redirected to Chief Deputy Timmons, the last person with whom he wanted to deal.

"We're working on it," Timmons said. "I'll let you know if there's any progress." Not *when*, Rudberg noted, *if*.

"Has the fire marshal completed his examination?"

"We don't have a report yet."

"It's been three days now."

"That's right, only three days. These things take time."

"I would expect the murder of a respected journalist to take a high priority."

"We haven't established it was murder. The only thing we know is that he didn't drown. It might have been an accident."

"Without any trace of whatever inflicted the fatal blow? I don't think so."

"There's lots of debris surrounding the dock and in the water. We're examining it all."

*I'll bet you are,* Rudberg thought. *There are all manner of explanations if one is sufficiently creative.*

"Do keep me informed," he said, "and I'll keep his colleagues at *The Floridian* up to date." It was the one bit of leverage he could think of.

"I'll do that," he said and hung up.

Rudberg called Lucius Martin and was immediately put through.

He repeated the conversation. "The sense of urgency is underwhelming," he concluded.

"This is Hampton County. They do things their own way and dare anyone to tell them different. If necessary, we may have to go around them, but not until we're sure it's necessary. No point in making enemies we don't need."

---

The initial euphoria Rudberg and Aisha experienced over gaining access to Mathew's work quickly evaporated. Besides his final, unpublished column, Mathew had left only fragments of what was a work-in-progress—two chapters and parts of a third.

At least these bits and pieces showed they were correct. Mathew had been trying to solve Alonzo Taylor's murder. The first chapter chronicled the man's education and professional life, his transition into activism, and the meeting in a Jacksonville church with other voter rights organizers on the day he was murdered. Mathew had talked with three living participants who detailed what had been discussed and why the day stretched into the early evening. "We were all worried for him," one said. "The bishop urged him to stay over, but he wouldn't leave his family alone."

In the second chapter, Mathew reconstructed what he'd learned about the murder itself. Aisha sucked in her breath as she read how a pair of grade school boys had discovered the man's body on the floor of his disabled automobile, his head torn open by twin blasts from a 12-gauge shotgun. She wept softly, shaking her head as she read, and hurried them on to a third chapter, an unfinished history of Hampton County and a portrait of Palatine as it existed in 1955. Mathew had sketched out the government and industry in the area, but the narrative trailed off, ending as a list of businesses and individuals, but giving no indication of why any of this was important.

"This isn't much to go on," she said. "You'd think he would have typed up his notes after each meeting."

"He was eighty-one and of the old school. I suspect he kept his notes in longhand."

"And they are gone." She sighed in exasperation.

Rudberg tapped away at his computer, muttering to himself for a few seconds. "Here's something," he said. "He stored his calendar in this cloud account. There are names, a few telephone numbers, and some addresses—people he either interviewed or intended to interview."

"Look how things stopped in September," she said. "Irma brought everything to a halt up and down the river. He'd just started making appointments again."

"He left us a few breadcrumbs. It's better than nothing." He sighed, running his hand through his hair. "I'd like to get his cell phone records. If we put all these things together, we may be able to follow his trail."

---

Aisha asked about his wife and family. "Stephanie's an executive with Victor Apparel in Portland. She scouts factories for them throughout the world. Son Eric has a business developing fitness apps in San Mateo. And you?"

"David's a lieutenant commander serving on the *Vicksburg* out of Mayport. He's a thirty-year man or will be two years from now. They're deployed right now. We have two kids. Rebecca is a teacher at Westside High School—that's the one that was named after the founder of the Klan until last year. Sam followed his father into the Navy; he's stationed on the *Eisenhower*."

"I'd like to meet them someday," Rudberg said.

Aisha didn't respond.

They shared an early dinner. Rudberg returned to his room and turned on the TV to watch the Seahawks host the Eagles. The evening news was on. Supreme Court Justice Bertram Marshall had died after a long battle with prostate cancer.

The news in itself was not surprising since Marshall was eighty-one, but Rudberg knew it would set off a scramble between those hoping to fill his seat and those who wanted to prevent their doing so. Beyond the political catfight, the justice's death did not seem significant.

# IF YOU KNOW THEY'RE OUT
# TO GET YOU, IT'S NOT
# PARANOIA

**M**athew's calendar listed twenty-seven contacts, only one of which Rudberg recognized. Some contained telephone numbers, but most did not, and Aisha tried to find them online. Rudberg separated the list into five groups—*Background*, *A-A leaders*, *Taylor family*, *Witnesses*, and *Unknown*. The majority fell into the latter group, but he hoped to reclassify most of them as he spoke with others on the list.

He started with the middle group. If Mathew had been in touch with the children and grandchildren of Alonzo Taylor, he might have kept them informed of his progress.

An August entry read *Alcee Taylor, son*. Rudberg found his number in the online directory. He got a grunted hello. He introduced himself and explained who he was. "I'm trying to pick up where my dad left off."

"They killed him, you know."

"Yes, I ordered the autopsy."

"Not that it will do you any good. They know who did it, and they won't let you near him."

Rudberg was no longer sure whether Taylor was referring to his father's death or Mathews's. He decided to just let the man talk. "They know? Who was it?"

"I don't know, but they do. That's the way things work here. They run the town to suit themselves and get rid of anyone who's in their way. That's how it's always been."

"Mr. Taylor, who is *they*?"

"Who d'you say you are?"

"Alan Rudberg, Mathew Rudberg's son. You spoke with him."

"I did, but how do I know who *you* are? You say you're picking up his investigation, but you don't know who *they* are."

"Could we meet somewhere, sit down and talk? I can prove my identity. I'm serious about finding out who killed your father."

"They know who killed my dad, and they'll never let you prove it." Again, Rudberg asked who *they* were, but Taylor responded, "They know."

"Please meet with me. I'll come to wherever you are, whenever it's convenient. I need your help."

"I told your father everything we know—the family."

"Would you tell me? His notes were either taken or destroyed."

Alcee Taylor gave it a moment's thought. "You see? They won't let you get near it. They know who did it, and they're still protecting him. It's no good opening this again. It's too dangerous for us, and it upsets Mother something fierce."

"Your mother is still alive?"

"Ninety-eight years old. This still haunts her. Not a day goes by she doesn't talk to him. She's waiting to join him. No, this won't do no one any good. Leave it alone."

Rudberg thanked him and hung up, uncertain whether the man was frightened or defeated.

———

Rudberg was trying to match names to phone numbers when Aisha called. "I'm emailing you a spreadsheet of his phone records." She had scanned the printed statements and parsed them into a spread-sheet. She explained how to sort it and also sent a link to a reverse directory.

"You're amazing," he said.

"This is pretty standard stuff, but you're right. I am amazing."

Following her instructions, Rudberg sorted the list by phone numbers and marked those most frequently called. He searched for them in the reverse directory and entered the names of those he found into the spreadsheet. It was drudgery, but as a young reporter he had spent hours sifting through public records of expenditures and contracts, documenting corruption. Electronic tools made it easier and faster.

Among the top six names, two were Taylor family members he had already identified. Another was in the 912 exchange. Georgia, his computer told him. He entered the number in the reverse directory but found nothing. Unlisted, he decided.

The rest were in 904, which was Jacksonville, and 386, which included Palatine. He entered one of the latter in the reverse directory and again came up empty. He sighed, covered his eyes in frustration, got up and went for a walk.

Do something, he told himself. On returning to his room, he dialed the 386 number. A guarded voice answered.

"My name is Alan Rudberg. I'm the son of Mathew Rudberg, with whom you talked several times over the past month." There was silence. "I've taken up where he left off. I wondered if we might get together and review what he told you."

"Let me call you back," he said.

"That's fine. My number is—"

"I have it."

The man ended the call. Rudberg did not expect to hear from him again, but five minutes later, his phone rang. "This is Purty," the voice said.

"Yes, Mr.—" He looked down his list. "William. Thank you for returning my call."

"You can't be too careful. I had to check the caller ID to make sure your name matched what you were telling me. Still," he said, "you could be someone else. They do these things, you know. Called spoofing. They can even spoof your phone number. That's why I wanted to call you back."

Rudberg hadn't a clue what he was talking about. "I am who I say I am. Call the *Oregon Examiner* and ask them if they had a guy working there named—"

"That's okay. I believe you." Rudberg remained silent. "Your father said he wouldn't quote me, that he wouldn't keep a record of what I told him."

"I found no notes," he said, tiptoeing around the cusp of truth. "I don't know why he talked to you. I found you through his phone records. He called you five times, so whatever you told him is important."

Silence at the other end. "Mr. Purty, I'm flying blind here. I need you to take the blinders off. Whatever confidentiality my father promised you goes for me too."

"He said he wouldn't quote me and wouldn't use what I told him unless he got it from someone else."

"Deep background," Rudberg said. "Okay. Same deal here. But I need your help."

A long pause. "There's a place called Shay's Diner, big red sign on US 17 about a mile south of Palatine. I'll be there tomorrow morning at eight. Come alone."

---

Shay's was an entry on Mathew's credit card statement. He had visited three times during a four-week period beginning in mid-October, his last on the Wednesday before his death. Rudberg marked the connection on the list.

Taking a chance, he dialed the 912 number. "This is Barstow," a deep voice drawled. "I'm probably out, so leave a message." Rudberg hung up before the recording started.

*J. S. Barstow, Deputy.* Rudberg checked the name off the list, writing *Waycross* after it, and marked the connection on the credit card entries. He would need a larger whiteboard. He called the office supply store and ordered one to be delivered.

Mathew had called two others on the list almost as many times. He dialed both, getting a voicemail at one, and no answer at the other. *This is not smart,* he told himself. He'd been lucky with Purty and, to some extent, with Barstow, but he couldn't continue making random calls without knowing why his father had sought these people out. They were likely to become defensive, and he could miss something important. Purty might be able to identify some of these names and, he hoped, Barstow others.

He had to be methodical and patient. Still, he couldn't afford to waste time. Caution fought urgency. What to do? With some hesitation, he called the one name on the list that he'd recognized earlier, which he'd now matched with a phone number.

"Hello, Alan," Sonja Lansberg said, her voice lowered to a purr. "I hoped I'd hear from you."

"The wonders of caller ID," he said, not for the first time that day.

"I thought you were leaving town."

"Not just yet. I'm following up on some conversations my dad had with people in the area. The two of you talked on several occasions. I'm wondering what it concerned."

"Palatine," she said. "Hampton County. I told you I was a reporter here."

"Was he after anything specific?"

"He was curious about the power structure, who runs things, who does what to whom."

"Could you share it with me?"

"Certainly. When can you come down?"

"Where are you? I have a breakfast meeting in Palatine tomorrow. We could meet for coffee or something."

"Not in public. Come to my home when you're through. I'm just south of downtown." She gave him the address. Because Rudberg was wary of her flirtatiousness, he preferred not to meet her alone, but he didn't see a way around it. Was he misjudging her motivation? Perhaps she suffered from the same fear that infected everyone else. And why not? Two people were dead. You don't need to be paranoid to be cautious.

---

Someone had gone wild with the color scheme. A long red counter ran the length of Shay's Diner, green and blue bar stools before it. The walls were a bright yellow and adorned with a Pabst Blue Ribbon clock and an array of bumper stickers that ranged from *Jesus Loves You, But I'm His Favorite* to *Don't Believe Everything You See on the Internet —Abe Lincoln.*

Rudberg was ten minutes early. He sat in a booth opposite the counter where he could see the parking lot through the long row of windows, ordered coffee, and told the waitress he was expecting a friend. He felt a pang of guilt commandeering the only remaining booth.

A white pickup truck pulled into the lot and a balding man in jeans and a plaid shirt got out. Rudberg sat up in anticipation, but the man sat down at the counter with his back to him and showed no interest. Four men at the next booth paid their bills and left.

Fifteen minutes passed. An aging Dodge van pulled into the parking lot, but the driver thought better of it and left. Perhaps the odor of bacon grease and onions had chased him away. That, Rudberg thought, and an undefinable odor that underlay everything, as though Shay needed to open a drain and flush the place down with a fire hose.

Rudberg's phone chimed. The counterman was yelling orders into the kitchen so loud that he couldn't make out what his caller was saying.

"I said I can't come in," the voice said.

"Why not?" Rudberg said.

"Someone's watching you. It's too dangerous." His voice trembled as he spoke.

"Who?" Purty hung up.

Rudberg sat for a moment, trying to appear nonchalant. He paid his bill and edged toward the counter, asking for a cup to go. He fumbled with his phone and pretended to speak into it. "Hello? Yes. Sure, I'm on my way." All the time he snapped photos of the man seated at the far end.

The man rose and started to leave, then turned and faced Rudberg. "People here don't take much to strangers," he said, "particularly those who ask too many questions." He got into the pickup truck and backed all the way into the street so that Rudberg couldn't get a look at his license plate.

His first impulse was to call the sheriff's department, but he realized how ludicrous he would seem. "A man comes in, minds his own business, and when you try to take his picture he tells you people here don't like strangers," Deputy Timmons would say. "Is that about it?"

Rudberg didn't care to add that the man's mere presence had frightened Purty away. He didn't want Timmons to know he was conducting his own investigation and certainly didn't want to betray Purty.

Sonja welcomed him in, looking lovelier than the first time he'd seen her. He told her about his encounter and showed her a photo he'd taken of the man, zoomed in to reveal as much detail as possible. She leaned over his shoulder to view it, letting her hair touch his cheek and giving him a whiff of lilac. He handed her the phone, but she didn't move. "It's not clear," she said, "but it's no one I recognize. He threatened you?"

"Intimidated is a better description. He scared off someone I was supposed to meet."

"Who was that?"

"I'd rather not say, and I don't know what he had to tell me." He waved off her offer of coffee, having had more than he'd planned at Shay's.

She covered much of the history of Hampton County, making note, as Lucius had days before, of the origin of the name. "Up and down the St. Johns, you see towns based on tourism, recreation, and fishing. Palatine is one of the few with an industrial base. Coupland Industries makes paper, pulp, and plywood. It's the largest employer in town and has been for many years.

"There used to be three mills here," she said, "but Thomas Coupland Sr., bought and merged them. Without competition, he could control wages. He built a political machine that allowed him to dictate much of what happened not just in Palatine, but throughout the county. No one got a government job or a contract unless Coupland blessed it. It was your classic company town, and no one dared cross him. He owned the local paper, a house organ for Coupland Industries, using it to limit what information got out about his company and local government. He became a state senator and served for years as Senate president. That spread his influence throughout North Florida—even downstate."

"But he's gone now," Rudberg said. "I saw his statue in the park."

"The company passed to his son, Thomas Jr. He's not as powerful as his dad was—times have changed in a lot of ways—but he still exercises considerable control. He shuttered the newspaper several years ago, but he served in the Florida House in the late nineties with two terms as speaker. He's getting up in years and is grooming his son to replace him, but Jeremy isn't as savvy and maybe not as hungry. My guess is he'll sell the mill when his father dies and spend most of his time sailing around on a yacht somewhere."

She'd prepared a shrimp salad for lunch and he readily accepted, having had nothing to eat since the night before. "So," she said, "why did you stay?"

"It's like I said, I'm following up on some things my dad left hanging."

"He was working on something, wasn't he? He didn't move here for the nightlife. He called me in late summer before Irma hit. I could tell something had grabbed his interest."

"And he didn't say what?" Rudberg said.

"He didn't. And you won't either, will you?"

"He left no records, so I'm having to piece things together." He asked her about several names from Mathew's list, but she recognized only a few. She identified one woman as a granddaughter of Alonzo Taylor, another as an executive with Coupland Industries.

"I read that he didn't drown. It wasn't an accident, was it? He got too close to something, and they killed him."

"That's one thing we're trying to determine."

"We?"

"You knew he had a daughter here?"

"No, I didn't. Mathew was all business, all the time. I knew nothing of his personal life. Speaking of which," she said, crossing her legs, "what about you? Married?"

"With a son," he replied.

"And your wife doesn't mind your staying?"

"She understands."

"Oh," she said, and he realized that his momentary hesitation had sent the opposite message. "I see."

When he left, she gave him a big hug at her front door, something between comradeship and passion, an embrace that suggested he was welcome to return. He thought, as he drove back away, that she knew a great deal about him, while he knew almost nothing about her.

―――――

He parked at the east end of Confederate Park and followed the Riverwalk along the St. Johns for a mile as it passed under the US 17 bridge over the Hampton River. The man in Shay's Diner had not just happened on him. He knew who he was and had placed himself at the counter to observe who came in. Rudberg had arrived first, the man had entered, then Purty had shown up and been frightened off. That meant that the man had followed Rudberg, not Purty.

How had he decided Rudberg was worth following and where to find him? He reviewed his calls of the day before and his conversations over the past week. Anyone could have tipped the man off. Palatine was a small town, and nothing could remain a secret for long. Yet who had he talked with here? Sonja Lansberg and the sheriff's office. Rudberg's money was on the latter. They had the means to follow him and, for reasons he didn't understand, seemed to have the motive.

What to do about Purty? He decided not to call him yet. The man had been skittish before and had sounded terrified over the phone. Rudberg would leave him alone for a few days and try to find another way to engage him.

He returned to his car, mopping his brow and pulling his shirt away from his moist skin. It was December, and winter was only two weeks away, yet the air was as heavy as a wet towel. What were these people thinking?

---

Back at his hotel, he hauled the new whiteboard and office supplies up to his suite and turned the anteroom into a war room. The board was double-sided, the whiteboard on one side, a cork surface on the other. He transferred his map to the corked surface, replaced his colored marks with pins, added new ones based on what Sonja had told him, and snapped a photo of the result.

He called the Coupland executive and explained his purpose, being as vague as possible since he didn't know why Mathew had interviewed her. "I'm sorry," she said, "but I don't have time to do this right now."

"Sometime next week, perhaps?"

The silence was deafening and her response, when she spoke, cold. "I don't think this would be at all helpful. Thank you."

And your refusal, Rudberg thought after she'd broken the connection, even less helpful. He marked the response in his notes, which he stored in Mathew's CloudBurst account where Aisha could also see it.

He dialed the number for J. S. Barstow, who quickly picked up the phone. Rudberg gave his introductory spiel, which he had honed into a succinct pitch of fewer than fifty words.

"Sure, I'll talk with you. I saw your father had died and feared that the investigation had gone with him. I'm glad you're taking it up."

He knew no more about how Barstow figured into the Alonzo Taylor story but reasoned it would be better to ask once he was in the door. They agreed to meet the following day.

He had two more calls that afternoon, the first to Stephanie, to whom he got no closer than another voice mail. The second was to his sister. They hadn't spoken since her sudden departure two weeks before.

He tried to tell her everything that had transpired since Thanksgiving, but she showed little interest. "I'm still so angry with him," she said. "I don't think I'll ever get over it. I don't even want to."

"If you'd read the letters he sent, you'd have a different view of him."

"I doubt it. Have you found out anything about those women?"

"Quite a bit. Do you really want to know?"

"Yes, since he left everything to them, leaving his family out in the cold again."

"Cheryl, they *were* his family. He was devoted to Grace Stewart and shared his life with her for fifty years. Aisha, her daughter, is our sister."

She launched a stream of invective both loud and unyielding. Rudberg was sorry he'd told her. He was learning all manner of things about his family, some of which he preferred not to know.

He drove to the airport and switched rental cars, then headed northwest on US 23 through sleepy towns like Callahan and Hilliard. He stopped twice to make certain he wasn't being followed. Ford F-150s had to be ubiquitous in southern Georgia, and half of them were white.

Waycross took its name from the confluence of six railroad lines near the center of town. Rudberg arrived a few minutes early, scouted out Barstow's home, and took a few minutes exploring the town. It was on flat terrain with brick buildings lining the main street—Palatine without the river. Signs pointed to the nearby Okeefenokee Swamp Park, and images of alligators festooned billboards and store windows.

He parked in front of J. S. Barstow's home a minute before his appointment. It was a two-story brick house surrounded by a screened-in porch that hosted wooden benches and chairs. He walked to the door, knocked, but got no answer. Returning to his car, he drummed his fingers on the steering wheel while pondering what to do. He felt conspicuous sitting in front of the man's house.

He was about to leave when a vehicle pulled behind him. A slender but rugged man with close-cropped, receding hair got out, opened the passenger door, and helped an overweight woman to her feet. As she shuffled up the front walk, the man looked over his shoulder. "Mr. Rudberg? Sorry we're late. C'mon in."

The interior was clean but dated, the furniture Victorian, heavy and dark, much of it antique. Barstow led him into a side room that served as an office, then disappeared. A stuffed bookcase contained volumes on history and criminology, many of them textbooks.

"Make yourself comfortable," Barstow said, reentering the room. "Clara has to go for dialysis three days a week. Sometimes we have to wait." Rudberg felt like an intruder, but Barstow leaned back in his swivel chair and folded his hands over his stomach as though he had all the time in the world.

"I knew your dad. We met years ago, back when I was on the force in Palatine." Rudberg, who had been considering how to triangulate the man's role, thanked whatever gods might be for this offering. "Then, a couple months ago, he looked me up. He came up twice to see me. He became interested in this case long before I got involved, back in the mid-eighties, as I recall."

"What was your role in it?"

"I was a young deputy back then. The state attorney asked us to re-investigate the case, so we did. I was working with a veteran, Lieutenant Bill Whiting. Good man, honest. He's gone now."

His wife shuffled into the room carrying a tray containing two ice-filled glasses and a pitcher of tea. Rudberg started to rise from his chair to help her, but something in Barstow's manner made him remain where he was. "Do you take lemon?" she asked. He did. She didn't ask whether he took sugar. This was assumed. He drank it and wore a sweet face.

Barstow took him through the case, the blind alleys, false leads, and closed doors they had encountered. "Even then—in 1988, this was—there was a code of silence in Palatine. One more black troublemaker, more or less, no one would waste time over it. If he'd been white..."

"So you hit a brick wall."

"Not exactly." Barstow thought for a moment, looked out the window at some distant point. Rudberg let the silence hang between them. Barstow knew the game. One of them would need to fill the conversational void.

"There was a young fellow in the county jail awaiting trial for armed robbery. He'd hurt no one, but he robbed a grocery store one Friday night, knowing there'd be a lot of cash on hand, and was foolish enough to bring a handgun with him. Someone recognized him, we arrested him, and a conviction was certain. He faced hard time at Raiford," he said, referring to Florida's state penitentiary.

"He came forward and offered us a deal—he'd give someone up if we forgot about the weapon and reduced the charge to simple robbery. For a dumb guy, he was pretty smart. He didn't use a lawyer, didn't complicate things, just 'you give me this and I'll give you that.'

"We asked him what he had. We didn't buy a pig in a poke, you understand. 'The guy who killed that black preacher,' he says. We asked a few questions and determined he was referring to Alonzo Taylor."

Clara Barstow entered the room with a plate of sandwiches. Rudberg sensed Barstow was grateful for the interruption. Seeing Rudberg follow the woman with his eyes as she left the room, he said, "She gets angry if I try to help her. She pretends nothing has changed." They ate in silence for a few minutes.

"Do you think your dad was murdered?"

"I'm convinced of it. It's classified as undetermined, but I had the University of Florida conduct a private autopsy, and it was conclusive. This was no accident."

"Private autopsy? That was smart." He gazed out the window for a moment. "Interesting after sixty-two years, isn't it? There's still something about that slaying worth covering up. Do you expect the sheriff's office to solve your dad's murder?"

Rudberg hesitated. "They don't seem to be making much progress."

"And I don't think they will," Barstow looked him in the eye as he spoke. *Do you get what I'm telling you?*

"This informant," Rudberg said. "What did he give you?"

"In the county jail, they threw a drunk into his cell one night to sleep it off. The guy started talking and wouldn't stop. He bragged about killing a black minister years before, said he'd driven him off the road and then shot him. He'd had someone with him, but didn't name him."

"So you had a suspect—"

"And nothing else." A long pause. "We brought the cellmate in—I might as well tell you since you'll ask anyway. I told your dad, too—Carl Trickett was his name. He died about ten years ago. We questioned him three times and tried to work backward across thirty-some years to check his connection to the murder and movements. We got nowhere. It was Trickett's word against the guy who'd ratted him out."

He paused as though that were the end of the story. "And?" Rudberg said.

Barstow sighed, taking several seconds before responding. "A new state attorney looked at what we had and dropped it."

"Did you keep any records from your investigation?"

Barstow thought again before responding. "I didn't," he said, "but I still have friends there. I'll see what they have."

---

Rudberg drove a few blocks until he was out of sight of the house. He called Aisha on his cell phone. "Find out what you can about a Carl Trickett," he said, spelling the name for her. "He died about ten years ago and lived in or near Palatine."

He summarized his conversation with Barstow. "He wouldn't name their informant, still respecting their agreement after all these years. I suspect it's Purty, though. I'll try reconnecting with him."

"Was he able to help you with any of the other names?"

"One fellow who was a guard at the jail, no one else. He said it's been too long since he left there. I learned other things, though. Dad was interested in this case since at least the mid-eighties. Alonzo Taylor's death must have been an obsession."

"That's the first time I've heard you call him Dad. You've always referred to him as Mathew."

He considered that. "Seeing him through other people's eyes has brought me close to him. No one has anything bad to say about him. Your mother loved him, and it seems he loved her. I've missed so much."

She did not respond, seemingly having no wish to make things easy for him.

"Two more things," he continued. "Barstow rattled on without my having to prompt him. Then he'd stop. He wanted to tell me something but held back. Or he was editing his words to avoid saying something. Either way, he didn't share all he knows. That's why we need to look at this guy Trickett. And Barstow has no use for the sheriff's department. He made that clear. He doesn't think they'll do anything about Dad's death."

"We don't expect much from small-town police departments and are seldom disappointed," she said.

*We*, he thought as he returned to Jacksonville. *Does that include me?*

Rudberg was not much of a drinker. He'd share a beer with friends when attending a soccer match. Stephanie was an expert on Oregon pinot noir, and on special occasions or when entertaining, they shared a bottle. Most evenings, however, he drank carbonated water.

This was not one of those nights. He bought a bottle of Scotch at a liquor store and had himself a pity party.

---

The bottle was three-quarters full the following morning. He was both glad of it and somewhat ashamed. Seven-eights would have been better—full, better still. He wasn't fogged in, but there were low-hanging clouds on his personal horizon.

After breakfast and more coffee than was advisable, he put in a call to William Purty. "I'm sorry about what happened Tuesday. I didn't realize I was being followed. I know that now. I'm being very cautious."

Silence. "I respect your caution. Everyone's been warning me, and I haven't paid attention. This isn't something that just happened half a century ago. It's real and present. I need your help."

"I can't afford to meet."

"I'll come to your place."

"No." His response was emphatic. "Not here." A dog barked in the background. Purty yelled at it to stop, then put him on hold while he let it out.

"I'm putting the pieces together," Rudberg said when he returned to the phone. "You took a courageous step years ago, and it didn't work out."

"Who told you that?" It was less a question than a cry.

"No one. I figured it out all by myself. I'm not as naïve as I seem—as I was two days ago. You tried to do the right thing once. It's unfinished business. Help me bring it to a close. I'm not in this alone. Others are helping me. We can win, but only with your help."

It took more stroking of the man's ego, but once Rudberg outlined a plan he'd been formulating, he agreed.

Rudberg called Sonja. "This may seem an odd question, but are you married?"

She laughed. "Do I act like I'm married? I'm divorced, happily divorced."

"How about a date, a little getaway, just the three of us?"

⸻

"Barstow here. I promised I'd try to get the records of Lieutenant Whiting's investigation. It was his investigation," he added. "I was just his partner."

Was he establishing deniability? Again, Rudberg got the feeling he was hiding something.

"But an odd thing has happened. Well, maybe not so odd. When we open a file, we hold on to it until the defendant dies, unless the case is unsolved, which was clearly the case here. When we reopened the investigation, the first thing we did was search for the old records. They were missing. That shouldn't have been the case, but things were kind of lax back in the fifties and sixties. By 1988, there were firm procedures. The case was unsolved when we left it, so they should have held on to the files we put together."

"Only they didn't," Rudberg said.

"Right. Everything's gone. It's as though we never looked into it. Someone's removed that file."

# TAKE GOOD CARE OF
# YOURSELF

"Carl Trickett was a white supremacist, a member of the Klan." Aisha was on the phone early Friday afternoon, telling him what she'd learned. "Americans United for Justice has a long file on him." Rudberg was vaguely aware of the AUJ, a civil rights organization that tracked hate groups from its Atlanta headquarters.

"He headed the Hampton County Klavern back in the fifties, brought a group to Jacksonville for Ax Handle Saturday in 1960, organized resistance to school desegregation in Hampton County—the list goes on."

"And in the late eighties, bragged about murdering Alonzo Taylor," Rudberg said. "He sounds like a wonderful human being."

"Who said anything about being human?" Aisha said.

She read what she'd learned about him—born in Palatine, educated in the public schools there, spent all his working life working at the paper mill, died of throat cancer in 2007, two children, Wade and Wanda—the latter now married to a man named Yarbrough. "But here's something interesting—Trickett has no arrest record. He lived in Palatine all his life, did all this rabble-rousing, but was never charged or convicted of a thing."

"Or, more likely, the records disappeared." Rudberg told her about the missing files from Barstow's 1988 investigation. "Someone in authority covered it up, made it go away."

"Thirty years after the fact," she said. "The truth was that threatening."

"And still is. That's why someone killed Mathew. An individual is so terrified about a six-decades-old slaying that he had to get rid of a retired newspaper editor who was looking into it. Who could still be vulnerable after all that time?" Neither of them had a clue.

Rudberg told her of his plan to meet with William Purty the following day, but not the labyrinthine steps he'd taken to avoid discovery.

"I'd like to take you and your mother out to dinner on Sunday," he said.

"I'm not sure she's up for that."

"Ask her, please. I want to get to know Dad better...and your mother."

"I'll see," she said. He recalled his sister's frequent complaint during their childhood. *We'll see always means no.*

---

What had seemed a good idea in theory seemed less than stellar in practice, but it was too late to change. Rudberg drove Sonja across the Coupland Bridge and up to St. Augustine. They checked into a luxury hotel overlooking the Matanzas River along Avenida Menendez, changed for dinner and, despite the cool weather, walked hand-in-hand to a Spanish restaurant on St. George Street.

After drinks, they ordered, then spoke in hushed tones as they awaited their meals, a precaution against being overheard that heightened the illusion of intimacy. "My ex is an engineer," she explained in answer to his question. "He traded me in on a new model, but I got the house and a generous settlement. And your wife? Stephanie, isn't it? How would she feel if she could see us now?"

"I'll tell her. She's a reporter's wife, so she understands the need for subterfuge." Both were lies. He wouldn't tell Stephanie, because she wouldn't understand.

"This person you're seeing, is he the same guy you were supposed to meet in Palatine?" When he hesitated, she said, "That's all right. You don't have to tell me. I'm just along for the ride. And the dinner."

"It's not just a matter of confidentiality," Rudberg replied. "It's fear. I'm worried I'm involving you too much as it is."

As they enjoyed a languid dinner, the skies opened, rain lashing the windows. He ordered a horse-drawn carriage to carry them back to the hotel. She'd had several glasses of wine, so hugged him for support as she alighted. Anyone passing them would have taken them for lovers whose weekend tryst was being rained out. Back in their room, she said, "Isn't this cloak and dagger business a bit overwrought?"

"I hope so," he said, "but he's the closest link I have to the matter my father was investigating."

"And that matter is?"

He didn't answer, and she didn't press him. They watched television for over an hour. "Are you sure you don't want to lie down and rest for a few minutes?"

"No," he said. "I appreciate what you're doing for me, but I can't afford any complications."

His phone beeped. "He's here."

Rudberg had changed into chinos and athletic shoes. Pulling on a rain jacket, he took the back stairs and found his way to Bridge Street. He avoided streetlights and, after a fifteen-minute walk, arrived soaked at a modest motel on the San Sebastian River. He took the interior stairway to the third floor and knocked at 312. William Purty opened the door, looking relieved to see him.

---

The room held twin beds separated by a nightstand, a built-in wardrobe and entertainment center, and a small table with two chairs. They sat across from each other at the table. Rudberg had brought the bottle of Scotch, and Purty accepted a glass.

He was a small man, only five feet, six inches tall, and wiry. He wore his thinning gray hair in a buzz cut, which was overdue for a trim. Rudberg put him in his mid-seventies.

"You're sure you weren't followed?" he said.

"As sure as I am of anything. A friend and I concocted an elaborate ruse. If anyone's followed us, they think we're shacked up in a hotel on the Intracoastal Waterway, but I don't think we were."

That seemed to satisfy Purty, but his eyes roamed the room as he rubbed his hands together, a hunted man.

"How many times did my dad meet with you?" Rudberg asked.

"Only the twice." An interesting construct, Rudberg thought. "Once at Shay's, and the second time at his place."

"How did he find you?"

"He talked to that former cop, Barstow, who told him my story. The cop didn't give him my name, but your dad went through court records and found a case like mine. That's what he said, anyway."

He led Purty through his story, which was much as J. S. Barstow had told it. He was arrested—he didn't say for what until Rudberg asked him—and held without bond pending a hearing. "There were four cells in the basement, so I had one to myself most of the time. But this one night, they threw a guy in with me. It was a weekend, and they were crowded. You could tell he'd been drinking. He reeked. I think he'd peed himself. And he was loud. He bragged about how some guy had started an argument with him. 'He won't be messing with me again.' That's what he said."

"He'd been in a fight," Rudberg said, trying to keep the conversation going.

"Yeah," he said, as though Rudberg were hard of hearing. "The man continued to talk and boast. 'No one messes with Carl,' he says. 'I'm the muscle.' He goes on about how tough he is. Something about breaking the arm of a union guy at the plant. It's been a long time. I don't remember all the details."

"Did he say which plant he meant?"

"There's only one. Anyway, all I wanted to do was shut him up. It was after midnight like it is now. I wanted to sleep. And he goes on raving about how macho he is. He says, 'I bet you don't believe me.' Like he was trying to pick a fight with me." He fixed Rudberg with an incredulous stare as if to say, "Who, me?" Rudberg grunted an acknowledgment.

"So then he says, 'We took care of that uppity preacher years ago, the one trying to organize all the colored folks to vote. We drove him off the road, and I let a guy that was with me finish him off. How he squirmed. Begged for mercy. We gave him mercy, all right. Two barrels full.' And he laughed."

"Did he name the pastor?"

"No, but I knew who he meant. Everyone knew about that murder."

"Even though the paper didn't report it at the time?"

"Like I said, everyone knew."

"And this drunk, did you know who he was?"

"No, never seen him before. I didn't live in Palatine back then. I had a bait and tackle shop across the river. Didn't make much money, but it was fun. I was my own man back then."

"What happened to him?"

"They came and got him, five, six in the morning. We were both asleep by then. A deputy comes into the cell and says something like, 'Okay, Carl. Off you go. Let's not see you back here for a while.'"

"And what did Carl do?"

"He smiled at the guy as though he owned the place. They all knew him. You could tell."

Purty poured lifted the bottle to pour himself another glass. "Don't drink it all now," Rudberg said. "You can take the bottle with you. Let's keep talking."

Purty said he'd approached the state attorney during a hearing and said he wanted to make a deal. "That lawyer they gave me, the public defender? He was useless. He just wanted me to plea so he could move on to the next defendant. They had me good and proper, and I needed to do something, so I went to the top and offered a trade —my information for a reduced charge. I thought they'd get this guy Trickett for murder, I'd get a light sentence, and that would be the end of it."

"But..."

"I told my story to the cop you talked to, Barstow, and his partner. But nothing came of it. They buried it."

"Buried it? Maybe they didn't have enough to charge him. You were the only witness. It was your word against Trickett's."

"I heard they found another witness, someone who saw him and his truck casing the preacher. Only it went no further. It was like the morning they walked into our cell and told him to behave himself in the future. I'm telling you, they just closed the book and let him walk. I know it."

---

"How was your meeting?" Aisha asked as soon as she and her mother were seated.

"He claims they dropped the case. I'll tell you more later."

"Figures," Grace said. They had a window seat at a riverfront restaurant on Independence Drive that served steak, seafood, and anything else one could imagine. As Grace studied the menu, he studied her. With silver hair pulled back in a bun, chocolate-colored skin, and angular features in an unlined face, she could have been the model in a retirement home ad. She was still beautiful, and Rudberg understood why his father had been attracted to her.

"I only came because Aisha asked me to."

"And I only asked you because I want to know the person my father loved. It's too late to connect with him, but I'm trying to connect to his life."

She said nothing and didn't look at him. "We've all lost something here. You lost a partner, and Aisha lost a father. I lost a family—the father I never knew and the mother I thought I knew. I'm looking for —something. What, I don't know."

A waiter took their orders, showing no surprise that a white man hosted two black women for dinner. Rudberg was old enough to remember blacks walking past empty seats in the whites-only section of a city bus to stand next to the crowded seats at the back. He remembered whites-only taxicabs. A few things had changed.

"Mathew was a lonely man," she said. "He lost his only son and his firstborn daughter. Though he had a new family, he couldn't show them to others, couldn't take them to a ball game, couldn't go for walks in the park on Sunday. It was pathetic seeing a man so devoted to others, unable to share everyday experiences with his neighbors. To live without happiness—that's a terrible thing."

"I cannot imagine."

It opened a floodgate. For thirty minutes, she talked while her meal sat untouched, telling stories of Mathew Rudberg and their shared, secret life together. "We didn't start as lovers," she said. "I applied for a job, and they turned me down. I may have told you they'd already filled the position when I came for the interview, but that wasn't true. The business department didn't want a black woman sitting in their office. It was that simple, and back then they could get away with it."

She seemed to consider it for a moment. "Maybe they can again. We seem to be slipping backward. At any rate, Mathew was in the interview. They were going through the motions, asking their standard questions without paying attention, but he was listening and following up. After they turned me down, he called and said he wanted me to come work for him. 'You're incisive,' he said. I've never forgotten that word. It stands for so much. He knew I'd know that word and what it meant. He was never condescending. 'You're incisive, and we need you here.' That was that. I started the next week, and he made people respect me. One day someone said—I wasn't there, but I heard about it later—'Let's have the girl look that up.'"

She tossed the line off with a slight sneer. Rudberg couldn't tell whether she was mimicking the woman or mocking her.

"'That's not a girl,'" Grace continued. "'She's a woman, and she's intelligent. You will treat her with civility.' He didn't say 'or else,' but the little ofay got the message. He didn't last, by the way."

"Ofay?"

Aisha and Grace glanced at each other and giggled. "She doesn't think you're one, okay?" Aisha said. "She doesn't think you're a cracker, either. Means the same thing."

They finished their meals, ordered desserts, then lingered over coffee while Grace Stewart continued her verbal memorial. As her mother visited the restroom before leaving, Aisha said, "She's started to trust you. I can tell. Just letting her talk about him was good for her."

"It was good for me." Changing the subject, he said, "There's something I'd like you to do for me—for us." He gave her a quick synopsis of what William Purty had told him. "So can you find out who was state attorney in 1988?" he asked.

"Consider it done."

Grace rejoined them, and Rudberg helped her into her coat. "Promise you won't let us down," she said.

"I promise *we* won't let you down."

———

Stephanie called him Sunday night, the first time they had spoken in two weeks. "I'm sorry you got upset."

There was no way to answer that. "We've learned what Dad knew—"

"Dad?"

"My father, yes. I'm trying to figure out what—"

"And who's 'we?'"

How to explain? "I'm working with a woman who knew him. She's a researcher and is helping to track—"

"When are you coming home?"

"Soon. I need to tie up loose ends here." An oversimplification, but it would have to do. "How was your weekend?"

"Quiet, uneventful. And yours?"

"Not quiet, eventful. I found a man who has vital information on the matter Dad was looking into. He—"

"Christmas is two weeks away. You'd better make arrangements." He promised to do so, which seemed to mollify her.

He spent much of the following day writing up notes and trying to decide what to do with what he'd learned. A white supremacist bragged to a cellmate about murdering Alonzo Taylor. Sheriff's deputies treated him like a friend and released him. The cellmate cut a deal with the local prosecutor. Investigators gathered additional evidence, but they didn't charge the man. That was one set of facts.

Even before this occurred, Mathew Rudberg had become interested in who had murdered Taylor. He wrote his penultimate column about the case. When *The Floridian* let him go, he sold his house, left his friends and family, and moved to Hampton County, where he could investigate it. Someone killed him, and Rudberg was convinced it was because he was asking questions that others didn't want answered—questions that still posed a threat sixty-two years after the murder.

How could he untangle a ball of yarn when he couldn't find the beginning or the end? He'd had to do that as a child whenever his mother began to unravel the ball from the middle. He'd lay the yarn across the floor and drape it over chairs, pulling the fiber through knots and tangles until, at last, it was one long strand.

On Monday morning Rudberg drove south to Palatine and stopped at the sheriff's office. Chief Deputy Timmons came into the reception area without inviting him back to his office. "There's nothing new. We've found no witnesses, no weapon. I told you I'd call if we made progress."

"I'm in the neighborhood. What about the fire?"

"It was arson. You can read the fire marshal's report for yourself.

Someone—teenaged vandals, we figure—doused the storage closet with gasoline and lit it. The flames spread up through the center of the house and it collapsed inward. What's your interest, anyway? It's not your property."

Rudberg wondered how he'd discovered that, why it mattered to him. "It was my father's, and whoever set fire to it was hiding evidence of his murder. You know that, and so do I." He left without another word, crossed the Coupland Bridge, and turned onto River Road.

The house was a pile of charred wood. At the edge of the debris, the remains of a television set rested incongruously, scavengers having gone through what remained. The fire had seared the trunk of an overhanging tree, denuding and blackening its branches.

He walked next door along the retaining wall and knocked at Henry Parker's door, carrying a six-pack he'd bought for the occasion. Parker invited him in and accepted the offering. He told him what he'd seen the night of the fire.

"Did you see or hear anyone around the house?" Rudberg asked.

"No, not a thing. I was watching the game."

"How about earlier?"

"Just you, that afternoon you came over and went inside." So Rudberg hadn't been as stealthy as he thought.

"Yeah, I was looking for some papers he left me. His attorney had them all the time. He could have saved me the trouble." Parker seemed to accept that. "Someone had stripped the place bare, emptied his file cabinet, taken his phone and computer. Did you see anyone around the weekend you discovered his body?"

"No, like I told you, I didn't see anyone coming or going."

Except me, Rudberg thought. Someone can commit a murder, ransack a house, and later return to torch it, and you don't see a thing. While I can't approach within a hundred yards...

"What did the sheriff's office ask?"

"Ask who?"

"When they questioned you after Dad's death and again after the fire."

"They didn't."

"I'm sorry. They interviewed you, didn't they? Took your statement?"

"No, why would they?"

Why, indeed?

---

Aisha called in midafternoon, her voice trembling with excitement. "This is incredible," she said. "In 1988, the Hampton County prosecutor died in office, and the circuit judge appointed a local attorney to fill out his term. This young attorney went on to win election to that office in the fall. His name is J. Morris Searcy."

Rudberg had heard the name, but couldn't recall where. "He spoke at Dad's funeral, the big guy with a limp."

"The judge," Rudberg recalled.

"Federal judge on the US Court of Appeals. He's the chief judge of this circuit. He's a big deal."

"A very big deal," Rudberg said. He took off his glasses and rubbed his eyes.

"Are you still there?"

"I'm thinking. He ended the investigation into Alonzo Taylor's death..."

"Killed it, your witness said."

"Yes, but that's his interpretation. He didn't pursue it, that much we know. Barstow was holding something back. I wonder if that's it."

He called Lucius Martin, who agreed to see him later the following morning.

Rudberg spent the evening puzzling over the disconnected bits and pieces of what he'd learned. A distinguished US jurist. Alonzo Taylor. Mathew Rudberg. What was the connection? Maybe there wasn't one. Maybe he was imagining things. Then he recalled the encounter at Shay's. *"People here don't take much to strangers, particularly those who ask too many questions."*

Martin greeted him warmly the following morning and led him into his spacious office, lined with law books and with stacks of file folders arranged on the credenza behind his desk. Rudberg summarized what he'd learned about the murder of Alonzo Taylor, then turned to the twin reasons for his visit. "The Hampton County sheriff is not investigating Dad's death. They keep telling me they have no leads and no witnesses, but I learned yesterday they never interviewed his next-door neighbor, the man who discovered his body and reported the fire. They resisted an autopsy, and they 'figure' that teenagers set the fire." He used his fingers as quotation marks. "They aren't doing a damned thing to identify his killer."

Martin rested his elbows on his desk and tented his hands, supporting his chin on them. "I'm shocked, truly shocked to find they're less than diligent down there. Welcome to the Deep South."

"How do I make them take this seriously?"

"You can't. Leave it to me. The front door leads nowhere, so we'll try the back."

"Also, what do you know about Judge Searcy?"

"I know I didn't like to try cases before him when he was on the circuit court bench. Extremely conservative. Not a great champion of civil rights...or of anyone's rights, come to think of it. Why do you ask?"

Rudberg told him what they'd learned. "Interesting," Martin said, "but it doesn't necessarily mean anything. I started my career as an assistant state attorney here. There are lots of reasons we declined to pursue a case. I'd think twice before assuming a cause and effect."

"And what does any of this have to do with Dad's death?"

"Perhaps nothing, but take good care of yourself. He's powerful. He could make your life difficult."

Rudberg didn't call in advance. He drove to Waycross and parked in front of J. S. Barstow's home at the same hour as he had six days before. Barstow answered the door, looked him over, and said, "You might have called."

"There've been developments," he said without apology. Barstow motioned him in, looked up and down the street, and closed the door.

"I drove around Hilliard for about ten minutes and pulled to the curb twice before coming to Waycross. I drove the length of town twice before coming to your house. I don't think I was followed."

"They use inexpensive GPS tracking devices nowadays. It's how trucking companies track their fleets. They don't have to follow you."

He described his initial attempt to meet with William Purty the week before in Palatine. "But you have talked with him since. That's why you're here."

Rudberg nodded affirmation, and Barstow emitted a long sigh. "How are you going to use this? Are you just after a story?"

"I'm completing a mission for my father. That's my priority. Everything else is secondary."

"Will you quote me? I don't know whether I can risk this. I—we're vulnerable." When Rudberg wrinkled his features in bewilderment, Barstow added, "I still do some work for the county, enough to qualify Clara for supplemental health insurance. Without it…"

Rudberg nodded. "I'm without coverage myself. I'm no longer a working journalist, so if they went after my source, I'd be on my own."

He and Barstow looked at each other, neither saying a word for a moment. "As I said, I'm not working on a story. This is personal. Let me tell you what I know, then you decide. You said last week you and your partner couldn't make a case so you couldn't bring charges. I think you had more than you're letting on. You were able to place a witness somewhere. Did someone pass the truck after they'd forced Taylor off the road?"

Barstow stroked the fingers of his right hand with those of his left. "You brought a case, and it got shelved," Rudberg said.

"That's most of it." He folded his hands and looked down for a few seconds.

"In Jacksonville, they took a group photo in front of the AME church. All the organizers stood on the front steps, everyone but the photographer. Since he couldn't be in the shot, he switched places with another man, who got behind the camera and took a second photo. I don't know how they intended to assemble the two, and it makes no difference. What's important is that the second guy wasn't familiar with the camera, so the photographer had to show him. He snapped a test photo. In that picture"—and here Barstow thrust out the index fingers of both hands as though they were a pair of six-shooters—"was a shot of a distinctive pickup truck whose left rear quarter panel was emblazoned with a painting of Lee's Confederate battle flag, the Stars and Bars. That was Carl Trickett's truck, and he can be seen at the steering wheel. He'd parked in such a way as to intimidate them. Several of the organizers remembered him."

"So you placed him at the meeting where, presumably, he followed Taylor back to Hampton County?"

"We did, but that's not all. The night that Trickett was arrested, the jailer who came on for the midnight shift heard him bragging to Purty. Whiting and I leaned on him a bit, told him we had other witnesses and if he didn't help us, we'd charge him with obstruction. He admitted he'd heard most of the conversation, enough to corroborate the outline of what Purty told us."

"It sounds like you made the case."

"That's what we thought. But the state attorney who'd reopened the investigation died in the middle of it. Warren Justice was his name. Helluva name, too. Anyway, he dies, and the circuit judge appoints a young attorney to fill out his term. That attorney takes one look at it, says we don't have enough to convict, and shuts it down."

"What did you do?"

Barstow snorted. "Whiting did the only thing he could do in those days. He dropped it. Put everything in a file and walked away. He retired a year later, bitter, disillusioned. I found my career over.

An outcast. Whiting told me I'd do better to move on, so I came here, was hired as a deputy, and eventually was elected sheriff. It was a good move. Nice little town here."

Rudberg thought it over. "There's a reason you didn't come out with this last week. This state attorney, who was he?"

"You've already figured that out or you wouldn't be here. He's now a federal judge, J. Morris Searcy."

---

The sun was setting as Rudberg left the veteran lawman's house, so he checked into a motel in Waycross rather than traveling through rural Georgia at night. He called Aisha and told her Barstow had confirmed that J. Morris Searcy was the state attorney who had closed their case. "He's convinced they had a case, that Searcy's ending the investigation wasn't just a value judgment."

She took a moment to process it. "So the man who shelved the investigation into one of the most infamous civil rights murders in Florida history is now the chief judge of one of the nation's appeals courts. Why would he do that?"

"I don't know, and Barstow didn't either. It doesn't make any sense." He lowered his voice as though the walls could hear. "This is significant. It's not ancient history, a six-decade-old murder covered up thirty years later. It is directly connected to Dad's death. Someone wanted to stop his investigation, too."

"Searcy," she said.

"Maybe, but I asked Barstow if he'd told Dad about Searcy's role. He said no, that he was totally focused on Carl Trickett."

"Maybe he learned it from your guy...?"

"Purty? No, I asked him the same question. Dad was trying to solve Alonzo Taylor's murder. He'd been after it for years. The botched investigation was a side issue."

"But we know it's important," she said. "Searcy figures into this somehow."

"I agree. Let's reconstruct his career. How does he go from a young lawyer who steps into a temporary role as a county prosecutor to a judge on the federal court of appeals? We need to learn everything we can about him. I'll work on that tomorrow. Meanwhile, Barstow said the guard on duty that night was a man named Graham. He didn't recall his first name. Can you track him down?"

"I'll work on it over my lunch hour."

He awoke after 3 A.M. with a confluence of questions. Had Searcy ended the investigation to protect someone? If so, who? And what about his father's death? It didn't seem logical that a respected jurist would order the murder of an aging reporter just because of a decision he'd made early in his career. Who else had Mathew Rudberg threatened when he launched his inquiry?

# AND THEN THERE
# WERE NINE

He was up early, typed notes of his conversation with Barstow, and saved them to the cloud account so Aisha could read them. He left at first light. Driving down US 23, something Barstow had said came back to him. South of Callahan, he detoured onto Florida 115 and drove to the rental agency at the airport.

"Are you turning it in?" the attendant asked.

"No, I'd like to exchange it for—" He thought for a moment. "Please go through this car and see if you can find anything that doesn't belong."

She looked at him with curiosity. "Can you give me a hint?"

"A small electronic device, perhaps beneath the car."

"Like a GPS?"

"Exactly." He entered the waiting room and poured himself a cup of cheap, watery coffee. Overhead, a TV set was tuned to a cable news channel. "That's what he promised when he campaigned," a talking head expounded, "choose from a list of ten highly qualified jurists vetted by the Judicial Society."

"All conservative," his female companion prompted him.

"*Reliably* conservative."

"And then there were nine."

"Yes, the president appointed Justice Yardley after his inauguration last year, so the list was down to nine." The screen was replaced by a graphic displaying the faces of nine white men. The talking head reviewed them quickly, as though he was giving the starting lineup at a NASCAR race. "Until this morning, when the White House announced that a tenth name is in consideration, Judge J. Morris Searcy, an appellate judge..."

Rudberg was on his feet, staring at the screen as the man briefly reviewed Searcy's background. "But all eyes really are on these four, Preston Madigan of Connecticut..."

"Sir. Sir?" Rudberg realized a woman was standing behind him trying to talk to him. Her name tag identified her as the manager. She held a small black object.

"I—I'm sorry. I was paying attention to—what is it?"

"We found this beneath the rear bumper. Do you have any idea how it got there?"

"Yes," he lied. Adjusting his bifocals, he turned the item over, looking for any markings that would suggest it had come from law enforcement. He stuttered as he spoke, his mind only half on the conversation. "My wife is a bit paranoid," he said, vamping. "She's suspicious of me—without cause, I should add. I took a business trip to Waycross yesterday. She said something on the phone last night that told me she knew about it..."

He stopped there since to embellish the explanation would make it seem suspect. He assumed the manager wanted to make sure she wasn't renting the car to a drug dealer.

"There was a similar device on the one you turned in two weeks ago."

He stammered out an excuse. "Ah, yes, that was just before my last Waycross trip." He hoped she would accept the explanation, even decide that his wife's suspicions were well founded. Let her think what she wished. He just wanted transportation—wanted desperately to get out of this office.

His cell phone chimed. "I need to take this."

"This is Lucius Martin's office. He wonders if you could meet him at the Florida Department of Law Enforcement on North Davis Street at two o'clock."

He assured her he'd be there. "Sorry about that," he said to the manager.

"So do you still need to switch cars?"

"Yes, if you don't mind. I'd like something a little bigger." More powerful is what he meant.

---

Lucius was waiting for him in the lobby of the FDLE field office. "You've heard the news?" he asked as he gripped the man's hand.

"Searcy? Yes. I'm appalled. I doubt anything will come of it, but if it does, at least one of our senators will resist it. The man's record on civil rights is appalling."

Before Rudberg could question him further, a tall, muscular black man stepped into the reception area. "Alan, this is Sergeant Barry Wheadon of the FDLE. I've told him what I know of your father's death, but he wants to hear the details from you."

Wheadon led them back through the corridor to his office, charging forward like a cat. Rudberg struggled to keep up, deciding he might have been a wide receiver in college. He gripped Rudberg's hand but did not smile, motioning the two men into government-issue wooden armchairs as he sat at his desk with a notepad before him.

Rudberg waited for him to ask a question, and when he didn't, said, "My father was Mathew Rudberg, the newspaper columnist." No reaction. "He died a month ago in what was originally ruled a drowning. In his retirement, he was looking into the death of a civil rights worker, Alonzo Taylor."

Rudberg paused, waiting for affirmation. "He'd been working on it for years," Rudberg added. "He was obsessed."

Wheadon glanced at Lucius Martin and some unspoken thought passed between them. Rudberg realized he was overselling his father's *bona fides* and felt foolish. *Alonzo Taylor was black, and you're black, and I'm white, but let me show you I'm one of the good whites.*

He rushed on, recounting his decision to ask for a private autopsy, the resistance of the sheriff's office, the subsequent fire, and his conviction that the Hampton County authorities were stonewalling. Through it all, Wheadon said little, posing an occasional question to put specifics to Rudberg's generalities and jotting down a few notes.

Rudberg looked from Sergeant Wheadon to Lucius Martin and back again, hoping for some reaction, but none was forthcoming. "And then there's this," he said, pulling the tracking device from his pocket. "The rental agency found it beneath the rear bumper of my car. They found another one two weeks ago."

He heard Lucius Martin suppress a gasp. Wheadon picked up the object and examined it. "Do you have any idea who placed it there?"

"None." He thought a moment. "I should tell you, this could have political ramifications."

"How so?"

"We've learned that an investigation into Mr. Taylor's death was reopened thirty years ago, but was shelved by a young state attorney." He paused for effect. "Morris Searcy."

Sergeant Wheadon remained impassive.

"Thank you for coming, Mr. Rudberg." That was it? Had he revealed too much or too little?

"Your father may have been poking around in something he shouldn't have," he said. "I'll look into it, but I ask you not to share this with anyone."

"My sister is working with me..."

"She's solid," Martin said.

"No one else, then. Let's keep this off the books for the time being."

Farris Ainsworth had spent two decades as Washington correspondent for the *Oregon Examiner*, before taking the newspaper's buyout offer two years before. Rudberg reached him at his home office, from which he wrote pieces for a political blog. The two had not spoken since Rudberg's termination, and Ainsworth spent several minutes reminiscing and offering his condolences.

"Thanks, Farris, but at the moment I don't need to be condoled, I need information. What's your take on the president adding Morris Searcy to the list of Supreme Court candidates?"

"Hilarious, isn't it?"

"Why hilarious?" Rudberg didn't see anything funny about it.

"He's just there for window dressing. The president loves drama. How many members of the Supreme Court have come from Florida?" Rudberg had no idea. "None. The closest they got was when Nixon named G, Harrold Carswell, and that was a disaster."

Rudberg remembered. The nomination of Carswell, an appellate court judge, came crashing down over racist statements he'd made during a campaign for office two decades before and his high rate of reversals during his service as a district court judge. When he was criticized for being mediocre, a Nebraska senator defended him by saying that even mediocre people were entitled to representation. It didn't help."

"How many have come from the University of Florida Law School?" Ainsworth continued. Even fewer." He laughed at his own joke.

"Judge Madigan has the inside track. He's Yale Law. The president loves that. Catholic, so he's pro-life. You go down the list, and Madigan checks every one of the administration's boxes. Ellsworth from Pennsylvania is also a possibility. He's Harvard Law, also pro-life. You detect a pattern here? But most bets are on Madigan."

"Why even put Searcy on the list?" Rudberg knew the answer but wanted to Ainsworth to confirm it.

"The president's throwing crumbs at the feet of his base, that's all. Besides not having the right curriculum vitae, Searcy's too old. Madigan is forty-six years, so he'll be on the court a long time. They want to remake the court for generations."

Rudberg hung up, feeling better, but not great.

---

"No luck." Aisha arrived late and out of breath. "Leroy Graham died in an automobile accident on May 17, 2002." They would get no corroboration from the guard who had overheard part of the conversation in the Hampton County jail. She dropped a stack of files onto the table in Rudberg's makeshift office. "This changes everything, doesn't it?"

"Because of Searcy, you mean? It does, though I'm not yet certain how." He told her what his Washington contact had said. "Still, Searcy's name is out there now, and it adds another dimension to our investigation."

He listed the questions that had been plaguing him since his meeting with J. S. Barstow. "Was Dad killed because of what he had discovered or because of what he risked discovering? Was that something the direct result of Taylor's murder or the cover-up of the 1988 investigation? Did Searcy end that investigation because he was covering for someone? If so, who?"

"And why is the sheriff's department impeding the investigation into Dad's death?" she added. "Who are they protecting?"

"Carl Trickett told Purty he had an accomplice with him the night they killed Alonzo Taylor, someone who pulled the trigger."

"So long ago," she said, echoing his thought of a moment before. They shared cups of coffee, drowning in their mutual ignorance. "I'm impressed with what you've done here," Aisha said, looking at the diagram he'd created on the bulletin board.

"Thanks. And that reminds me..." He snapped a photo of the

board and uploaded it to their CloudBurst account. "Every note I've taken is on our site, just in case."

"In case...?"

"In case something happens to me," he said. "I'm not being melodramatic. Someone has been tracking my every move over the past few weeks." He told her about the GPS devices found beneath his rental car.

"Alan, that's terrifying. You need protection. You're following your father's trail, and we know what happened to him."

He nodded an acknowledgment. "I'm equally worried about Purty and Barstow. More Barstow, at this point. I took extra precautions when I met with Purty."

They discussed the implications at length, but in the end, all they could do was keep digging. The only concrete information they had was that a young prosecutor, J. Morris Searcy, had ended an investigation into the death of a civil rights worker at the point where investigators had hard leads. They decided to start with him.

Two hours later, they had not only constructed Searcy's biography but charted his rise through the legal profession. "In 1985 he graduates from law school and is admitted to the Florida bar. Four years later he's appointed acting state attorney after the death of Warren Justice. He's twenty-eight years of age."

"Remarkable," Rudberg said. "Three months into his term he drops the investigation."

"That fall he runs for that office and is unopposed."

"There's a lot of that in Hampton County," he added. "Elected without opposition."

"He's appointed to the state circuit court eight years later and is soon elected to that seat. He's appointed a federal judge four years later and joins the appellate court after nine years on the federal bench."

"It's as though the hand of God were pushing him forward."

"Or someone else," she said.

On Sunday afternoon, Grace Stewart prepared dinner at her home—pot roast, mashed potatoes, creamed spinach, and a thick crusted apple pie. "I haven't eaten food this good since I was a little boy," he said and meant it.

She looked down and covered her mouth. "Mathew loved my cooking. He used to sit right where you are and rave about the food."

"He came here often?"

"Every Sunday afternoon. That was our time together." She looked up to include Aisha, her eyes sparkling with tears.

"Your neighbors must have seen him come and go. What did they think?"

"No one around here judges you."

"What I meant is you had to hide your relationship at the paper, but it must have been apparent to your neighbors."

"They knew him, they know me, and they know life is complicated. If Mathew had been anything other than a kind, loving man and devoted father, they might have felt different. But they saw him as a decent person doing good by his family, and that's all that mattered."

They made her sit while they cleared the table and washed dishes. "She likes you," she said. "She has confidence in you. That's quite an accomplishment."

"She senses how much shame I feel about rejecting my father."

"That, of course, but—she doesn't trust most white people." She paused for a moment. "Neither do I."

He started to say something, but she stopped him. "You want to tell me that not all whites are racist, that some are good, kindhearted individuals, etcetera, etcetera. I've encountered more of the other kind. Especially now. It's hard for a white person to gain our trust, and it's easy to lose it."

He took the dish she had been washing and rewashing as she

spoke, ran it under the tap water, and dried it. He didn't know what to say.

---

Rudberg called Searcy's office first thing Monday morning. He and Aisha had debated whether to approach him without having more facts in hand, but with no other living witnesses but Barstow and Purty, neither of whom were willing to go public, they didn't know how they could learn more. Searcy was in the news at the moment, which lent itself to a nonconfrontational approach.

Rudberg navigated a phalanx of assistants and aides until he reached a general factotum. He doubted that every judge had this level of support and suspected that Searcy had called in reinforcements.

He introduced himself as an independent journalist without stating that he was, at the moment, extremely independent and explained that he wanted to interview the judge to get background on his career. The factotum offered to provide anything he needed, so Rudberg tried another tack.

"He knew my late father," he said. "He spoke at his memorial service last month. He was engaging, humorous, entertaining. Readers might like to see a more personal side to him than the image of a staid jurist."

"Let me look into it and get back to you," he said. "How can we reach you?"

Rudberg scribbled questions on a notepad while he waited. If the summons came, it could be immediate. The aide returned his call over the noon hour. "Judge Searcy can make time for you tomorrow afternoon at four if you're available."

"At four? I'll move another appointment," he lied. "This is more important." Which was the truth.

His cell phone screeched at him. "When do you arrive?"

"I'm sorry?"

"When are you coming home?" Stephanie said. "I've had to do everything myself—the tree, the decorations, the presents. I need you here."

"I don't have a firm time yet..."

Silence. Then, "You haven't made reservations, have you? They will be impossible to get now. Everyone travels at Christmas."

"I'll make arrangements as soon as I—"

"Do it now. You've been completely absent, not just physically, but emotionally. This is not a marriage. You can't have one partner devoting herself to work and family while the other relives his childhood without a care in the world."

"I'm interviewing one of the Supreme Court candidates tomorrow."

He made the mistake of taking a breath.

"And you will share that with whom, precisely? You have no position and no interest in finding one."

"Stephanie, I will conduct this interview, which has ramifications you cannot begin to comprehend—"

"Don't patronize me."

"—because you will not listen. When I have completed it, I will take the first available flight and return to our happy home for what I am sure will be—"

"And I don't appreciate your constant sarcasm."

"—a joyous yuletide celebration."

"And it will be. David and Roxanne and Mark and Wendy are coming for dinner Christmas Eve. They're looking forward to seeing you and hearing about all your adventures."

"I always enjoy seeing your friends, Stephanie."</p>

"*Our* friends."

He did as he'd promised, finding a Thursday afternoon flight with a return on New Year's Day.

The federal courthouse was an imposing, multistory glass monolith on North Hogan Street. Rudberg found it more difficult to get through security than at the Senate and House office buildings in Washington, but he made it with time to spare and took the elevator to the seventh floor. The anteroom was, in fact, ant-like, with aides coming and going as though bringing nourishment to the queen.

Rudberg had been given an hour, but as 4:00 passed, his window narrowed, and he became less convinced that he would have the time to implement the velvet glove strategy Lucius Martin had helped him devise. He was not admitted to the *sanctum sanctorum* until 4:20.

Searcy stood to greet him, and Rudberg noticed his slight limp, a product, he now knew, of an injury he'd sustained as a halfback on the Florida Gators team. Rudberg thanked him for speaking at his father's memorial service.

"I was pleased to do it. He was a fine man." He sported a wide, toothy smile that never left his face as he spoke, though Rudberg suspected it was not the visage he donned along with his judicial robe. "Jeremy said you were working independently. Who are you writing for?"

"I'll share it with the AP," he said. Searcy's smile was not as wide, as though he knew he was lying, but he said nothing. Rudberg asked several questions about Searcy's family, education, and what he considered the key cases he'd decided until he thought the man was at ease.

"You began as a prosecutor," Rudberg said.

"I did. State attorney in Hampton County. I was appointed in 1987 and won my first term a year later."

"And from there to circuit court."

"In 1996, yes."

"When you were first appointed state attorney, do you recall the case of Alonzo Taylor?"

"Oh, that was a long time ago, back in the fifties sometime."

"It was 1955, but your predecessor reopened the case in 1987. Do you recall anything about it?"

"Not really." No smile now. "What's your interest after all this time?"

"Dad was looking into it." Searcy nodded and waited. "Two deputies were working the case. They found a witness who'd heard a jailhouse confession." Nothing. "They brought it to you, but say you declined to prosecute."

"If that's true, it's because we didn't have enough evidence to convict. You can't waste the court's time trying cases you know you can't win."

"One of the investigating officers is still alive. He says they had a solid case, photographs of the suspect staking out the church where the victim was meeting, a guard in the jail who overheard the confession—"

"One thing you'll learn if you cover criminal matters for long, cops always think they have a case tied up. Some become emotionally involved, which is always a problem. What excites them doesn't always hold up in court. One person says one thing, another says another. My office only had so much time. There was nothing to it."

"You remember it now. A moment ago you weren't sure."

"Well, you've brought it back. I've handled so many cases over the years. I could look at the record and refresh my memory if I had time. I don't right now. A lot's going on."

"There is no record. The file's been taken."

"Taken or missing? They're not the same. We've tightened up a lot of procedures since the eighties. I'm proud to say I had a lot to do with that once I got on the bench. It's not that they were careless back then, but there are new rules of procedure."

He glanced at his watch. Rudberg knew the game. Stretch out your answers, fill the available space with fluff, then say you've run out of time.

"The suspect was a man named Carl Trickett, but he had an

accomplice—the person who actually pulled the trigger. Did you ever determine who that was?"

"No, I don't believe they did. You'd have to ask the investigating officer. You know," he said, leaning forward, "this was a great tragedy —an injustice—a dark moment for Florida. But it happened a long time ago. It's ancient history."

"Not to his family. His son still thinks about the father he never had." *As am I*, Rudberg thought.

"Well, I'm sorry, but it's five, and I have another appointment." He rose to show that the interview was over.

"Thank you. I guess this case will be a hanging chad in my story."

Searcy closed the distance between them. "First, this happened when I was new to the office, just a young attorney. I made a value judgment based on the available evidence. Prosecutors do this *every day*. You can quote me, *but you won't*. That's the other thing. You don't have a story, because you don't have a newspaper. And you don't have much of a reputation. *Allston v. Oregon Examiner*. It's a well-known case. No one's likely to buy what you're selling."

Rudberg struggled to appear impassive, but Searcy's smirk showed he knew he'd hit his target. Searcy returned to his desk, tugging on the sleeves of his suit coat. That left nothing for Rudberg to do but return his notebook and pen to his laptop bag. He took his time doing it, while Searcy drummed a pencil on his desk. As he closed the office door behind him, Rudberg caught it with the toe of his shoe, turned, opened it, and peered in.

Searcy looked up, bewilderment clouding his face, and replaced the phone in its cradle. Rudberg nodded and eased the door shut. Whoever Searcy was about to call, it wasn't to wish him a happy holiday.

---

"He threatened you?" Aisha said.

"More or less. I lost a libel case several years ago. The story was true, but witnesses changed their stories, records disappeared, and the paper and I were left hanging. It's notorious within the profession and makes me damaged goods."

"So he's saying if you report what we know..."

"He'll say, 'This guy has made things up in the past. He's unreliable. Pay no attention to him.'"

"So what do we do?"

"We do what I should have done in the first place, we look for more evidence, something concrete." He didn't add that he had no idea where to find it. "It'll have to wait until after the holidays, though. I'm flying home Thursday afternoon."

"But you'll be back." He reassured her and ended the call.

What had he expected, that Searcy would admit everything, collapse to the floor and grovel for mercy? It was his own fault; he'd pulled the trigger too soon, succumbing to the pressure of time and his wife's badgering. He wondered why he was flying home. To celebrate Christmas? What was there to celebrate? To make her happy? She was only happy when she was unhappy.

As if reading his mind, Sonja called. "I haven't heard from you in a week. You must be one of these guys who gets what he wants from a girl and then drops her."

He laughed. He was beginning to like this woman. "Usually, but not this time. I've just been busy."

"Your top-secret investigation heating up?"

"Yes, and also cooling down. It's been an interesting week."

She waited, and when nothing more was forthcoming, said, "I'm going to a party Christmas Eve and need a date. Are you available?"

"I'd love to, but duty calls. I'm headed home."

"You're going back to Oregon?" She mispronounced it, hitting the "gon" as though it had departed. "Why?"

"Because my wife wants me to spend Christmas with her."

"And what do you want?" A pause. "You're not fooling anyone. You have this bland façade and think no one can see past it, but you're wrong. Your unhappiness shows in everything you do."

He stood speechless in the middle of his room. What had he said that was so revealing? Or was it what he hadn't said?

"Do what you have to do," she said, "but when you've done it, come back. Merry Christmas."

---

Bad news travels in packs. His phone chimed as he was removing the documents, string, photos, and notes from his whiteboard the following morning.

"J. S. Barstow here." They exchanged pleasantries, but Rudberg could tell from his authoritative manner that this was not a social call. "I'm afraid I misled you last week. Overstated, is more like it. I get angry when I think about this case. I don't like loose ends."

"What are you saying?" Rudberg said, knowing full well what was about to come.

"I've given it a lot of thought, gone over what we had back then and what we didn't. We couldn't have proven that case in court."

"You had"—he put a name to it—"William Purty, who heard Trickett not only confess, but give details only he could have known. You had this guard, Leroy Graham, who overhead the discussion. You placed Trickett at the church—"

"All hearsay and coincidence. Any judge would have thrown it out of court at the preliminary hearing."

"What about Searcy shutting you down? He could have said, 'Look, boys, you don't have enough here. Keep digging.' He didn't."

"Searcy was brand new. He'd never done this before. He had only two assistants as I recall. I'm sure he felt devoting more time to an old murder wasn't worth the time. He made a judgment call. Prosecutors have to do that every day."

*You read your line almost to the letter.* "Mr. Barstow, I have to ask this. Who got to you?"

"No one!" he shouted through the phone. "I'm my own man. Don't use me. Don't quote me. If you refer to me in any way, I'll deny it." He paused for a moment, then his anger dissipated and he made a plea. "You have to leave us out of this."

*Us.* He had no doubt what had happened. Barstow had outlined precisely how they could get to him, and they had.

Rudberg thanked him with less grace than he felt and collapsed into the swivel chair, staring at the whiteboard, now as blank as his case.

---

The receptionist called his room and told him someone was in the lobby to see him. A man, the receptionist said in response to his question. She didn't know who. Rudberg took the stairs down to the first-floor level. An overweight man in a sweat-stained, long-sleeve shirt and tie put an envelope in his hands, bearing the letterhead of a Jacksonville law firm. "You've been served," he said.

Rudberg ran his finger under the back flap of the envelope, unfolded the letter, and read:

Dear Mr. Rudberg:

This CEASE AND DESIST ORDER is to inform you that your actions regarding certain allegations made against the Honorable J. Morris Searcy are intended to harm his reputation and career. You have been informed that they are without merit. You are ORDERED TO STOP any further investigation immediately and to refrain from uttering or publishing any such baseless allegations.

You must send me written confirmation that you will cease such activities. You risk incurring severe legal consequences if you fail to comply with this demand.

To ensure compliance with this letter, and to halt any legal action we may take against you, I require you to sign the attached form and mail it back within 10 days of your receipt of this letter. Failure to do so will act as evidence of your infringement upon our legal rights, and we will immediately seek legal avenues to remedy the situation.

Sincerely,

George T. Randolph, Esq.

---

When he'd arrived in Florida five weeks before, he had three months' severance pay. He'd spent two-thirds of it and had little to show for it. It was going to be at least two months before the probate court finalized Mathew's estate, and probably longer. He had managed to prove that his father's death was not an accident, but the resolution of that mystery was in the hands of the FDLE agent. He lacked the resources to do it himself.

As for his father's quest to resolve Alonzo Taylor's slaying, he was at a dead end. He knew who had murdered Taylor—or at least one of the two—but that suspect was now dead, and there was no way to confirm it. He had no proof, no witnesses, and no path forward.

As dispiriting as that was, he was facing disparagement and humiliation at home. He was tempted to cancel his flight and spend the week with Sonja, but he had nothing else to stay for. The clock radio in his room poured out an a cappella rendition of *In the Bleak Midwinter*—someone's cruel idea of a joke. He turned it off.

Checking his email, he found a message sent half an hour before. "We are seeking a candidate for an important editorial position. You come highly recommended by your former colleagues. Please call me to discuss this at your earliest opportunity."

Here was good news. He had never heard of Monford Publishing Company or its managing editor, Philip Grimley, but called without Googling either name.

Grimley asked if he knew the company, and Rudberg admitted he did not. *Some reporter*, Stephanie had called him, and because he had not taken the time to research the firm, he appeared too anxious. Grimley was reassuring. "I'm not surprised. We're a chain of small, local dailies spread through Kansas, Oklahoma, and Texas. We're based in Fort Worth, but all our papers serve rural communities."

He described the job, which seemed to be a roving columnist of some sort, making connections between diverse Midwestern locations. "You know how this business is nowadays. We can't afford to fill every column inch of a small-town newspaper with locally produced content, and readers don't turn to us for what they can get from cable news. We need regional content that connects at the local level. I know this sounds vague, but that's because it is. I'm looking for someone who can translate our business need into good editorial content. Do you want to talk to us about it?"

He did. It might be an interesting job that would carry him through to retirement. At worst, it was a prospect to dangle before his wife's judgmental friends at dinner Sunday night. And someone wanted him.

---

"What are you saying?" Aisha asked.

"We have nothing." He stood in her front room, his roll of accumulated notes and documents held in his arms like an infant. "We have no sources, no evidence, and he's threatening me with a lawsuit."

"Searcy can't win," she said. "He's a public figure. He's trying to intimidate you."

Rudberg's Portland attorney had told him the same thing, but with a catch. "He can't win, but he can pull me into court and cost me legal fees I can't afford. All that and dredging up the libel case at a time when I'm trying to find work. That's how the game is played."

"He won't move against you as long as he's a candidate for the Supreme Court. He'd end up publicizing the suspicions about how he handled the Taylor investigation."

"But *if* we say something publicly, and *if* he loses the nomination over it..."

"He won't be nominated. That's what you said."

"And William Purty is missing. I've been calling him ever since I got off the phone with Barstow. We have nothing," he said, repeating his original argument.

"So you're dropping us." Her arms were folded, her eyes flashing. Rudberg felt small and defenseless in the face of her mounting rage. "How can you run out on us at a time like this? You promised!"

"I'm not dropping you. I simply don't see a way forward right now. And I must find work. I'm interviewing for a job in Texas. I fly there on January 2. Then, we'll see where we are."

"We'll see always means no," she said. Just what his sister said. A gift from their father?

He'd never forget the look on her face, a mix of disappointment and anger.

## DOGS USE HYDRANTS

O ver breakfast on his first day home, Rudberg tried to brief his wife on the events of the past few weeks, but she changed the subject, launching into a diatribe against a Vietnamese factory owner. Stephanie gave no details—she never did—but grumbled that she would have to fly there after the holidays to straighten him out.

He got the message. *If you think you have problems, you should hear what I'm up against.* For the next two days, he kept out of the way, shopping for a present for her, battling crowds at the local grocery store as he planned the Christmas Eve dinner, and doing odd jobs around the house.

He arrived home on Saturday afternoon to find a truck parked out front and two workers carrying cardboard boxes up the steps. They had erected a tall tree in the living room and were unpacking what appeared to be brightly colored shoes. "What is all this?" he asked.

"It's my Christmas tree. I bought it at the World of Trees Auction."

"Why the shoes?"

She sighed. "You remember the auction. I made you go last year. Companies sponsor trees, which are decorated to reflect their businesses. Patrons buy tickets, have dinner and drinks, then bid on the trees. The money goes to charity, and everyone has a good time."

"But shoes on a Christmas tree?"

"Victor Apparel makes shoes. I thought you knew that." He ignored her sarcasm. She'd outbid everyone at her table on the company tree. It was as simple as that. How much had she spent? Rudberg knew not to ask. It was her money, she'd imply.

On Sunday he arose early, salting the beef tenderloin, chopping parsley, scallions, and cornichons for the sauce, roasting garlic for the mashed potatoes, and peeling asparagus stalks. He selected four of the best bottles of Oregon pinot noir from their cellar. Stephanie flitted from one concern to the next, bossing their maid, whom she'd coerced into working on Christmas Eve—a Sunday, no less—trying on different outfits, and fussing with the hair she'd paid over two hundred dollars to have done the day before. He stayed busy so as not to intersect her orbit.

Mark and Wendy Fisher arrived first, Mark bearing a cardboard carrier with four bottles of wine. "You're doing beef tenderloin again? You don't want pinot noir with that. I brought cabernet, Alcorn Heights, 2014. The finest." He was one of Portland's leading neurologists and let no one forget it. "I hope you have horseradish sauce instead of that parsley thing." He made for the living room while Rudberg kept his refuge in the kitchen.

"Beautiful tree," he said. "It looks even better than it did in the hall. Wendy, I told you about the tree..."

But Wendy had peeled off and joined Rudberg in the kitchen. "How are you doing, Alan?"

"Fine. Thanks for asking. I've been in Florida..."

David and Roxanne Galloway were fashionably late, which was just fine with Rudberg. David had something to do with insurance, exactly what Rudberg had never divined. He removed the tenderloin from the oven and let it sit out. "Shouldn't it be served warm?" Stephanie asked.

"Room temperature," he said. *Same as last year. Same as every year.*

Mark the Neurologist had opened two bottles of cabernet and returned Rudberg's unopened bottles to the kitchen. Rudberg opened one and returned it to the dining room along with a bottle of horseradish. Seconds later, Stephanie marched into the kitchen bearing the container. "You are *not* putting this on the table."

"Mark wants it."

"Put it in a dish and add sour cream to it."

"I'll let you attend to that."

"Where's the sour cream? What's gotten into you?"

Rudberg dressed the serving platters and brought everything to the table. Mark poured the cabernet. Rudberg set his aside and poured a glass of pinot.

Stephanie chattered about the tree. "My house is just made for Christmas. When I bought it, Alan couldn't understand why I wanted that high ceiling in front of the bay window. I told him, the tree will go there."

After several minutes of desultory conversation, Mark asked, "How was Florida?"

"Interesting, challenging, puzzling. I went there thinking my father had drowned. It turns out he was murdered."

There was a collective gasp around the table, but Stephanie said, "Now, you don't really believe that."

"I do, and so does the Florida Department of Law Enforcement. We—"

"I don't think this is table conversation," she said.

"But it's fascinating. Tell us about it," Wendy said.

"More wine anyone? Alan, pour more wine." He did as he was told.

"I hear you're going into politics," Mark the Neurologist said.

Rudberg held the bottle in midair, staring at Mark over his glasses. "No, who told you that?"

"It's just a joke." He tried a laugh on for size. "Didn't Frank Sherman suggest you run for office?"

"Alan has a job offer," Stephanie interjected.

"Oh," Mark the Neurologist said. "It's in Dallas, isn't it?"

"The publishing company is in Fort Worth. I'm not sure where I'd be based. *If* I take it," he added.

"Of course, *I* wouldn't be moving there. We'd be a bicoastal couple." Stephanie chuckled, ignoring the inaccuracy.

Rudberg returned to the kitchen, bringing his wineglass, which he'd overfilled. He restocked the serving platters, taking his time while the conversation continued without him. He could hear David and Mark debate Portland's homeless problem. "They should put them on buses and send them back to Arizona," David said.

Rudberg reentered the dining room with more food. "They could camp out in the Rose Garden," he said. "It doesn't get much use in the winter." The Rose Garden was two blocks from where they were sitting. They ignored his provocation. He returned to the kitchen for his glass.

When he returned, the conversation had turned a corner. "All lives matter," David said. "It's not just black lives. All lives matter."

"But black lives do matter," Rudberg said.

David looked at him as though seeing him for the first time. "But it's not just black lives. All lives matter."

"To say 'Black lives matter' is not to suggest that those of others do not. It's only black lives that are being systematically threatened at the moment," he said. "No, not just at the moment. For as long as I can remember. That's what my father was after. It's why he was killed. He was trying to solve the murder of a black man back in the fifties whose only offense, as far as I can determine, was trying to help his fellow African Americans register to vote. We were picking up his investigation."

"Who's we?" Stephanie asked.

Rudberg studied her for a moment, regarding her as he would an amoeba under a microscope. "My sister."

"I thought she went back to Austin."

"I have another sister. Her name is Aisha. I didn't know of her existence until a few weeks ago. I've enjoyed getting to know her. I wish she were here now."

The table went silent. Mark and Stephanie exchanged a glance while the other three looked down at their plates.

David Galloway broke the silence. "Anyway, I just don't know what they want."

---

"You were horrid tonight." When he didn't respond, Stephanie added, "You had too much to drink."

"Not nearly enough."

"What is wrong with you?"

"I dislike those people. Mark is an arrogant ass. David's a racist. Roxanne is plastic, and I don't just mean her chest. Wendy's okay. I'll make an exception for her. She's the only person at that table who expresses interest in anything beyond her own little world."

"They are my friends, and I will thank you to treat them with respect."

"Your friends in your house. I prefer never having to interact with them again."

"David and Wendy are having their big New Year's Eve party. Perhaps I should leave you here."

"That suits me," he said, "because *I just don't know what they want.*"

---

He called Aisha the next morning, but got no answer. It was early afternoon there. He hung up and thought about it. She might be genuinely busy or just unwilling to speak with him. He called again and waited for the tone at the end of her voicemail message.

"This is Alan. I'm calling to wish you a Merry Christmas. And to apologize. I know I've let you down. I'm under a lot of pressure here at home. If I'd stayed in Jacksonville, I don't know what we'd do next. I'm out of ideas."

He took a deep breath before plunging on. "We had guests for dinner last night. It was terrible. Something off about the whole evening. I don't know what. I told them about you and said that I miss you. I do. I wish I were with you and your mother today instead of—"

Another pause while he searched for a way to conclude the conversation. "If I think of something, I'll call. Please don't lose faith. I'm still here. I'm just...lost."

He dialed William Purty's number for the second time since he'd left Florida, but got no answer. His worry over the man's welfare was nearing panic, but there wasn't a thing he could do about it from a continent away.

He and Stephanie exchanged presents. She'd bought him a new wallet, which he needed. He'd bought her a jacket that he found stylish. She asked if he still had a gift receipt. They had little to say to each other until midafternoon when she broke the silence.

"Tell me about this sister of yours—half sister, I guess." He told her about Mathew and Grace and about Aisha. "They're black?" she said.

"Yes. That's the whole point. That's why they could never marry, at least not while they both worked at the paper."

Her face conveyed no emotion. He described his growing sense that his mother had betrayed him and robbed him of his father.

"No wonder you were so cranky," she said.

"That wasn't what bothered me. It started the minute Mark walked in and started changing the wine and the menu. He acted like he owned the place."

"He was trying to help."

"And why did you tell him Sherman suggested I go into politics?"

"So what? That's what he suggested."

"He was laughing at me, or didn't you notice?" She turned her head away, hiding whatever reaction she had. "I'm going out to the coast for a couple of days."

"What for?"

"To think."

"Haven't you thought enough?" It was his turn to respond with silence. "You're not leaving today. It's Christmas, and it's freezing."

"It can't be any colder there."

---

Though plows had shoved aside the snow over the Coastal Range, black ice covered those stretches of US 26 shielded from sunlight by the Douglas firs towering over either side. Rudberg drove cautiously, relieved when he descended from the pass and headed north on Highway 101 as darkness fell.

Past Seaside, he turned at the traffic light into Gearhart, a small residential community with only a restaurant and grocery store at its crossroads. Alan and Stephanie had purchased their two-bedroom, oceanfront condominium during the real estate bust. It was now worth twice what they'd paid for it.

He dropped his suitcase and computer at the entrance and opened the drapes to see the Pacific Ocean roaring and frothing across the line of dunes. He placed leftovers from last night's meal in the refrigerator where a half carton of eggs and jars of condiments from previous visits rested, along with a half-empty bottle of wine that had presumably gone to vinegar. He wouldn't need anything tonight. He'd had quite enough to last the weekend, thank you.

He didn't mind the solitude, even on Christmas Day. If anything, he felt more comfortable being on his own, thinking his own thoughts without having to parry Stephanie's verbal thrusts.

Where had their relationship gone sour? He couldn't pinpoint one date or incident. As she had risen in her company, she had begun to hide things from him—not maliciously, but because anything she told him about Victor Apparel could eventually fit into a story the

*Examiner* was doing on Portland's largest private employer. By the same token, he had never shared details of his work with her. It was in the nature of his job and, he had to admit, his personality to keep the stories he was working on to himself. Just like his father, he realized.

Slowly, inexorably, they had drifted apart—she with her business secrets and circle of friends made through various public events for the company, he with his newspaper colleagues and circle of sources, all of whom were now gone.

Everything around him was washing away like the eroding shoreline. He had no job, his marriage was empty, and the ties that had bound him to his mother and sister for more than a half century were frayed. Even the cause to which he'd devoted himself for the past month-and-a-half seemed lost, along with the relationship he had formed with his new sister.

Monford Publishing offered him not just a new job, but a new beginning. He opened his notebook computer to research the company. It owned twenty-three small newspapers scattered across the lower Midwest. None had a circulation exceeding 10,000. He couldn't imagine how they kept going, except that in many communities they were the only sources of local news, the local radio stations having been absorbed by media conglomerates that spat out music content originating from some disinterested, disconnected studio in God-knows-where.

All Monford's newspapers published web editions, but the sites had a standardized look, suggesting that they were produced at some centralized facility. The content gave little indication of what the chain would need from him. *Lions Park Improvements, Free Homebuyer Workshop,* and his favorite, *Midget Wrestling Comes to Brimfield.* Really?

The following morning he began searching larger newspapers in the region, making lists of topics that seemed to have universality. Most were related to agriculture, many concerning public policy. Opioids were a frequent topic, and both Oklahoma and

Texas were dealing with the consequences of constricted public funding. The parsimonious streak in state legislatures affected education, law enforcement, infrastructure, and public health, which, in turn, exacerbated the opioid epidemic. He made notes of this and posed questions. How free would he be to make these connections in print? He found several other themes he could introduce into his interview the following week, but he couldn't imagine that these newspapers had not dealt with them extensively.

The weather was just above freezing, but he bundled up and walked the beach. Logs and detritus formed a dark line against the dunes, the residue of one or more winter storms that had already battered the coast. He trudged on, a solitary figure leaning against the wind, shielding his eyes against the glare and blowing sand.

When he returned an hour later, shivering but invigorated, he knew no more than when he'd left. What did Monford Publishing want, and why did they want him to do it? It made no sense.

---

Henry Parker heard them before he saw them. With no other cars on the narrow dirt road at that hour, it was hard not to. Two Chevy Tahoes pulled into the lot next door. He couldn't see who got out, but he heard their voices. Parker would ordinarily walk out to his back deck and cross the retaining wall to investigate, but something told him to stay put this morning. Nothing good would come from getting involved.

For nearly a quarter hour, he saw nothing, but heard the low rumble of conversation. Then, from his living room window, he saw two black-clad figures enter the water wearing oxygen tanks. He watched them enter the water, knowing why were there. It was raining and cool, and he couldn't imagine how they could stand it.

He lost interest after a while and turned on his television to find something to watch. He made himself a sandwich and opened a beer, noticing as he did so that he was nearly out. He'd have to do something about that.

A knock at the front door interrupted him. The uniformed man standing there was black. He wore a broad hat and a black raincoat from which water cascaded in rivulets. He introduced himself as Sergeant Wheadon from the Florida Department of Law Enforcement. He showed his ID and asked to come in. Parker stood aside, and the man entered, carefully doffing his hat and raincoat and hanging them on a peg near the door.

"We're investigating the death of your neighbor, Mathew Rudberg. I understand you knew him."

"Not well, but I'd seen him around," Parker said.

"Didn't he come over to watch football on occasion?"

"Well, yes. What I mean is, he didn't tell me anything about his business. He'd just moved here when it happened."

"I see." The detective looked at him for a moment without any expression. It made Parker uncomfortable.

"He was a nice man," he said. "It's too bad what happened to him."

"And what do you think happened to him?"

"When I found his body, I thought he'd drowned. But then I heard maybe not. I don't know. I didn't see anything."

"What made you look for him? The dock was torn up by the flood, there was debris everywhere—still is." Wheadon looked at him, taking in his weight. "It couldn't have been easy picking your way through all that."

"He was supposed to come over and watch a game with me. When he didn't show, I went looking for him." He looked at Wheadon and, getting no response, added, "I thought something might have happened to him, that I should check on him. He would've done the same for me."

"You could have called."

Parker shifted uncomfortably. "He didn't answer the phone?"

"Is that a question?"

"I can't remember if I called him or not, but I could have, and if he didn't answer, I might have decided to go looking for him."

Again, the dispassionate stare, which Parker felt menacing.

"Your window looks out over the dock. You've been watching our divers. It was Saturday evening, the weather was good, you were home. Are you sure you didn't see anything?"

Parker didn't speak, looking around the room for help.

"You wouldn't want to impede our investigation. You'd better tell me what happened."

Parker buckled. "There were two of them," he began.

---

Rudberg awoke certain that he was about to vomit. He bolted for the bathroom, kneeled in front of the commode, and waited. Nothing came, no acidic taste in his mouth, no heaving in his stomach.

He relaxed and reclined against the wall.

It was a dream. A bad dream. A dream so fresh and vivid he could recall every detail.

*He's at a baseball game, the Jacksonville Suns at Wolfson Park. It is late afternoon and shadows creep across the field. He is sitting in a lower tier of the grandstand beneath the sheltering roof, midway between third base and home plate.*

*His mother is sitting alongside him, but his sister isn't there. He doesn't know why. Perhaps she is too young.*

*A man sits to his left. He keeps up a constant banter, explaining what is happening, why the infield has moved toward the plate, why the coach at third base keeps talking to the runner.*

*The man keeps buying food, first popcorn, then a watery cola. A vendor waddles up the aisle balancing a rectangular disk that holds paper cones filled with pink froth. The man buys him a cotton candy without asking.*

*He gets sick and throws up. The man hustles him up the stairs and into the bathroom.*

It was real. They had to leave the ballpark. His mother was angry not at him, but at the man who, he now recalled, was his uncle. He tried to recall his name.

Rudberg made coffee, threw on a sweatshirt, and sat on the deck, watching as the sun rose over the Coastal Range and bathed the clouds floating over the ocean in gold.

What was he doing here? What was he doing with his life?

---

Henry Parker sat in the interrogation room shivering. The air conditioner vent was aimed squarely at his back, and no amount of shifting or repositioning his chair got him out of the blast. He rubbed his eyes. He had been sitting there for nearly an hour, first going over his story as the sergeant approached it from every angle, now staring at a computer screen as images of scruffy-looking men paraded across it. One had begun to look much like the next.

"Do you need a break?" Wheadon asked. It was the first kind word he'd spoken to him.

"No, let's get this over. How many more are there?"

Wheadon said nothing since there was really no good answer. There were dozens, hundreds, thousands even, until they got to the right one. He clicked the mouse advancing to the next photo, then another, two more, four more. With each, Parker shook his head, sometimes muttering, "Nope."

Suddenly he paused, looked closely at the screen, first the front view, then the side view. "That's him," he said.

"You're certain."

"That's the guy. He dumped Mathew's body in the water, then came by two days later."

Wheadon asked him to repeat what the man had said. "Like I explained, he just thanked me for reporting the drowning and asked if I'd seen anything."

"Was he a police officer?"

"I thought so at first."

"Did he show you an ID?"

"No, he didn't come right out and say he was a cop. He just tried to act all official-like. But he wasn't. He didn't come across as professional."

"Did he threaten you?"

"Not in so many words, but he just gave the impression, you know, that anything I saw I was to keep to myself. Of course, back then, everyone thought it was a drowning."

"But if you'd come forward then..." Wheadon said. He didn't have to finish the thought.

———————

It was Rudberg's last day at the coast, and he had run out of inspiration. He drove north to Astoria and walked the length of the river trail, watching pilot boats guide container ships up the Columbia River to Portland's Swan Island. He had a late lunch of razor clams at a restaurant perched on a pier over the river, drove to the top of Coxcomb Hill, climbed the Astoria Column.

It had started to rain, hiding the view of the Oregon coast and Saddle Mountain to the south. To the north, the Astoria-Megler Bridge disappeared in rain and fog as it crossed to Washington State.

It was late afternoon when he returned to the condominium. He changed out of his wet clothes and called Aisha. There was no answer. It wasn't like her. She was avoiding him. He opened his computer and began typing a message to her, then thought about it and got an idea.

He opened his father's email account and composed the message anew. If she received a message from Mathew's account, she was certain to open it out of curiosity. As he worked, email messages began appearing in the left panel.

He stopped writing and began paging through them. There was a lot of spam. He remembered a technician from the *Examiner* establishing a new email account one day and showing him how these unwanted messages began appearing within minutes. He began deleting them, then gave up.

Rudberg paged back through December and the last two weeks of November, beginning to pay more attention as he passed the date of his father's death. He found messages to Grace and Aisha, read two, found them to be of a personal nature, and ignored the rest, not wanting to pry.

Several emails were confirmations of accounts Mathew had opened at online services and the local library. That made sense. His father had been doing research.

He paused at one from an account listed as *ecannon*. The name seemed familiar. The subject line read "Dad's recap."

On the phone, I told you Dad once wrote a summary of his investigation. I found it last night and scanned it. It's hard to read because the typing has faded, but it gets the point across. It doesn't come through in his writing, because he had a just-the-facts approach, but I can tell he was angry. I hope this helps. Elizabeth.

Elizabeth Cannon. It was one of the names from Mathew Rudberg's calendar that Aisha had been unable to identify. He opened the attached file.

It was a straightforward account of the 1988 investigation into the death of Alonzo Taylor, written in the dry, unmodified style of a professional investigator. Rudberg scrolled to the end and found a scrawled signature and a date. "William Whiting," it read, "July 18, 1999." J. S. Barstow's senior partner in the investigation, the man to whom he had deferred when discussing the case.

Rudberg read the account. It began when the state attorney appointed them to the case in late 1987, detailing the steps they had taken and witnesses they had identified. Up to a point, it added nothing Barstow had not already told him. Then he reached the last few paragraphs.

Before he died, Mr. Justice and I agreed we lacked sufficient evidence to bring a case against Carl Trickett. We questioned him twice. Confronted by the photograph taken in Jacksonville, he admitted being present but claimed he was merely "hassling" the civil rights workers. He denied any knowledge of or involvement in the murder of Alonzo Taylor.

Mr. Justice nevertheless agreed to bring charges against him. Our hope was that in so doing we could pressure him to confess and identify his confederate. Whenever we asked who had been with him on that day, Trickett had grown nervous. He was eager to protect him.

Mr. Justice died before we could execute the plan. We had to postpone it until he was replaced. Shortly after Mr. Searcy was appointed, I met with him and presented a history of our investigation, including our plan to charge Trickett.

Mr. Searcy refused. I made several attempts to change his mind over the course of the next few weeks, but he was adamant. He finally ordered me to drop the case and said he did not want to hear of it again.

My next several months were made very difficult for me. I was no longer assigned important cases. Others in the department avoided me. I had my thirty years of service and left the sheriff's office ten months later.

I believe that I was ostracized due to my investigation of Alonzo Taylor's death and that Mr. Searcy was responsible for this treatment.

Rudberg swore to himself. He stared out at the ocean for several minutes, then returned to the dining room table and composed a message to Aisha and to Lucius Martin using his father's email account. Under the subject "READ THIS," he wrote an explanation of what he'd found. He ended it by writing, "I confronted Searcy too soon." He attached the file and sent it.

He took the half-empty bottle of wine from the refrigerator, sniffed it, and poured himself a glass. It wasn't bad, not a bad way to celebrate a good day's work.

---

Rudberg was up early Friday morning and threw his laundry into the washing machine. He made himself breakfast and called the housekeeping staff to give the place a thorough cleaning and change the bedding.

He checked email and found a note from Lucius Martin to call him. There was nothing from Aisha on either his email account or his father's.

"You made quite a discovery yesterday," Martin said. "It's a damning indictment of Searcy. I'm just not sure what to do with it."

Rudberg agreed. "He has his defense all mapped out: he was new to the job, faced competing priorities for prosecutorial resources, the case against Trickett wasn't solid. It's still a case of one man's word against another's. Before we do anything, we need to check with this Elizabeth Cannon to make certain she is his daughter and that the document is genuine."

"Establish the chain of custody," Martin said, "and see if she'll give us the original. You'll do that?"

Rudberg hesitated.

"Alan, you need to return. The president's going to appoint his nominee early next week. Searcy is still in the mix. If he's named—"

"What are his chances?"

"No one's mentioning him. They're all focused on the guys from the Second and Third Circuit Courts. Still, we can't ignore him."

"Even if the president nominates someone else, he's a judge on the federal court of appeals," Rudberg said. "Given what we know, he doesn't belong there."

"So you'll return?"

"Lucius, I have a job interview in Fort Worth on Tuesday. I'm running out of money and have to find work. And things here—my marriage is not good. I just don't know that I can do that."

"Aisha is upset."

"She's angry, I know."

"She's hurt. She thought you were different."

"What do you mean? I *am* different."

He sighed. "You cannot begin to understand how African Americans view white people. We've seen folks like you smile to our faces and stab us once we walk away. We've seen sunshine friends turn their backs when storm clouds gather. Trust takes a lifetime to build and a single incident to destroy. I don't know if you can ever win hers back—or Grace's."

When Rudberg didn't reply, he added, "You owe it to your father's memory."

"I'll think about it," he said, but promised nothing more. He hung up disheartened. He dressed to take a last walk on the beach, needing one more chance to clear his head.

Before leaving, he began to transfer his washing to the dryer. He was surprised to find a small pile of clothing in the drum. He removed the items and sorted through them, carried them into the bedroom and began to fold them, examining each item in turn.

His hands shook. He sat down on the bed and thought for a moment, returned to the kitchen, opened the garbage bin, stared into it, removed an item, stared at it. He put his wet clothing in the dryer and left for his walk, sorting through memories of the last few days—of a Christmas tree and abundant wine and scattered conversation. On his return, he checked with housekeeping and with the front desk to be certain of his facts.

Satisfied, but dissatisfied, he packed his own things and made a small package of the clothing he'd discovered in the dryer. He left the condominium and the coast, not certain whether he would see either again.

Mark and Wendy Fisher owned a sprawling house on the shore of Oswego Lake. Their driveway was full, and cars lined the opposite side of Lakeshore Drive. Rudberg let Stephanie off at the driveway and parked a block away, carrying a wrapped present with him into the house.

The party was underway. Loud voices competed with louder music, making it impossible for anyone to hear the front doorbell. He let himself in and handed his coat to a member of the catering crew, stashing the package in the hall closet.

"You'll watch what you drink?" Stephanie said. "You're driving, and we don't want a repeat of last weekend."

"I'm not having a thing," Rudberg said. He had stopped trying to convince her that his anger on Christmas Eve had little to do with three glasses of wine.

They drifted among old friends, acquaintances, and people they'd never met. A former colleague from the newspaper, herself cashiered, asked Rudberg how he was doing. He lied to her and suspected she knew it.

Stephanie had drifted off somewhere, searching for a circle of her own friends to impress. Rudberg drifted onto the rear deck, which ran the length of the house, and looked out at the lights from homes across the lake.

"You'd best come in before you freeze." Wendy Fisher joined him, carrying a glass of champagne. "Can I get you something?"

"No, I'm driving, and I'm fine."

"Are you?" she said.

"I want to apologize for Christmas Eve. I know I seemed a bit—" He searched for the right word.

"No need. You weren't the problem. Everyone else was playing little games. You said what was on your mind. We need more of that. I meant, how are you doing—you, yourself. Beaten and bruised, but still fighting?"

"Still fighting," he agreed. They moved into the kitchen and sat in the breakfast alcove, disregarding the bustle of caterers just a few feet away. He filled in the details of his job offer. "I don't know much about it, but I'm heading to Fort Worth tomorrow to find out."

She wished him good luck, and he knew that she meant it.

"It's a busy time, isn't it?" he said. "No lull over the holidays."

"It's been worse this year. He's had two weekend trips." She looked away, tears in her eyes, and he became convinced that she had sought him out, was hiding from the dozens of her guests mingling, socializing, flirting, and sharing the joy of their own self-importance just rooms away.

"You're a special person, Wendy. Mark is lucky to have you."

She continued to stare at the wall. Tears cascaded down her cheeks. She reached out and grasped his hand. "I'm sorry. I'm being maudlin."

"It's the season," he said. "Happy New Year, and all that."

A guest staggered through the kitchen looking for something stronger than wine and champagne. "What are you two up to?" he said.

"Move along," Rudberg said. "There's nothing to see here."

He mingled and socialized with the best of them for over an hour, grazing at a table filled with cheeses, meats, seafood, and desserts, sipping bottled water, and wondering at the sheer cost of it all. At 11:30 he found Mark and Stephanie in a small semicircle of mutual friends. "Do you have a minute?" he said. "I have something for you."

Rudberg took the package from the coat closet and led Mark upstairs into one of the bedrooms. Stephanie, curious, followed behind.

"It's a little something I picked up for you at the coast," he said.

He stood back while Mark unwrapped it. "U-dub," Mark said, as he spotted the University of Washington logo on the sweatshirt. "How thought—what's this?"

"It looks like underwear to me. I found it in the dryer at our condo."

He looked at Rudberg, then glanced at Stephanie, who stared at the floor. "Stephanie was nice enough to let me use your place."

"Oh, she was very thoughtful," Rudberg said. "She drove all the way to the coast so she could ask the front desk to have housekeeping clean up—not once, but twice—two weekends ago and the weekend after Thanksgiving. So accommodating."

Mark again turned to Stephanie for help, but she had become fascinated with her shoes. "Don't tell Wendy. Please."

"I would never hurt her," Rudberg said. "She's the only decent person in our little crowd. But she knows. She may not know with whom, but she knows. And how could she miss it? You've been dropping little hints ever since I returned. '*The tree looks better here than at the auction. I hear you're going into politics. It's in Dallas, isn't it?*'" Rudberg gave a bad imitation of Fisher's pompous tone. "Your clothes in the dryer. A half bottle of Alcorn Heights in the refrigerator."

The room was silent. "Dogs do that on hydrants," Rudberg said. "People tend to be more circumspect."

# PART TWO

## JANUARY-FEBRUARY, 2018

# REMEMBERING UNCLE CHARLIE

F ort Worth sprawled in the winter sunlight, both larger and more modern than he remembered. It retained its self-image as the nation's largest cow town. Tin-roofed barbecue pits with oilcloth-covered picnic tables thrived in the shadow of steel and glass towers bearing the names of energy companies.

Monford Publishing Company occupied a corner of one of these buildings on a lower floor—a low-rent operation in a high-rent location. As he entered the small, sunlit lobby, Rudberg was confronted by a large oil painting of the company's founder, "Colonel Bob" Monford, flanked by portraits of the US president and vice-president, images incongruous in the lobby of a news organization.

"We're proud of our nation and its leaders," Grimley said as he saw Rudberg glancing at the photographs. He was a well-built man in his midthirties, short blond hair parted and shellacked, his skin toasted to a permanent crimson by hours spent on the golf course.

"I am too," Rudberg responded, "to the nation and its institutions."

Grimley led him through the three rooms that constituted Monford's headquarters, most of which seemed devoted to sales and accounting. He spoke in clipped tones about outsourced web operations, centralized advertising sales, and cost-containment.

"The small, local daily is in decline," he said, "some would say dying. We are not. Monford is a sustainable business model that allows local businesses access to their customers. We have nearly a dozen outlets in three states and constantly add new properties. We buy small newspapers in thriving Midwestern communities at fire-sale prices, impose our business model, and make them profitable."

He led Rudberg into his office, a modest, almost spartan workspace with a desk, file cabinets against a wall, and a small table surrounded by four chairs. There were no bookshelves and none of the framed images of notable front pages so typical in the publishing business. "We're privately held," he said, "giving us the freedom to do business as we please."

"Impressive," Rudberg said, though he was losing his enthusiasm with every sentence. "Where do I fit in?"

"As I explained when we talked, I'm looking for someone who can provide engaging, but generalized content to our readers. Pieces based on regional themes that have local appeal."

Rudberg outlined some themes he'd researched, looking for a reaction. "That sounds fine," Grimley said, though he didn't seem that interested.

"Why is basketball so big in Kansas?"

"I don't know," Rudberg said.

"Neither do I, but wouldn't our readers like to find out? It's huge."

"Why me? That doesn't sound like anything I've ever written, not that I can't. I can write about anything."

"You come highly recommended. You have a great reputation among your colleagues. Just the sort of person we're looking for."

"And Allston?" Rudberg said.

"I'm sorry, but who's that?"

"A series I once did. Many people know of it."

"Hmm. So what do you think? Are we the kind of company you'd like to work for?"

"Can you give me some details? What's the salary? Where would I be based?"

"You could work here in Fort Worth or perhaps in Wichita. It's right at the seam between the agricultural and petrochemical Midwest. Have you been there?"

"It has a sailboat," Rudberg replied. "A big boat that won the America's Cup, only it's on dry land along the river." He had nothing else to offer about Wichita. Grimley appeared not to have listened.

Rudberg pressed him to provide more specifics about the position, but Grimley repeated his bare outline, adding, "We're looking to you to define the position. You have plenty to work with. It's a big region, and we're constantly expanding." Shifting gears, he said, "Are you working on anything else right now?"

"No."

"No stories you have in development?"

"None to speak of. Just the ideas I outlined."

Grimley cupped his hands and looked at him. "Well, that's good. We've drafted a contract for your consideration. Look at it and sign it if you think you'd be a good fit."

He leaned across his desk. "*We* think you'd be an excellent addition to the Monford family. You have just the skills we're looking for. Let's make this happen."

"I'd like to," Rudberg lied. "Let me look over the contract and make certain I have no questions."

"Do you need an office?"

"Here? Now? No, let me go back to my hotel and study it. My attorney looks over everything I sign."

"The terms are straightforward."

Rudberg rose. "I'll be back to you by the end of the day. I'm sure it's fine, but this is a major commitment."

In his room, he read it over and spotted what he thought were deal breakers. He scanned a copy in the hotel business center and emailed it to Lucius Martin, following it with a call. Martin was back to him within thirty minutes.

"First off, there's no contract here from your point of view. Any party can cancel the agreement on two weeks' notice without cause. That means they can fire you anytime they want, and you have no recourse.

"From their end, however, it's an ironclad agreement. It prohibits you from doing any outside work of any sort. Any work you've done since leaving the *Examiner* becomes their property. The financial penalties for any violation are steep. Do you need me to explain this?"

"No, thank you. It's what I thought. We both know why it's in there and why they want me."

"Catch and kill," Martin said.

---

"It is my honor and privilege to nominate Judge Preston Madigan to the United States Supreme Court." The president's face filled the screen in Rudberg's hotel room. "He is a man of outstanding integrity and a strong respect for our Constitution and laws."

A young, fresh-faced man stepped to the microphone, a broad, toothy smile breaking the even plane of his face. The president gave him a bear hug. Senators from the president's party grinned and applauded like spectators at a concert. Shutters clicked, a few firing frames in volleys.

Judge Madigan reached behind him and motioned for a dark-haired woman dressed in blue to step forward. Her two children joined her. They smiled and waved at no one in particular as the applause continued, but to Rudberg Madigan's wife seemed uncomfortable. The judge opened his mouth to speak.

"Thank God!" Rudberg said. He turned off the set, killed the light on his nightstand, and had his first restful night of sleep in weeks.

"I'm glad you've come," Cheryl said as she greeted Rudberg at her door, "but I wish you'd given us more notice."

"I didn't decide until yesterday afternoon," he said. "I had a job interview in Fort Worth and drove down for a visit. It's cheaper to drive to Austin than fly, and you don't have to go through security."

"How was the interview?"

"Not good. They are less interested in what I can write for them than in what I can't."

"I don't understand."

"It was an involved scheme to keep Dad's investigation from going public. They want to take ownership of my notes and anything I've written, even in draft form, so they can bury it." If Grimley had acted more like a journalist than a businessman, if he'd offered more appealing terms, if he hadn't been so insistent on a quick sale, Rudberg might have signed his life away without looking at the fine print. He was hungry.

"Be nice to Mom," Cheryl said. "She's not in the best of health."

"I will," he said. "I want to say hello, make sure she knows I care and clear a few things up."

"Such as?"

"Do you remember Uncle Charlie?"

"Charlie? We don't have an Uncle Charlie." She stared at her brother, awaiting an explanation, but he didn't elaborate. She showed him to her guest room and fed him lunch. After she'd placed a call, they drove to their mother's retirement home near Barton Creek. From the front entrance, he could see a spacious pool advertising the carefree life that awaited newcomers, though no one was lounging around it in Austin's cool January weather. They took the elevator to the third floor and knocked on Margaret's door. She answered immediately, and Rudberg realized she'd been watching the parking lot from her window.

Cheryl fussed around her mother, asking her whether she needed tea, a pillow, anything to make her more comfortable. She looked fine, Rudberg thought, gray-haired, but alert and spry. She'd walked without a limp from the front door and settled into a chair by the window without difficulty. Her principal malady seemed to be Cheryl's over-mothering.

"So what brings my Alan all the way to Austin?" she said.

"I came to see you."

"He was interviewing for a job in Fort Worth," Cheryl said from the kitchenette. "It didn't work out."

"Oh, why's that?"

Rudberg gave her a varnished version of the truth and inquired into her health. She asked about Stephanie, and Rudberg lied. He was becoming an accomplished prevaricator. They chatted about nothing for nearly an hour, then Rudberg came to the point. "I had a dream the other night. We were at a baseball park, and you were there. I got sick."

"I remember."

"A man was with us. Uncle Charlie, you called him." His mother became quiet. "He wasn't our uncle," he said, delivering it as a statement.

"I don't remember an Uncle Charlie," Cheryl said.

"Who was he, Mom?"

A long sigh. "A friend of the family. He liked you, took you places. He was good to you."

"He was your friend, wasn't he?"

"Well, he was good to me, too. Your father had left us—"

"No, this was before Dad left. I'm sure of it." Sensing he was getting nowhere, he said, "Tell me why you and Dad parted."

"You know that. He left our family and provided no support. He was no good."

"Cheryl and I have letters he sent us for years. You wrote 'Return to Sender' on them. He saved them."

Her eyes darted around the room, looking for help. "He left us high and dry, no child support, no alimony. He lost the right to be part of your lives."

Cheryl had joined them, standing alongside her mother. He wasn't sure whether she was there to listen or to referee. He spoke softly, barely above a whisper. "Here's what I know. Dad didn't leave us. You left him. Far from abandoning us, he sent you money every month, never missing a payment. Don't argue," he said, as she protested, "I have the bank records."

It was pure bluff, but she didn't argue. "He sent support payments while we were still in Jacksonville and continued them after we moved here. Do you understand, Cheryl?"

"Alan, leave her alone. You're badgering her."

"I'm asking her to tell us the truth for the first time in her life. Either listen or leave." Turning back to their mother, he said, "You left him for this man Charlie, didn't you? Or he found out about Charlie. Which was it?"

"Charlie Scott had nothing to do with it," she said, her tone a mix of sarcasm and anger. "He was a friend. We had—we enjoyed each other's company. In the end, he was no good, either. He went back to his wife."

Rudberg lowered his voice. "Then why did you divorce Dad? Why break up this family?"

"He humiliated me!" she shouted. "I was born and raised in Jacksonville. My friends were people I'd known since high school, grade school, a few even earlier. He sat there at that newspaper and wrote about all these coloreds whining about their schools, trying to change the government to suit themselves. And your father took their side. They all made fun of us. 'Who's that man of yours, that nigger lover? Why don't you get him in line?' I went nowhere without hearing about your father and his crusade. All my friends!"

"I can't imagine how hard that must have been," Cheryl said.

"Christ!"

"Don't you take the name of the Lord in vain! I raised you better than that."

"So you divorced him. You threatened him through a restraining order—"

"He was abusing me."

"He was not. He was a decent man, a good father who loved us. Even you."

Cheryl wept. "Stop it!" he said. "Stop feeling sorry for her. Look what she's done. She took our father from us and told us lies about him. She started lying when we were children, kept lying until we were adults, and didn't stop until ten minutes ago. One more question, Mother. Why did you move us here?"

"Isn't it obvious? I had to get you away from him, from his influence." Her right lip curled up in a sneer. "Once he took up with that—"

"Don't use that word in front of me ever again, understand?" Getting no response, he forged on. "After the divorce, he began a relationship with Grace. You learned about it—how?"

"A friend heard it from her maid. She couldn't wait to tell me—came out with it in front of friends at a church social."

"Oh, not at church!" Rudberg said. "Heavens!"

"You laugh, but then they had that little black bastard!"

"Our sister, a lovely person."

He got up. He'd had enough. Cheryl took him back to her house, where he collected his things and drove to the airport. He walked among the counters until he found a flight.

---

"I can explain," Stephanie had said during their drive home during the early hours of New Year's Day.

"No, you can't." Those were the last words he'd spoken to her before boarding his flight to Texas. Now he called her at her office. She didn't pick up. If he were having a heart attack, he would either have to go through her assistant or leave a message. This morning he did the latter.

"I'm in Jacksonville. There was no job offer. It was a bribe of sorts, hush money and not much of it. Which means there's something worth hushing up, so I've returned here to unhush it. When I do, you'll be the second to hear." He did not say goodbye, wish her well, or send his love.

Rudberg found a furnished room online. No lease, no down payment, just a room. Checking out of the hotel near the airport, he picked up a car, drove to Southside, and rented the room, paying two weeks in advance. He left a message for Lucius, who was in court that morning, and drove south to find Elizabeth Cannon, *ecannon*.

She was a slight white-haired lady with an engaging smile who lived on the edge of Palatine—south edge, of course—and who wielded a sharp pair of garden shears as she had Rudberg hold a paper bag. "You might have called first," she said.

"I was afraid you wouldn't see me."

"And why wouldn't I? I'm happy to talk to anyone about my dad." Talk she did, regaling him with stories of her father's career, his triumphs and frustrations.

"He didn't let much get to him, except unsolved cases, of course. Dedicated officers never get over those. This was different. You had to know him to understand how angry he was when Searcy ended their work. It never left him."

"Did he ever speculate as to Searcy's motivation? Was it racism?"

"That and more. He thought Searcy was covering up for someone."

"For whom? Did he have any idea?"

"If he did, he took it to his grave." She finished her gardening and invited him into her home, asking him if he'd care for iced tea. He accepted to keep the conversation going, not relishing the sugar shock he was about to receive. "Sweetened or unsweetened?"

"At last, civilization. Unsweetened, please."

"I'm diabetic," she explained. "Is he headed to the Supreme Court?"

Rudberg made the leap. "No, the president appointed Judge Madigan Monday night."

"Then why did Searcy fly to Washington this morning?"

"I have no idea. Some judicial matter, I suppose."

"He left suddenly. Everyone's speculating he's in line for something. What else is there but the Supreme Court?"

"Are you sure? Where did you hear this?"

"He's from Palatine. Everyone here knows everyone else's business."

Rudberg asked if she would give him the original of her father's memorandum. She declined but, showing she was no fool, said, "Let's find a notary and get you a certified copy. You will stop him, won't you? He's a bad man."

"I'll do my damnedest."

---

Rudberg placed a call before leaving Palatine. "Hi, there," Sonja Lansberg said. "I wasn't sure I'd hear from you again. Which coast are you on, or is it somewhere in between?"

"I'm here. Less than a mile from your house, in fact."

He heard a sharp intake of breath.

"What are you doing here, or shouldn't I ask?"

"I'm doing what I was doing before that I couldn't talk about then and can't now."

"Things not working out at home?"

He debated how much to share and opted for discretion. "What you always get over the holidays—a week of parties, friends sharing their ignorance, much talk but little conversation." He weighed whether to say what was on his mind, then plunged ahead. "I'd like to see you."

"Me too. I'd invite you over, but I can't right now." Did he imagine that she'd just lowered her voice, or was she purring?

They made a date to meet in Mandarin Friday evening. Rudberg drove north, wondering if she'd had someone with her. Why not? She didn't owe him anything.

---

They met in the smaller of Lucius Martin's two conference rooms, Martin at the head of the table and Rudberg and Aisha on either side. Aisha folded her arms beneath her breasts, avoiding his gaze. "Alan is back with us," Lucius said, "and we all have things to share. I hope this little meeting will get us back on track."

"Will he stay this time?" she said, posing the question to the attorney as though Rudberg were not sitting across from her.

"I went home for Christmas. Is that all right?"

"You said you were giving up."

"I said I didn't see a way forward. Now I do."

"All right, you two. Let's cut the crap. Alan, are you willing to see this through?"

"To the end, whatever that may be."

"Do you accept that, Aisha? Can we move on?"

"What's changed?" she said.

"You already know about the memo that William Whiting wrote after he left the sheriff's office. I have a certified copy from his daughter, who also tells us that Searcy is in Washington today."

"I've also heard Madigan will withdraw his name from consideration," Lucius said.

"What? Why?"

"Officially, his wife fears the effect his confirmation hearings will have on his children. The opposition is lining up. Unofficially"—he looked from one to the other—"word is he had a fling with at least two of his clerks and paid one to get rid of the resulting complication."

"Men," she said. "Men in power."

Rudberg recalled how uncomfortable Madigan's wife had seemed three nights before when she'd stood alongside her husband.

She knew. He shook his head. She knew, yet he was prepared to put his family through this.

"Point is," Lucius said, "I can't discount the possibility that Searcy is under genuine consideration. Alan, please share your news with us."

"What Lucius also knows, but you haven't heard, Aisha, is that there was an elaborate attempt to end my role in this investigation." He told her about his visit to Monford Publishing Company and the terms of its contract.

"So we have written confirmation of what J. S. Barstow told us three weeks ago, what appears to be a successful effort to silence him, and this elaborate effort to prevent me from writing anything about it. Where there's smoke..."

"What do you propose to do with it?" Lucius said.

"I've been keeping a running narrative of what we've learned. It's sequential now, but I could pull it together into a tight story this afternoon. I'd like to submit it to *The Floridian* under a joint byline, Mathew and Alan Rudberg."

The two of them exchanged noncommittal glances. "It's a long shot, but we have no other platform. How do we share what we've learned, in a blog post—stand on a soapbox in Hemming Park? We need a media outlet to give us a voice, and because this started out as Mathew's story, *The Floridian* might serve that purpose."

Lucius turned to Aisha again, then said, "Would you be willing to write it up and share it with us before submitting it?"

"Because you don't trust me."

Aisha stared at the table, saying nothing.

"We're a team now, right? You're the reporter, but Aisha's your researcher and I've been acting as your attorney. The team needs to be together on this. Okay?"

"All right," he said, unable to conceal his resentment.

With that hurdle surmounted, Martin called on Aisha. "I have nothing as concrete," she said, "but I've been thinking about that timeline we built of Searcy's career. I'm convinced of something, though I can't prove it.

"Florida elects its circuit court judges, but when there's a vacancy, the governor fills it until the next election. The Judicial Nominating Committee provides a list from which he must choose, but he has the final say. Remember that Searcy reached the state attorney's office through appointment and then ran for office at the next election. That's how he became a circuit court judge."

"You're suggesting he had political pull," Rudberg said. "I think the same thing."

"Four years later, he's plucked from this position in which he's a relative newcomer and appointed to the federal bench. So, yes, I'm saying he had some powerful friends pushing him from behind."

"Or pulling him from in front," Martin said. "I can tell you, he's had an undistinguished judicial career. He had lots of reversals and some questionable calls. It surprised those of us in the local bar when he was appointed to the appellate court, but you don't go around criticizing judges if you expect to try cases before them."

Suspecting a hidden hand was not proving it, and identifying the body attached to the hand could be even tougher. They discussed how to go about it for several minutes but came to no conclusion. Rudberg had an idea but decided to pursue it on his own.

As they broke up, he asked Aisha to stay. "What's going on between us?" he asked. "You're acting like I'm the enemy."

"Are you?"

"Please tell me why you're so angry."

"It was the way you went, Alan. You don't know what Dad's death has done to my mother. She puts on a brave front, but she's been disconsolate. You come along and give her hope that at least she will have justice. Then, the moment there's a setback, you run."

"I didn't run. I had to go home. And I had to step back and think about what to do next."

She took a deep breath and stared at him with an intensity he found unnerving. "It is impossible for you to get into the head of a black person. Do you wake up each morning saying, 'I'm white?' Of course not. You are what you are, and the world around you looks the same, so you're comfy in your white skin and don't think about it."

She leaned forward as though imparting an intimate secret. "It's different for me—for us. When I step out each day, I enter a white world that judges my every action and statement against its assumption that I am somehow different."

"I don't look at you that way."

"Yes, you do, whether you realize it. I'll tell you how it works. I'm sitting at a table in a restaurant and a white man smiles at me. He's not coming on to me. He's trying to make me comfortable by welcoming me *into his world.*

"A white lady stops a black mother and makes over her child. 'What a precious little girl,'" she said, aping a southern white voice. "Why is she doing that? She doesn't make eyes at a white child. Does she genuinely find this child attractive, or is this strategic—an effort to prove to the mother she is not like all those other whites around her?"

Aisha lowered her voice and leaned toward him. "This is the way our lives work. We have to analyze everything, even everyday interactions that you might take as simple acts of kindness. We're suspicious, and we have a right to be."

She leaned back, her voice taking on an aggressive note. "Now when you, Mr. Reporter, promise my mother that you're—that *we're* not letting her down, suggesting a familiarity with me that I do not share—and then leave a week and a half later without a word to her, I have to wonder about you. That's how you've trained me.

"I'm along for this ride because the destination is important but I'm watching you as you drive. Keep your eyes on the road and your hands on the wheel, and we'll get along just fine."

She didn't wait for a response, and he had none. He sat alone at Lucius Martin's conference table, feeling as though she had struck him.

He'd picked a restaurant on Julington Creek, half an hour's drive for him, an hour for her. Crowds packed it in summer, sitting out on the long deck, drinking beer and peeling shrimp. In winter, everything moved indoors, and the place was quieter, particularly now, the first weekend after the holiday and an unseasonably cold night.

Rudberg arrived first and amused himself by studying the pen and ink drawings of fish that dotted the walls. Sonja arrived just as he began to doubt she was coming, muttering something about an accident on the Shands Bridge. He tucked his glasses into his jacket pocket and kissed her on the cheek. She embraced him, pressing her right breast into his arm.

They sat by the window, studied the menu, and ordered grouper, knowing it was the last of the season. Rudberg added a bottle of pinot gris from "back home."

"Be honest with me. How are things between you and your wife?"

Rudberg sighed and averted her gaze. "She's having an affair with her best friend's husband."

"You know this?"

"I confronted them."

"That must have been painful."

"It wasn't," he said. "I hope his wife doesn't find out. Wendy Fisher's her name. A good person—trustworthy, loyal, helpful, friendly, courteous, kind, obedient—not so cheerful these days."

"A good scout."

"A very good scout. He's a neurologist, so he has a lot of nerve."

"Haha. And so what happened?"

"Nothing. We didn't fight, if that's what you mean. We added it to the endless list of things we never discuss."

"What happens now? I'm not asking out of curiosity."

He studied her for a moment, conscious that this was no mere flirtation. "Each of us is waiting for the other to call the question. It's been this way for some time."

Loud voices came from the bar, then cheering and applause.

Rudberg had a view of the television screen and knew they weren't watching a sporting event. He walked closer and saw a local newscaster with a photo of J. Morris Searcy over his shoulder. He listened for a few seconds and returned to the table.

"The president has just nominated Judge Searcy to the Supreme Court." He cupped his mouth in his hand, sighed, and shook his head.

"I know what you're up to. You're looking into Searcy's past." He looked out at the creek without responding "Alan, if we're going to have a relationship—"

"Are we going to have a relationship?"

"Don't be flippant. It won't get you where you want to go, and we both know where that is. If we are to have a relationship," she repeated, "you must let me in. I'm a reporter. I know all about keeping your story to yourself until you're ready to publish. I also know this town—better than you do or ever will. I can help. Want to help. But I can't do a thing unless you're willing to share with me."

He considered it for a moment, then told her everything they'd learned and suspected—about Mathew's death, Alonzo Taylor, Searcy's role in derailing the cold case investigation, the efforts to silence Rudberg—while she stroked his hand. "We need to know who's behind him and why," he concluded.

"I'll ask around, try to find out," she said. "And thank you for trusting me."

They sat in silence for a few moments, watching the moonlight dance across ripples in the creek as it flowed into the St. Johns. "I grew up in Hampton County. No one taught us this story. I'd never heard of Alonzo Taylor..." She trailed off, letting the thought hang unspoken.

"Where are you staying?" she said at last.

"I have a room on Southside with a private entrance. It's the best I can do right now."

"Do you want to stay with me?"

"Yes, but I won't."

"We can keep it on the sly until your divorce comes through."

"I will not do that, Sonja."

"You're trustworthy, loyal, helpful..."

"And married. If I were to sleep with you now, you would get a man who slept with another woman while he was married."

"Talk to her, then."

"And I need to find work, produce income, pay my own way. Stephanie has a gift for making it appear that I'm living off of her. I'm not, nor will I live off you."

He drove back to town nursing a hangover of ecstasy and trepidation. What was he doing with this woman?

# A SIN OF OMISSION

Rudberg worked on the story at first light. He wrote quickly, pulling full sections from the narrative he'd been assembling. Just after 9:00, he placed a call to J. S. Barstow in Waycross. Clara answered.

"No, you can't speak to him. He's in the hospital. He had a heart attack three days ago," she said in response to his question. "The stress you people put him under got to him."

"I don't understand. He told me about an investigation he did years ago in Palatine, then called and took it back. I wasn't happy that he backed out, but I let it go. I haven't involved him and haven't talked with him since."

She seemed mollified. In a quavering voice, she said, "Two men came by a week before Christmas. It unnerved him. I haven't seen him so wrought up in years. I thought he'd left all that behind him when he retired."

"Do you know what they said to him?"

"No, they spoke outside. I asked him what it was about, and he wouldn't tell me. 'I'm in the middle of something I don't understand, and I have to end it.' That's all he would tell me."

He asked her several more questions, but either she knew nothing more or wasn't saying. Two men had come by, talked to Barstow outside their house, and left. He had then called Rudberg to say he'd reconsidered. The man had sounded frantic. "You have to leave me out of this."

"Mrs. Barstow, I was calling to tell him that there may be a story. His partner left a written account of their investigation. I wanted him to go on the record, but I'll manage without him and will do my best to keep his name out. Wish him well for me."

He slumped at his keyboard. How was he to write a story based on what Whiting had written without revealing he'd had a partner? Putting on his editor's hat, he posed the questions he would have put to a reporter. *Did you contact the partner? What did he say? Why won't he talk?*

Rudberg placed another call to William Purty but got no answer. He rubbed clammy hands on his pant legs. *I put him in this position. I need to find him, make certain he's all right. But how?*

He had no idea where the man lived. What had he told him? *I didn't live in Palatine back then. I had a bait and tackle shop across the river.* So he now lived in Palatine. Rudberg thought back to his attempt to meet Purty at the diner little more than a month before. He had pulled out of the diner's parking lot and called Rudberg less than five minutes later. Had it sounded like he was calling from a cell phone?

He thought back to the last time he'd talked with him by phone, the day he'd arranged the furtive St. Augustine meeting. Was he imagining it or did he recall Purty stepping away for a moment — to let the dog out?

Rudberg got in his car and drove south, passing through Palatine until he reached Shay's Diner. He drove north for three minutes, returned and drove south for three more. Back at Shay's, he headed east toward the river. Homes here were too expensive for a man with Purty's background. He returned and drove west, reaching a lake less than a mile away. In less than fifteen minutes, he had staked out the limits of an area within which he suspected William Purty lived. Starting at the north end, he drove down roads and up side streets, examining the names on mailboxes.

In one neighborhood, lined by house trailers on cement blocks, he stopped to ask two residents if they knew William Purty. He came up empty and drove on. Not four blocks east of US 17, he prowled through a similar neighborhood. Dogs strained their tethers and barked. A woman in a shapeless shift glared at him, eyeing his late model car with suspicion. *A stranger. What did he want here?* Rudberg reached the end of the lane and headed back, struggling to make out the names on each forest of mailboxes. Growing weary of the hunt, he became sloppy, looking for a pattern rather than reading the scrawled name. *Pay attention. You've come this far.*

Then he saw it, six letters slapped onto one of four mailboxes. *W. Purty.* He parked, got out, and walked down a dirt path that passed two house trailers on either side. He knocked at the first and got no response. Went to the second, heard a TV blaring at full blast, but still got no answer. Crossing the path, he knocked at the third. A teenaged boy came to the screen door, its webbing torn at the bottom. A small, scrappy dog stood at his side, presumably the source of the torn screen.

"I'm looking for William Purty," he said.

"Who wants him?"

"I do. I'm a friend. I met with him last month in St. Augustine. I haven't been able to reach him since." The teenager inserted his right finger into his nose, withdrew it, and examined the result. Rudberg looked at the other trailers. "Please. Which one is his?"

Again, no reaction. "Is your dad home? Your mom? Purty may be in danger. I need to warn him."

"Uncle Bill took off."

"Where'd he go?"

He scratched his left ribcage with his right hand. "Dunno. He just took off. Didn't say where he was headed. Asked me to look after his dog." He nodded toward the mutt at his side.

"When was this?"

"Week before Christmas," he said. "I gotta go." He turned to retreat into the trailer.

"If you hear from him, please ask him to call Rudberg. *Rudberg.* Can you remember that?"

"Redbird?"

He sighed. "Just ask him to contact the guy he met in St. Augustine."

The kid grunted and went back inside.

Lucius Martin picked him up after church on Sunday and drove south to a rendezvous he had arranged. "Searcy's nomination will change everything," Rudberg said. "Reporters will scramble all over this, digging into his background and career, talking to his colleagues..."

"Yes!" Martin shouted, showing Rudberg his fist and expecting a bump. It dawned on Rudberg that his interests and Martin's were at cross-purposes. While Rudberg lived in fear of being scooped, Martin welcomed information from any source. He decided not to raise the point.

"The clock is ticking," Martin continued. He outlined what Rudberg already realized, that the nomination was on a fast track. Embarrassed and angry over Madigan's sudden withdrawal, the president had reacted with characteristic abandon, nominating a man from a state he'd need to carry in the next election without consulting his party's leaders. Stuck with a *fait accompli,* they rushed to repair the damage. The chairman of the Senate Judiciary Committee said he could begin hearings in a week and could send the nomination to the Senate by the end of the month. The majority leader promised to send Searcy's name to the floor as soon as he received it.

Leaders of the opposition warned against "a rush to judgment," but they lacked the votes to slow the process. Both Florida senators had endorsed Searcy's nomination, hailing the chance to put the first Floridian on the high court, and many newspapers had endorsed him in their Sunday editions. "It's like a runaway train," Rudberg said.

Martin parked in front of a white, two-story structure with green trim and faded olive-colored awnings in Palatine's north end. A heavy wooden swing, also in green, hung at the front porch. They walked to the door and knocked.

The attorney introduced Rudberg to Alcee Taylor, a tall, gaunt man who walked with a slight stoop and appeared to be in his early seventies. Taylor invited them in, introducing them to his wife, two grown children, and his mother, a frail-looking woman with snow-white hair who sat in a rocker, moving a cane back and forth in rhythm to the chair. Her eyes were milky. Rudberg suspected she could barely see through her cataracts.

"We've come here today," Martin said, "to learn your story. You helped Mr. Rudberg's father when he first became interested in Alonzo Taylor's life. Someone destroyed his notes of your conversation. Alan is picking up where his father left off, and I'm helping him.

"This is painful for you, but Alan is a good man. He's come to listen, to understand, and to tell your story to the world."

Taylor looked at the two men, then reached out his arm, encompassing the room. "My mother is Mrs. Minnie Taylor. She was widowed sixty-three years ago. She raised three children on her own. It was hard going. Nobody helped her. She had no husband to share the burden."

Taylor paused, staring at the threadbare rug as though he would find strands of memory.

"She spent a lifetime on her hands and knees, cleaning for the white folks south of the river," he said. "No healthcare, no retirement, no nothing."

The woman showed no reaction, continuing her slow rocking.

"Alice, my sister, lives in Jacksonville now. She was too young to remember much about her father. Seth, our brother, died in Vietnam. He was only eighteen and sent over there for nothing. I'm the oldest. These are two of my children. They never had a grandfather, and their children never had a great-grandfather."

He paused and looked at them. "What else do you want to know? What else is there to say?"

"Your father was a minister?" Rudberg began.

"On weekends and many nights he preached in the little AME church on the corner down there," he said, pointing. "By day, he was a printer. Owned his own shop. Built it from nothing. That's how he supported his family. He always worked, never took a day off. Preaching and printing. That was his life."

"Remarkable," Rudberg said, "and still he found time to register voters."

"Printing was his business, preaching was his calling, and voting was his cause. He got involved with a statewide group—"

"The Florida Voting Rights Project," his mother said with pride. "He was one of four organizers. They started it up after Harry Moore's murder. You've heard about that?"

"Yes," Rudberg said, recalling the details from his father's column, "a founder of the Florida NAACP and one of the first voting rights organizers. They bombed his house, killing him and his wife."

"They did," she said. "So my Alonzo and three other brave men picked up the banner. They soon had nearly twenty men working all over North Florida, then down as far as Kissimmee. This was before Montgomery and Dr. King. They were pioneers."

"And they were working to register voters..." Rudberg prompted.

"So they could break the back of the white power structure," Alcee Taylor replied. "Everywhere you looked in Florida, whites had organized the government to run things as they saw fit. Paved roads in white neighborhoods, dirt roads for blacks. Sewers in white neighborhoods, ditches in black—"

"You should have smelled Jacksonville back then," his mother said. "You'd drive up the toll road through town and cross that creek —what was it, Alcee?"

"McCoy's Creek, Mama. You wouldn't believe it. It stunk like a skunk. You had to hold your nose just to drive through town. Just shit, flowing right into the St. Johns. That was good enough for black neighborhoods. And the worst were the schools," he said. "Nice, concrete buildings with big windows to let in the breeze in spring and fall, green laws extending all the way to the street, baseball diamonds, a football stadium, you name it—all that on the south side of Palatine. Over here, a big box with windows that didn't shut in winter—year-round ventilation, even when you didn't want it—all grades in one school. No sports facilities, hand-me-down books—"

"The white kids used to make nasty little drawings in the margins when it was time for them to get new books," his mother said. "Alcee, you remember that little stick figure—"

"Yes, Mama. You pasted blank paper over it hoping I wouldn't see it." Taylor was warming up, no longer reticent about delving into the past. "And our science textbooks still had only eight planets. This was in the fifties, mind you. Eight planets while the white folks got nine. Well, guess who turned out to be right!"

They all laughed at his joke. "Say, you want something to drink, maybe? Some iced tea? Something stronger?"

Both men declined, happy enough that Taylor no longer saw them as intruders. He recalled the night his father had not returned from his meeting in Jacksonville, the following morning, the last Monday before school started, when he and his brothers and sister sat in the front room as the sheriff's deputies told their mother they had found their father, the sadness that enveloped them, ending the joy of summer not just for that year, but for the rest of their lives.

"Why did they kill him?" Rudberg asked. "Just because he was trying to get African Americans to vote?"

Taylor snorted. "Those voters posed a threat. Have you been through this town? It's half white and half black. If you got all those black voters to the polls, you could change everything. I mean *every-thing*," he said, his eyes flashing.

"There's one industry, and back then, almost every job depended on it. A third of the town worked at that paper mill, and the other two-thirds worked in businesses that depended on it. Senator Coupland ran the mill, and he ran the town. He set wages, and if you didn't like what he paid, there was nowhere else to go. At city hall, he made the rules. If he wanted to dump chemicals in the water, no one would stop him. He got himself elected to the state senate and then became Senate president. No one at the state level would cross him."

"And to keep the machine running, he had to keep brothers from voting," Lucius Martin said.

"You got it. Coupland called everyone together at the plant and told them, 'You boys love your jobs because they feed your families. We wouldn't want anything to happen to that.' On election day, they threw up every possible roadblock. There were three car dealerships in town. They kept their mechanics working all day so they couldn't vote, so most didn't bother registering."

He paused, shook his head, his hands shaking with barely controlled rage.

"Dad wanted everyone to vote. He figured that they needed our backs and our shoulders. They couldn't run the plant, the power station, or any of the local businesses without us. 'We have the power,' he said. If everyone registered, he told them, they couldn't single out anyone to fire."

"And so?" Rudberg said.

"So they got rid of him. Murdered him. It was as simple as that."

---

Rudberg arrived at *The Floridian* unannounced at midmorning. He'd been up since dawn incorporating edits Aisha and Lucius had proposed and adding Alcee Taylor's background on his father.

"Will you include their suspicions about why he was murdered?" the attorney asked.

"No, we don't have enough to go on yet. I'm just shaking the tree to see what falls at our feet," he said, repeating one of his favorite metaphors.

He asked to speak with Mike Flynn. The managing editor made him wait for half an hour before admitting him. Rudberg explained his purpose, and Flynn said, "We don't accept local stories from free-lancers."

"Dad wasn't a freelancer. He was one of you."

"Your dad wrote this?"

"Co-wrote it. He began the research while he was still doing his monthly column. He was working on a book. I included some of what he wrote."

Flynn extended his arm, and Rudberg handed him the file folder. He read it without speaking, but as he marked it up, Rudberg grew encouraged. When he'd finished, however, he handed it back and said, "Pretty thin stuff."

"It's one of the great unsolved slayings in Florida history," Rudberg protested, "a modern-day lynching, and a man who's nominated to the Supreme Court—"

"You're late," he said. "Judge Searcy met with the editorial board Saturday morning. He told us this story and predicted you'd try to sell it to us. He feels, as we do, that you've embraced Mathew's fixation with this case as your own, perhaps as an act of contrition. I'm not a psychologist so I couldn't say." He sniffed, cuffed his chin in his hand, and appraised Rudberg.

"The point is, Judge Searcy was a young attorney, thrust into a role with which he was unfamiliar, asked to make an important decision during his first days in office. The evidence was thin, just as your story is—hearsay and nothing more. If he is guilty of anything it was an error of omission. I'm not even sure about that."

"I have to hand it to him. He did a real number on you."

"I resent that. Judge Searcy has served our region faithfully and honorably. He devoted his life to public service rather than seeking personal gain in private practice. The president has nominated him to the nation's highest court. No justice of the Supreme Court has ever come from Florida.

"You, however, left Portland under a cloud. No one wants to touch you. You'll do well to remember that before you go peddling your story elsewhere."

---

"'You have meddled with the primal forces of nature, Mr. Beale, and I won't have it. Is that clear?'" Rudberg stood at one end of the conference table, his arms outstretched, palms up, just as he recalled the scene.

Aisha and Lucius looked at each other over their box lunches as though he had taken leave of his senses. He lowered his arms and sat down, returning his eyeglasses to his face. "You've never seen the movie *Network*? You're both too young. Go watch it. There's this scene where the network president excoriates the anchor..." He dropped the explanation. You had to be there.

"Anyway, that's what he was saying. Judge Searcy is a devoted public servant, while you, Mr. Beale, are nothing. And should you have the temerity to speak ill of him or of us in public, we will grind you into dust."

"I take it they're not printing it," Martin said. They smiled at his gallows humor but didn't laugh.

"But seriously, folks, that's their position, the one Searcy staked out weeks ago, and it's a valid one. Maybe I need to remove myself from whatever we put forward."

"Forget it," Martin said. "They've read the story and will tie it back to you, even if Aisha holds a news conference at the corner of Main and Duval at high noon."

"Particularly if I do it," she said. "Besides, this is your story. We're in this together."

He tried a smile on, but she wasn't humoring him. She was only stating the truth as she saw it.

"Excuse me," Rudberg said, reaching for his phone, "I have to take this."

He listened for a moment, then said, "I didn't. I would never hurt Wendy." Rudberg left the room while Martin and Aisha sat puzzled. When he returned a few minutes later, his hands and voice trembled with rage.

"That was my wife. About an hour ago her best friend got a call from someone who told her that her husband and Stephanie are having an affair. That's true. I uncovered it during my trip home. It was not a happy holiday."

They muttered their sympathy. "That's not the point. They weren't discreet, so it was easy enough for someone to uncover, but why would they do that?"

"To intimidate you," Aisha said.

"Yes, but why bother? Searcy has his story down. He sold it to *The Floridian*. A sin of omission. Everyone else will buy it, particularly since Searcy is smart enough to raise it himself. Why the overkill?"

The answer grasped him like a drowning man. "We are looking at this through Dad's lens. Racial injustice consumed him. Every time he used his nostalgic column to explore something consequential, it concerned race. Good for him. Someone needed to do it. But it's affecting how we look at Searcy."

"It's not just Alonzo Taylor..." Aisha said.

"There's something more," Lucius Martin finished for her.

They spent a few minutes speculating what other secrets Searcy was hiding and how they could uncover it. "Perhaps it's something in his early decisions on the bench," Martin said. "We subscribe to an online database that tracks every legal action—from filing to decisions through appeals—through every court in the land. I can set you up at a terminal and show you how to use it."

Aisha had to return to work, but Rudberg sat down while a paralegal took him through the program. He spent the rest of the afternoon going through Searcy's decisions as a circuit court judge. He made little headway, getting trapped in cases that seemed to have little significance. At the end of the afternoon, he took Martin out for a beer. "I don't see how we'll get through all this," he said. "I'm uncertain what we're looking for, and there are too many places to look. It's discouraging."

Martin studied the foam in his glass. "We need a surge," he said. "Let me think about it."

Rudberg, meanwhile, worried about something else. How had Searcy's forces learned about Stephanie and Mark?

---

Sergeant Wheadon greeted Rudberg and led him to a conference room. He offered coffee, which Rudberg accepted, the single-shot unit in his furnished room offering a bland, flavorless brew that might have been sitting in a warehouse for weeks.

"It took two weeks to get approval to take this on," Wheadon said. "We don't get involved in a local case unless we're invited or have evidence that local authorities aren't doing their jobs. We have a long history of the latter with Hampton County, so it didn't take much."

"What have you found?"

"I can't say much yet, but we recovered a cell phone and notebook computer from the water near the boathouse. We've submitted it to the lab, but we may not get any usable evidence after six weeks. However, we have a witness who saw your father's body dumped in the river. We've placed a subject at the scene. That's where we need your help."

Wheadon explained what he wanted and brought up images on the computer before him. He turned it around to face Rudberg and paged through mug shots of white males, all in late middle age. Rudberg said no as the first few images flashed on the screen, then stopped speaking and shook his head. He paused at one and stared at it for several seconds.

"This one," he said.

"You're sure?" Wheadon said.

"Yes, that's the guy."

"Let me show you one more." He brought up another photo.

"That's the same guy, just younger, isn't it?"

"You're certain this is the man who approached you in the diner in Palatine."

"That's him."

Wheadon allowed himself a rare smile and closed the screen. "We'll need a statement," he said,

"Who is he?"

"I can't tell you that. I don't want to compromise this investigation. But we're continuing our inquiries, and we'll bring him in for questioning once we have a few more pieces in place."

---

Aisha was engrossed in research by the time he reached Lucius Martin's office. She took the day off from the historical society, got a quick lesson from the paralegal, and quickly mastered the software. "There is so much raw material here," she said. "I don't know what's important."

"I found the same thing yesterday. Circuit judges handle everything from felonies to divorce cases. Lucius told me it wasn't always that way. Florida used to have separate criminal and civil courts, long before Searcy got on the bench. Now it's a mishmash."

They worked on their own for an hour, then brought in sandwiches. He related what Wheadon had told him about the investigation. "Who is this witness?" she asked.

"He wouldn't say, but it has to be his neighbor. Parker saw everything that happened there. He must have seen the murder—perhaps just the tail end of it—and been frightened."

They returned to work with their lunches unfinished, bowing to the pressure of the Senate confirmation process. "What if we find nothing?" she said. "What if his record is spotless?"

"And his act in shelving the Alonzo Taylor investigation was just what he claims it was, a judgment call?" He considered it for a moment. "I don't buy it. They wouldn't go to so much trouble to silence me unless there's more hiding in this haystack."

"Here's something," she said. It was late afternoon, and they were both tired and discouraged. "How common is it for an appellate court to overrule a judge?"

"It happens. That's why they exist, but I'm finding so many that it seems excessive."

They compared notes, left their screens, and walked down the hall to interrupt Lucius Martin.

———————

Wendy called while he was having dinner. He wasn't enjoying it and was glad for the excuse to push it aside, speaking to her in the restaurant's confined entry area. "You knew about Mark and Stephanie on New Year's Eve, didn't you?"

He described how he'd uncovered the affair and his confrontation with them. "Why didn't you tell me then?" she said.

"Mark asked me not to. Once I'd found them out, I thought they might break it off. And I didn't want to hurt you."

"I wish you'd just come out and told me." When he didn't respond, she said, "It's not the first time."

"For Mark or for Stephanie?"

"Stephanie. She had a thing going with one of her assistants for a while. Didn't you know?"

"I'm clueless," he said, trying to conceal the tension in his voice.

"She'd take him with her on these factory tours to China, Vietnam, and wherever." She spat it out, abandoning sorrow for anger—for revenge.

"And *you* didn't tell *me*."

"I didn't want to violate her confidence."

*At least my instincts were noble.* "What's his name, the guy at work?"

"Stephen." He'd heard the name, heard it many times—Stephen this and Stephen that. "He's no longer at Victor," she said. "Something happened, I don't know what, and he left the company."

Stephanie had betrayed him, but so had Wendy. His sympathy for her collapsed like the shards of a broken window. "What will you do?" he asked.

"I've started divorce proceedings. I don't put up with that. Not with anyone, but particularly with someone who I thought was a friend."

"They may get over each other."

"And you'd take her back?" she asked.

"I don't think she wants me back." She was the dominant party in their relationship and wouldn't abide his having leverage over her. "For what it's worth, Wendy, whoever called and told you about them wasn't trying to hurt you...nor Mark or Stephanie. He was trying to get at me."

"She. The caller was a woman. Nice voice."

Rudberg gulped. "Wendy, was it a local call?"

"The caller ID read Unavailable."

---

Rudberg spotted the headline in the online edition of the *Washington Journal* and stared open-mouthed. He stopped at a newsstand on his way to the law office and found the same story in the *New York Herald*. His lips compressed in a grimace, he handed it to Lucius and Aisha the moment he entered the room. "They're way ahead of us."

Martin glanced at it. *Searcy Had Record Reversals*. The story reported that while a federal circuit court judge, Morris Searcy had been reversed by higher courts more than any other judge in the circuit.

"This is great," Martin said.

"Look at all this!" A smile danced across Aisha's features.

"I can't believe you two. We've been working on this for weeks, and two national newspapers step in and grab the headlines."

"And that bothers you?" Lucius Martin fired back. "This is a hell of a lot bigger than who gets the story first. We're investigating a man who may not belong on the US Supreme Court. It's a lifetime appointment. He can do damage for years. I don't care if it's in every newspaper in the country."

Rudberg took a deep breath, began to protest, then conceded the point. "I'm a neutral observer. I don't take sides, don't get invested. I take on a public issue to get behind the façade, understand the super-structure, and explain it to others. What we're doing is advocacy. I'm not used to it."

"Advocacy is my life," Martin said with a laugh. "I can't imagine standing on the sidelines watching the game unfold when I have the skill to score goals."

"And look, Alan," Aisha said, "they have details on all these cases in which he was reversed. This may give us a place to dig deeper."

"All right," he said at length. "An advocate, not just an observer. I need an attitude adjustment. So what's our next step?"

"Keep at it," the attorney said. "I have a luncheon meeting with someone who may help us." He gave no details, but Rudberg detected a bounce to his step.

---

Aisha had taken another day off, and they worked together through the morning. While no single decision by Judge Searcy stood out, Aisha noted a trend that troubled her. "He's been quick to hand out the death penalty," she said. "A disproportionate number of those he sentenced are black."

"Isn't that true throughout the country?"

"Yes, there are as many blacks on death row as whites, even though we're only twelve percent of the population. It's legalized lynching. Black defendants are four times as likely to get the death penalty as whites. Even by that standard, this looks abnormal. Look," she said, showing him some cases on which she'd made notes. "These are five death sentences in a row, and all of them were black."

She sighed. "I need to research every murder case over which he's presided. How will I find time to do that?"

At noon they brought in sandwiches and watched the news. The president appeared on the screen, flanked by Florida's junior senator and the Judiciary Committee chairman.

"I have full confidence in Judge Searcy," he said. "He is one of our most outstanding legal minds, has served our country with honor, and deserves a seat on the Supreme Court."

They heard a cacophony of shouted questions, none of which was distinguishable, but the context was clear from the president's answer. "I'm not troubled by that. He's handled some of the most difficult cases imaginable, and he heard more cases than any judge in the circuit during his time on the federal bench. You put yourself on the line often enough, you will take shots."

More shouted questions. "They knew all this when they approved his nomination to the appeals court. He's had a sterling record there. It's just another witch hunt by dishonest media."

"We'll give him a full, thorough hearing," the judiciary chairman said. "Every member will have their opportunity to pose questions. I'm sure he'll answer them and will justify the president's trust in him."

"We'll stage a show and send him on to the Senate floor," Rudberg said, his voice dripping with sarcasm.

———

Lucius Martin grinned as he entered the conference room. He

brought with him a short, balding black man in his early sixties. "Meet Dr. Harold Stansell," Martin said, "*Professor* Stansell is dean of the law school at Florida Northern University."

Florida Northern, Rudberg knew, was a state-owned institution once known as Florida Normal, the "separate but unequal" university for black students heading for teaching careers. Though it was now integrated, FNU continued to serve a predominantly African American student body, but in addition to educators now turned out scientists, engineers, physicians, and lawyers.

Stansell greeted them as Martin made the introductions. "Lucius has told me about your project," he said. "We'd like to help. Classes for the spring semester began Monday. I'm setting up a special project to help with your research. We'll recruit a small group of students to work with you."

"We'll use this conference room," Martin said. "I'll need one of you to coordinate their work, dividing Searcy's career into time periods, the different benches on which he's served, the types of cases he's tried—anything that makes sense."

They discussed logistics. All knew time was precious. Dean Stansell would issue invitations to a select group of students that evening, interview them the following day, and try to have at least two begin work on Friday. "By Monday," he said, "we should have a full working group and can look at every case he's ever decided."

As to who would lead them, Rudberg took a pass. "I've organized team reporting," he said, "but it's not my strength. You're the researcher, Aisha. Can you oversee this?"

Aisha had two weeks of vacation coming and would ask the historical society to allow her to take them now. "What will you do?"

"What I should have been doing all along—what I know best. You said last week that powerful friends seemed to be behind him. I'll find out who they are."

He wanted to talk to Sonja, but it would have to wait. As Rudberg returned from another lonely meal, his phone chimed. He picked it up and got an immediate blast.

"You hypocrite! You sanctimonious liar!"

"What's this all about?"

"Who is this woman you're seeing?" Stephanie asked. "You pretend you're working on some super-secret project of your father's, you confront me at a New Year's Eve party, humiliating Mark, and all the time you're seeing this—who is she?"

Though Rudberg knew full well who she was referring to, he played dumb. "Why don't you tell me what this is all about?"

"You deny this?"

"Stephanie, someone's been handing you a story. Please calm down and tell me what you're talking about."

"Pictures, Alan. Photographs. I have a package of photographs of you and some woman—"

"Describe her. I've met many people here."

Stephanie provided an accurate description. "That sounds like Sonja Lansberg," he said. "She's a former reporter from Palatine. She knew Dad and is helping me piece together this story."

"Alan, you're going into a hotel room with her. Are you denying that?"

"She was a decoy. If you check our credit card statement, you'll find I booked two rooms that night. One was for her, the other was for my witness. Sonja and I made a big show of checking into that hotel in St. Augustine so anyone following me would think we were spending the night together. I slipped out before midnight, met my informant at another hotel, got a few hours' sleep, and returned to her room before dawn. Nothing happened."

"And I suppose she's holding your hand in that restaurant to read your palm."

"No. I was telling her what Dad had discovered, and what I'd discovered about him. It's complicated but innocent. Someone wants to make it seem more than that. They're the same people who called Wendy. It's a warning. *Drop what you're doing and go home.*"

She was silent for so long he thought she'd ended the call. "You can talk to her. She'll tell you the same thing."

"Oh, I don't doubt that."

"I am not having an affair with her. I leave that sort of thing to you."

"I want a divorce."

"What?"

"It's time, Alan. I don't know whether you're being truthful, but it makes no difference. I want out, and I think you do, too."

"All right, if that's what you want, I won't stand in your way." *All I feel is relief. Thank you for making the choice for me.*

"We have an agreement, you know. You won't be left with much."

The prenuptial agreement. She'd produced it out of nowhere when she'd moved into the C-suite at Victor and now was holding it over him.

"You remember, Alan?"

His temperature rose. "Yes, I do. Infidelity invalidates it. You remember that?" *Check.*

Now it was her turn to pause. "You can't prove that anything went on between Mark and me, any more than I can prove something went on between you and—what's her name?" *Check.*

"I wasn't thinking of Mark. It was Stephen I had in mind." Complete silence at the other end.

"Who do you mean?"

"You traveled with him to China, to Vietnam... He worked for you at Victor—used to carry your shoes for you. That Stephen."

"I don't know how you heard about that, but it was a long time ago."

"Not so long. He left the company. But still..."

"No one knows about that. They mustn't." Another pause. He let silence float between them like a balloon, knowing she would have to puncture it. "He told you, didn't he? That little bastard! After all I did for him. I'll make him repay every cent." *Checkmate.* She had paid for his silence, probably from her own pocket.

"I don't think you will, Stephanie. And be glad I'm not vindictive. Get with your attorney. Make me an offer. Include the beach place. Think about the improvements I've made to *your house.* I'm sure we can act like adults."

She got the last word in—the last two words. He allowed her the satisfaction and ended the call.

## WHEN JUSTICE DIED

Sonja reached him over breakfast Thursday morning. She asked how he was, and he gave her a vague reply. "Will I see you this weekend?" she asked.

"There's nothing I'd like better," he said, "but we need to be circumspect for a few weeks."

"Sneaky."

"It's more than that. We can't see each other." He told her about his wife's call—her accusations, the photos, and her demand for a divorce. "I can't afford to give Stephanie any ammunition until we reach a settlement."

"Pictures of us? Who took them? How did they get them?"

"I wish I knew. I have a handle on the why but the how is another matter. Are you being followed?"

"I haven't looked, but no, I don't think so."

"Sonja, I have to ask you something. A woman called Wendy Fisher Monday morning and told her Mark and Stephanie are having an affair. Was that you?"

"How can you accuse me of doing something that hurtful? I've been in that position and don't wish it on anyone."

"I'm asking only because I thought you might have wanted to

nudge things along. If you didn't, someone else did, and I'd like to know who."

"Well, I didn't," she snapped. "I wouldn't even know how to reach her."

Rudberg had wondered the same thing. Like most doctors, Mark's home phone was unlisted, but that's a low barrier to a good reporter.

"I'm sorry. I had to ask."

"All right." She still sounded frosty, and Rudberg didn't blame her. "How's your investigation coming?"

"We discovered his record of reversals before the big newspapers had it. We were just outgunned. But we're getting reinforcements." Still obsessing over scoops. He couldn't stop himself. He told her about the FNU law students joining the project. "Have you discovered who's behind Searcy?" he asked.

"I have some ideas, but can't prove anything yet. I'm working on it. If we could get together..." He repeated why that couldn't happen, and they agreed to stay in touch. "I miss you," she said.

"And I miss you. This will all be over soon."

———

Three new faces greeted him as he entered Martin's conference room Friday morning, a black woman and two men, one white and one black. Aisha greeted him with uncharacteristic warmth. She'd covered a whiteboard in notes, dividing it into three columns corresponding to the phases of Searcy's judicial career.

Lucius Martin made the introductions. "Our adventure began when Alan returned to Jacksonville following his father's death. You may remember a local journalist, Mathew Rudberg." They nodded in unison. Rudberg found it remarkable that three young law students all remembered a retired journalist older than their combined ages.

The attorney gave them the CliffsNotes version of their investigation and discoveries—nothing about Alan's estrangement from his father nor the circumstances of his death. "Aisha is Mathew's daughter. She's a trained researcher and will lead your work."

Aisha reviewed Searcy's career and made preliminary assignments. "Charise, you'll dig into Searcy's decisions as a circuit court judge; Alan and I have already done some work so you won't start from scratch. Brendan will focus on his years as a federal judge; if you need help, Mr. Martin will assign one of his attorneys. Bryan, you and I will concentrate on the ten years Searcy has spent on the appellate court."

Rudberg beamed, signaling his appreciation of her calm, direct manner. He'd done well to leave the organizational task to her. "We don't have time to delve into every single case," she said. "Searcy's Senate opponents are looking at the same records we are, and they have more hands on deck. We must focus our work. We'll concentrate on his criminal docket. You heard from Mr. Martin that, as a young prosecutor, Searcy quashed an investigation into the murder of a black civil rights worker. He handed down the death penalty to a disproportionate number of African American defendants. Let's pay particular attention to cases in which race played a role."

Rudberg thought she was missing areas with equal potential, but he'd made it her show and chose not to interfere. He repeated to the three students what he'd told Aisha two days before. "I'm looking into the sources of his political power. That means going back to the beginning, to his days as a prosecutor."

"Great," she said. "A fourth member of the team will join us Tuesday, and I'll assign her to help you."

Turning back to the law students, she said, "Monday is Martin Luther King Jr. Day. The Senate Judiciary Committee begins hearings the following day. We're racing against their schedule."

Lucius rolled his eyes and shook his head while Rudberg nodded in agreement. Searcy had been busy on Capitol Hill, meeting with every senator on the committee. All members of the majority had endorsed him, and one member of the minority appeared favorable. Searcy had now moved beyond the committee, meeting with other senators of both parties. The majority held a two-vote margin, both Florida senators had come out for Searcy, and minority members from three battleground states—Ohio, West Virginia, and Missouri—had indicated their openness to his nomination. Unless this group came up with something ruinous, Searcy seemed assured of at least fifty-five of the hundred Senate votes.

---

Rudberg moved his base of operations to the downtown library, He searched the index for articles from *The Floridian* in 1989 and 1990, finding two dozen listings for Searcy and several more for the race for state attorney. He ordered up the microfilm records and began the tiresome investigative work.

He read through the stories on Searcy's appointment to the position in 1989, searched for and found nothing about the Alonzo Taylor investigation, but uncovered several articles on three murder cases Searcy's office had tried during that time. One was of a white man convicted of killing his wife. Two were of black men, one for a murder connected to an armed robbery, the second for a stabbing death following a bar fight. Searcy had asked for life imprisonment for the white man and the death penalty for the two blacks. He'd won all three cases. Rudberg took down the details and paid for printed copies.

He found accounts of trials for a variety of assaults and robberies. Searcy had a sterling track record in his first year as a prosecutor, but to Rudberg's less practiced eye black defendants appeared to receive more severe sentences than whites. While judges handed down the sentences, most tended to go along with the prosecutor's recommendation. Searcy was a hard man.

He jumped to the story on the November election in which Searcy had won his first term. He had run unopposed. This wasn't unusual for an incumbent, but Rudberg backed up to read his announcement the previous spring. "Searcy faces strong opposition from former assistant state attorney Bradley Henderson," he read.

Then, two months later, "Henderson Drops Out, Endorses Searcy." The story gave only the barest details. "After considering the toll this campaign would take on my family and the need to abandon my private practice, I have decided to withdraw and support Mr. Searcy," the article quoted him as saying. Most endorsements conveyed enthusiasm for the surviving candidate, but Rudberg found no trace of that in Henderson's statement.

He made copies of both articles and shut down the viewer. He searched for an attorney named Bradley Henderson and found a current listing in Palatine. It took a moment to get the lawyer to the phone, and when Rudberg had explained his business, he said, "That wasn't me. That was my dad."

"Oh," Rudberg said, noting the past tense and feeling deflated.

"He may be willing to talk with you about it," he continued. "It still grates on him." He provided his father's phone number, adding, "Don't count on it, though."

Rudberg placed the call and waited while the woman who answered brought her husband to the phone. He introduced himself and offered his father's name as a reference. If the man recognized Mathew, he didn't say. "I'm looking into the career of Morris Searcy," he said. Silence. "You ran against him back in 1990, but you dropped out rather suddenly." Nothing. "I wonder if you'd tell me why."

"Who are you?"

Rudberg reintroduced himself and was about to give the man the entire history of his inquiry into the career of J. Morris Searcy when he responded.

"Maybe you better come over. Where are you now?"

"I'm in Jacksonville, but I can be there in an hour."

"Make it two. I was about to take a nap," he said and hung up. Rudberg had to call his son again to get the address.

He used the extra time to call a Portland divorce attorney. Their family attorney handled Stephanie's affairs, and he needed his own hired gun. As he unrolled the recent history of their relationship, she stopped him and said, "This is too much for a phone call. When can you come see me?"

He explained that he was on the opposite coast and unlikely to return soon. They set a follow-up call the following Monday when, she said, "Everything here will be closed."

The rain was pelting down for a fourth straight day, and he left for Palatine early so he wouldn't have to rush. As it was, he arrived five minutes late.

Bradley Henderson greeted him at the door. He was burly and fit, his full head of white hair suggesting a human polar bear. He offered coffee and left to fetch it himself, moving with an incongruous lightness.

He led Rudberg into a Florida room looking out on an expanse of green lawn above the river. "So Mo is headed to the Supreme Court," he said. "Old Senator Coupland must be chortling in his grave. Man," he said, "this country is going to hell."

Rudberg concealed his ignorance. "Let's go back to the campaign of 1989," he said. "You were the assistant state attorney, Warren Justice died, Searcy was appointed to succeed him..."

"And his first act was to get rid of me," he said. "He wanted no one hanging around who was smarter than he was, so he showed me the door. I liked nothing about him, so I was happy to agree. It was tough, though. We were newlyweds, young Brad was on the way, I didn't have the proverbial pot. But I had standards. Laura's parents helped us, I launched my practice, and within a year I was making my way. Never looked back."

"But you filed to run against him," Rudberg said.

"Like I said, I didn't care for him. There are two types of prosecutors—those who pursue victories and those who pursue justice. I'm the latter."

"Why did you drop out?"

Henderson spread his hands. "Senator Coupland told me to. It was that simple. He called me into his office one day, sat me down, and said, 'You will not be the state attorney of Hampton County. Drop out now.' No 'please,' no 'I'd appreciate it.' Just do it."

"And you...?"

"Me?" he replied, as though the question didn't bear asking. "I did what he said. That's the way things worked here. Still do, to an extent, but nothing like when Senator Tom was running things."

"Did he offer you something in return?"

"A bribe, you mean? More like a reverse bribe. 'You build your little practice. I'm sure you'll do fine.' It was his way of saying I would not do well if I crossed him."

"What would have happened if you'd refused?"

"First, he would have buried me. Lots of ad money for Searcy, much of it negative toward me, maybe enough to ruin my reputation. A solid block of Searcy votes from his workers and those who depended on contracts, which meant most of the town. After my defeat, word would go out not to retain me."

"He had that kind of power," Rudberg said—a statement rather than a question. "Where did Searcy figure into all this?"

"His boy. He prosecuted those that needed prosecuting and protected those that needed protecting. Coupland owned the mill, the town, and now he owned the justice system. Or at least a key part of it. A few years later, he boosted Searcy into a judgeship, and he'd circled the wagons."

Henderson showed no sign of slowing down, so Rudberg led him in a related direction. "What do you recall about the reopened investigation into the murder of Alonzo Taylor?"

"'Reopened,' you say? They never opened it to begin with. His murder was never seriously investigated when it happened. Just one less colored troublemaker. Who's to care? Anyway, my boss—Warren Justice was his name—he read up on it and had a couple of sheriff's deputies assigned to look into it. Bill Whiting was one of them. A terrific cop."

"What became of that investigation?" Rudberg asked, though he knew the answer.

"They found an informant who put them on the trail of one of the killers. Guy by the name of Carl Trickett. He's gone now, but his son's still around, Wade Trickett. A dangerous man."

He shook his white mane as he thought about the man.

"Trickett had a partner the night of the killing, but they never got him to tell who it was. Anyway, they were about to charge him with the murder when Justice died. That's a good one. Justice died. And that's what happened."

"So they appointed Searcy to replace him. Then what?"

"Then nothing. Searcy ended the investigation. I'd left by then. I think that was one reason he forced me out. I was too close to it." He stared out the window at the rain sweeping across the lawn, remembering.

"Why did he do that? What was so important about a thirty-year-old killing?"

"I suspect he was protecting the killer, Trickett's accomplice." Seeing Rudberg frown, Henderson said, "Nothing else makes sense. And whoever it was, Senator Tom knew about it. Nothing significant went on in Searcy's office without his asking by-your-leave."

Rudberg interrogated him until he ran out of questions, but Henderson had nothing to add. "We have a team looking into every criminal case that ever came before him."

"Good," Harrison said, "but don't limit yourself to criminal cases. Look into civil suits—employment, environment, taxes—anything that affects Coupland Industries. Senator Tom put Searcy on the bench for a reason and rewarded him for good behavior. A lot's at stake here, more than you realize."

---

Rudberg cruised Palatine until he found a seafood restaurant near the river. Rollier's consisted of a deep wood-paneled dining room with tables on both sides and up the middle, divided by a wood and plastic panel that afforded little privacy.

The hostess looked him over and, despite there being a table for two near the front door, placed him at a four-top at the rear, near the kitchen. From here, the Friday night noise was a cacophony, table conversation struggling for dominance over shouts from the kitchen and the crash of dirty plates colliding with each other as servers dropped them into bus tubs.

He studied the menu. Fried oysters, clams, shrimp, scallops, and the inevitable sides of hush puppies. Why did Floridians have to bread everything from the ocean and immerse it in grease? An insert told him the catch of the day was grilled bass. Salvation, he thought.

While he waited for a server to find him, he thought about what Henderson had just told him and how it meshed with Alcee Taylor's description of Hampton County. He and Aisha needed to expand their legal excavation. Searcy had been placed in office to protect the interests of Coupland Industries, whose footprints would wander far beyond the intersection of crime and race.

Ten minutes passed with no sign of a server—not even a glass of water. He studied the wall concealing the doors to the restrooms. It held a large image of an alligator flanked by two fishing rods that had served their purpose and gone into retirement. Fish camp *kitsch*. He tried to flag down a server, recalling a Carol Burnett skit in which the waiter studiously ignores her while she ratchets her efforts to be noticed to comic extremes. Tonight, he seemed to be the joke.

Twenty minutes after his arrival, he approached the hostess. "I've been sitting at that back table for some time. Could someone take my order?"

She looked at him with undisguised contempt. "You're that guy that's poking around, asking questions about Judge Searcy, aren't you?"

Rudberg couldn't hide his disbelief. "How do you know who I am?"

"Everyone knows," she said, "and everyone here respects the

judge. If you're hungry, you'd best head north to colored town." She stared at him, daring him to respond. He nodded and left, drawing his rain jacket around him as he ran to the car.

"Damn!" he said. All four tires of his rental were flattened, the back window was shattered, and his backpack was missing, along with his notebook computer.

He returned to the restaurant. The hostess smirked. "Nice work," he said. He looked around the restaurant. Every guest was looking his way and smiling, some laughing. "I need to call the police," he said.

"This phone is only for business calls," she said.

He took out his cell phone, dialed 911, was asked to state the nature of his emergency, and was patched through to the Palatine police. "Is this an emergency?" the officer on duty said.

"It is to me," he replied. He explained his predicament, and the officer promised to send a patrolman by "as soon as he's available." Rudberg got the picture. He dialed the rental car agency, told them what had happened, and said he needed a replacement. "You'll have to bring the car in," the agent said.

"I can't. It's not drivable."

Several minutes of back-and-forth ensued until she agreed to dispatch a tow truck and bring his vehicle to their Orange Park location. "You can ride with the driver and pick up a replacement vehicle there."

He thanked her and hung up, knowing it would take over an hour for the truck to reach him. He waited inside the restaurant for a few more minutes, but the stares and snickers of the diners intimidated him, and when two burly men collided with him as they made their way out the door, Rudberg left.

He took shelter beneath the awning of an antique shop across the street, affording him a view of the restaurant's parking lot. No police cruiser came by. The wind drove the rain beneath the overhang, and the temperature dropped into the low forties. He stood and shivered, rocking from one foot to the other, defenseless and exposed.

He considered calling Sonja, confident she'd take him in, but rejected the idea. His concern was less for the effect on his impending divorce as for her. These people meant business, and he would not involve her more than he already had. The same went for Alcee Taylor. And the rental office had told him to stay with the car. All he could do was stand there and shiver.

Minutes turned into hours. Cars and pickups drove past, and he imagined that they slowed as they passed, concealed eyes studying him. Had he seen that white pickup truck before? He was certain he had. It circled the block, its driver pretending to look elsewhere, came around once more, disappeared for fifteen minutes, and came back. He tried to catch the tag number, but the driving rain fogged his glasses.

Whenever diners emerged from the restaurant's entrance, he imagined that they looked across at him. Someone slammed a car door in the parking lot, and he jumped back, startled. He had to urinate, but didn't dare; he couldn't summon a cop with a phone call, but if he peed on the sidewalk, he felt confident one would arrive.

Three hours after he'd entered the restaurant, the tow truck arrived. The driver loaded the rental car onto his trailer and let Rudberg climb into the cab. "You're soaking wet," he said, as though Rudberg were unaware of the fact. He turned up the heater until Rudberg stopped shivering.

At the rental agency, he filled out stacks of forms, then took the only vehicle available, a huge Cadillac SUV. He promised to exchange it at the airport the following day, solving the problem of how to spend his weekend.

In his room, he took a shower long enough to empty the hot water tank, donned pajamas, and pulled the blanket up to his shoulders. They had done it, he thought. They'd run him out of town. He shivered again, marveling that he'd escaped with his life.

# YOGI WAS RIGHT

The Senate hearing was to begin in an hour, and Aisha was sick. She was a specialist in old documents—treaties, journals, maps, family letters. She dug out details of historical events, separating the significant from the mundane, cataloging what she found, and helping others to mine it.

Aisha didn't know the legal world and lacked the background to know which court cases were significant. Yet here she was, leading a group of students—law students, but still students—in a search that could have consequences for decades.

Against the Goliath of a presidential nomination and a Senate committee, Aisha Stewart Moser was a David who had never used a slingshot. She leaned over the toilet bowl and heaved until nothing came up. She stood at the washbasin and wept, watching tears cascade down her normally inscrutable features.

With great effort, she pulled herself together, patting her tight, black curls into place, drying her eyes, restoring the thin coat of lipstick, her only armor against the world.

She walked into the conference room, allowing the group, which now numbered four, a small smile of recognition and began. "Good morning. This may be the most important week in our lives."

Rudberg had attended MLK services with her the day before. He'd seemed uncomfortable at first. She knew what he was thinking: would he be the only white face in the crowd? Aisha could relate. She experienced something similar every day.

As the service began, he warmed up. He craned his neck to see the children's choir, swayed in time to the chorus of adults, and wiped his eyes with a handkerchief as speaker after speaker stood to bear witness to what Martin had meant to his people and his country.

It was one of two handkerchiefs he'd brought for the occasion. The other he held to his nose. The man had a nasty cold, and over lunch, he told her why. "That must have been terrifying," she said.

"I admit I was frightened," he said, "but it had its upside. I got a new computer out of it." Aisha worried aloud about the security of the information they had gathered. "Nothing is on the computer," he assured her. "I've stored everything on our cloud account, and you know how complex that password is." He silently thanked his son for insisting on these precautions.

Rudberg related what Bradley Henderson had told him about Thomas Coupland's role in promoting Searcy into the position of county prosecutor and his suspicions that Coupland had played a role in getting him his first judgeship. "That's why we need to broaden our investigation," he said. And that is when she sensed the enormity of what lay ahead and her own inadequacy.

---

J. Morris Searcy stood at the witness table, raised his right hand and swore to tell the truth, brushed his tie into his suit coat, and took his seat at the witness table. Camera shutters clattered like castanets.

He read an opening statement, thanking the president and vice president, various senators, his parents, wife, and children, and all the ships at sea. Searcy spoke of his humble origins in "a small river town in North Florida," which was a stretch since Rudberg knew he had come from a solid upper middle-class background.

He launched into a description of his judicial philosophy—conservative but not rigid, faithful to the Constitution, but open to changes necessitated by changing times— a piece of clay ready to be molded into whatever shape would get him confirmed. Rudberg admitted it was adroit, the sort of statement he would have written had he been a flack. He knew what would come next. Senators would take turns tossing bouquets or throwing punches, depending on their philosophy; Searcy would accept or deflect, depending on the situation.

It was all an act. Searcy had the votes, and all the players knew it. Rudberg switched off the set and left his room. He had a more urgent task ahead of him.

He had spent the weekend rebuilding his life, swapping rental cars, purchasing a new computer and restoring his files, and engaging in a long phone conversation with the divorce lawyer. She recommended that Rudberg file first "to let them know you're serious," but he demurred.

Early Monday afternoon, he got an idea. Going online, he found the names of all nine members of the Judicial Nominating Commission who had recommended Searcy for a Florida circuit court seat in early 1997. Four had passed away, he found no trace of two more, and focused on the remaining three. Of these, two declined to speak with him, but the third was willing, though cautious.

"Commission meetings are open," James Gardner told him once they'd settled into seats at his dining room table, "but I found aspects of this nomination unsettling."

Rudberg sneezed into his handkerchief, apologized, and asked him to describe the nominating process. "I'll get to that," he said, "but this vacancy should never have come before the commission. We're mostly there to recommend candidates for vacancies on the Florida Supreme Court and the district courts of appeals. We get involved in circuit court appointments only when the governor requests it, and that *normally* happens only when a vacancy occurs well before the next election. That wasn't the case here."

"There was a vacancy," Rudberg said.

"True. Judge Oliver Spencer resigned in January. He cited poor health, but he lived another sixteen years, so I found that excuse curious. The more important thing was, there were only ten months until the next election, so the governor would *normally* have left the seat unfilled."

It was the second time Gardner had emphasized the word "normally." He peered over his bifocals until he was certain Rudberg had gotten the message. "We're required to produce three to six candidates for the governor. Here, we offered only three."

Rudberg considered several questions, but waited, sensing that the veteran attorney would get to the point. "One had been a vocal opponent of the governor, another was older than the man he would replace..."

"And that left Searcy," Rudberg finished.

"That left Searcy," Gardner echoed, "who'd been championed by the six members of the commission who came from his district and who'd been nominated by a prominent political force there."

"Let me guess. Thomas Coupland Sr."

"The same. I never considered Searcy the best-qualified candidate, but he was the most qualified of the three they allowed us to forward to the governor." Turning to the television set tuned to cable news in the next room, he said, "History repeats itself."

---

"You won't believe this," Brendan Foster said.

Aisha sighed. "I probably will." It was the third time she'd heard similar words that day. The first was a divorce case in which Searcy had ruled in favor of the husband, a local attorney whom his wife had accused of domestic abuse. The second was a rape case in which Searcy had allowed the defense untrammeled access to the victim's sexual history. Both suggested that he was a misogynist, but Aisha doubted they were enough to derail his nomination.

"It's a case called US v Coupland," the student continued. "The government sued, claiming that Coupland Industries had harmed the environment by discharging dangerous chemicals into the St. Johns River. Coupland argued the government lacked jurisdiction because the discharge was into the Hampton River, which it claimed is not a navigable waterway and thus not subject to EPA jurisdiction."

"That's absurd," she said. "The Hampton flows into the St. Johns."

"That's what the appeals court said. The ruling was unanimous."

"Brendan, I want you to cross reference the search words 'Coupland' and 'Searcy' and see what you find. This is great work."

Aisha's sense of inadequacy had lifted. She was continuing to search capital cases on which Searcy had ruled while still a state district judge. There was abundant evidence of racial bias.

As the second day of hearings began, the verdict from national media was that Searcy had done well. Several senators had directed pointed questions to him regarding reversals he'd suffered while a federal district judge. Searcy had swatted them away like flies.

A black senator had posed pointed questions on his views on race. Searcy's response was worthy of Martin Luther King Jr.—all it lacked was music in the background—and the senator had no specific cases with which to challenge him. The chairman had brushed aside the minority's demands to postpone the hearings while they researched the judge's background, and their resulting lack of preparation was evident. Searcy was dancing through the hearing in a cakewalk.

Rudberg and Aisha had breakfast together and shared their discoveries of the previous day. "Brendan found three more cases he tried involving Coupland Industries," she said. "One concerned an effort to unionize the plant. Another was a wage dispute. The third was a gender discrimination suit from a group of female employees. Searcy ruled for Coupland in all three cases. All were reversed."

"We should share this with Lucius," Rudberg said. "He may want to get this to a member of the committee." She agreed to do so while he headed back to the library.

Florida maintains a database of campaign contributions dating from 1996. Rudberg looked up Searcy's 1997 race in which he'd run for a full term as circuit court judge against one opponent. He detected a pattern. Among many smaller individual contributions, there were nineteen of exactly three thousand dollars. Two names he recognized—Thomas Coupland Sr. and Jr. Their wives had made identical contributions. So had Oliver Spencer, whose resignation from the bench had created Searcy's opening. The other fourteen were unknown to him, but one name stood out. It did not make him happy.

Rudberg printed out the record and circled those who had made the largest contributions. He checked Florida law, confirmed his suspicion that three thousand was the most one individual could legally contribute.

He searched for Oliver Spencer's obituary and found the names of three children listed. One was deceased, but the other two still lived. From a coffee shop, he called Spencer's son, also an attorney. He was in court that morning and unavailable. Rudberg left no message.

He called the daughter, whose last name was now Chandler, introduced himself, and told her he was working on a story about Judge Searcy's nomination. "We're very proud of him," she said.

"He got his start filling your father's seat on the bench." She acknowledged the fact but offered no further information. He asked a few perfunctory questions about her father's background and whether he'd known Searcy—he had—then said, "Why did he leave the bench? He was still relatively young."

"He never talked about it. He said it was his health, but he was fine. It was Mom who was having issues back then, although she passed away only last year. He may have felt he needed to lower his time commitment and bring in more money to help her."

"I understand," Rudberg said. "What did he do when he stepped down?"

"He became general counsel to Coupland Industries. Senator Coupland needed someone right away and made Dad a generous offer."

*I'll bet he did*, Rudberg thought.

There was no sense putting it off. After lunch, he returned to Lucius Martin's chambers and asked for a private office. He called Sonja, who expressed sympathy when she heard his raspy voice. "I got caught in the rain," he explained, offering no further explanation. They exchanged pleasantries until he ran out of ways to forestall what he had to ask.

"I want to run some names by you," he said. "Tell me what you know about them. Chloe Evans?"

She paused a beat before answering. "She was Senator Coupland's private secretary for many years. I believe she's passed away."

He read the next name, then another. Both were executives with Coupland Industries. The next was a prominent local attorney who, Rudberg suspected, had angled for a favorable reception before His Honor by placing an unsubtle bribe into the campaign coffers.

He read two more names, both of which had Coupland connections. "David Kelson," he said.

Her pause was palpable. "He's an engineer with Coupland," she said. When Rudberg waited, expecting more, she said, "He was my husband. I think you know that."

"And Sonja Kelson," he concluded. "These are people who made the maximum allowable personal contribution to the judicial campaign of Judge J. Morris Searcy." He waited for her to say something, and when she remained silent, said, "Why didn't you tell me this?"

"I had nothing to do with it. It was a condition of employment. They told all top executives and their spouses to contribute. A few weeks later, the employee received a bonus for the full amount. I didn't even sign the check. He did. I had nothing to say about it. That's one reason I'm no longer married to him."

"I'm sorry. I'm just trying to figure out where you stand."

"You have to ask that?"

"Yes," he said. "Odd things are happening—information getting out that shouldn't—and I need to protect the investigation."

"Well, go ahead," she said. "And thank you. If there's anything I don't need, is to trade one sanctimonious ass for another."

She hung up. Rudberg covered his face and sighed. Had he lost his only friend here? He called her back, but she didn't answer. He left a message apologizing.

Then he remembered her promise to help him. *She hasn't given me anything, other than when we first met and she described Palatine as a company town. But that's no great secret. I would have figured that out on my own.* <!$Scr_Cs::o>He no longer knew what to believe.

"Are you all right?" Aisha said when he entered the conference room.

"No, but I can't talk about it right now." He sat at a terminal and searched the records of Searcy's cases as a prosecutor. He felt like a fool—a sanctimonious ass.

---

The headline in *The Floridian* startled him. *FNU Students Join Effort to Reject Searcy.* Rudberg sat at the lunch counter and gagged as he read.

Law students at Florida Northern University have joined an effort to provide opposition research on Federal Judge J. Morris Searcy, the president's nominee to the US Supreme Court. A source close to the project said its goal is to develop negative information that will cause the Senate Judiciary Committee to reject Searcy's nomination.

If confirmed by the Senate, Judge Searcy, who now serves on the federal appeals court, would become the first Floridian to serve on the high court.

The effort to derail his nomination is led by Alan Rudberg, a former journalist and son of the late managing editor of *The Floridian*. Rudberg, who was fired late last November by the *Oregon Examiner* newspaper, was previously found to have libeled a public official there.

A clever narrative, Rudberg thought. He had libeled a public official, been fired by his newspaper, and come to Florida to libel another one. Who would believe someone like that?

The accompanying editorial was worse. Under the headline, *FNU Must Stop Biting the Hand that Feeds It*, the paper drew a connection between the university's public funding and an effort to "deny Florida its first-ever seat on the US Supreme Court." Now the entire state was under attack.

The editorial called on Dean Harold Stansell "to withdraw from this taxpayer-funded effort to besmirch the reputation of a respected jurist." The editorial also mentioned him by name. "Alan Rudberg, a discredited former journalist, offered a story to *The Floridian* last week that attacked Judge Searcy's record while he was Hampton County state attorney. This newspaper investigated the story and found it baseless."

He rushed the few blocks to the law office, where he found Lucius and Aisha sitting at the conference table in dismay. Both had read the story and the editorial. "Dean Stansell called me at home before I was up," Martin said. "He's withdrawing their students from the project."

"This is my fault," Rudberg said.

"Nonsense. They're just using you to divert attention from Searcy's record. Kill the messenger."

"I know that, but I'm responsible for—"

"The question," Aisha said, "is what we do now."

She was right. Recriminations could come later. The question was how to reorganize their work without the extra hands the law school had provided. "Were you able to contact a member of the committee about Searcy's ties to Coupland Industries?" he asked.

"I can't go to either of our senators. One won't listen, and the other's not on the committee. I contacted Senator Hooker from New Jersey, but only reached an aide. He found the whole relationship to Coupland too layered. They're looking for something that screams that this guy's unfit."

"The questioning is over," Rudberg said, "Searcy's off the stand. They will spend today and tomorrow listening to witnesses. It's over."

"I'm telling you guys, it's in the criminal cases. Whenever the defendant is black, he throws the book at them. He's a racist. We just need the right case to prove it."

"Maybe so, Aisha. You keep working the criminal cases, and Alan—"

"I'm on his prosecutorial record. I see the same evidence of racial bias, but there's a lot more—"

There was a knock at the conference room door and a face appeared. "Hello, Brendan," Aisha said.

"Is it okay if I still work on this?"

---

By midmorning, all four students were at work. While they couldn't devote as many hours to the project as they had when it was a sanctioned project, Brendan Foster recruited four new students and said there were more if needed. Aisha felt overwhelmed, but Brendan helped organize them into teams so that one could hand off to the next without a break.

Rudberg kept a low profile, convinced that Sonja had been the source of the leak on FNU's involvement in the study. He began writing a list of occurrences that matched things he had told her but dropped it after several minutes because it revealed his own stupidity. He would have to confess to Aisha and Lucius but now was not the time. He had work to do.

He continued cataloging murder cases Searcy and his office had brought while he was a prosecutor, expanding his search to other violent crimes, such as armed robbery. Searcy's office had demanded the death penalty in almost every murder case in which the defendant was black, and most judges had agreed. In cases of violent crime, he demanded the maximum penalty for black defendants, while white defendants accepted plea bargains and never went on trial. It was as clear a case of unequal justice as Rudberg had seen, but it was subjective. He could envision Searcy saying, "My office simply made a recommendation. Judges handed down these sentences."

In early afternoon, a call from his attorney interrupted him. "We have an offer from their side," she said. Stephanie proposed that he keep the condominium at the coast, she keep the house, and that she give him $150,000 for his share. "That's not much," she said. "You paid for the condo, so the cash is her only concession to the prenup."

"It's enough," he said.

"We should hold out for more. She is so intent on keeping the affair with her former aide a secret, she's demanding that you sign a nondisclosure agreement. I suspect you're right that she paid him hush money. We can uncover all this by demanding her financial records. You have considerable leverage."

Rudberg suspected whatever had gone on between them could cost Stephanie her job, but what good would it do him to hurt her? "Counter by telling her she's paying your fee, and let's move on," he said. "I'm tired of it, and I'm tired of her."

The truth was simpler. He was tired of everything. He couldn't recall a time when he'd been more alone and depressed.

---

"Look at this." Aisha and Rudberg huddled over the conference table. It was covered with small stacks of printed records, each tagged with a yellow note in her neat handwriting. "In 2003, a defendant on Florida's death row filed an appeal of his conviction in federal court, claiming he got an unfair trial. Because," she continued, emphasizing the word, "during deliberations, a juror expressed the conviction that, after studying the Bible, he'd concluded that black people don't have souls."

Rudberg read over her shoulder. "'Defendant's constitutional right to an impartial trial was violated,'" he read aloud.

"The federal district judge disagreed and threw the case out. That judge was J. Morris Searcy. It was one of the first cases he heard. A three-judge appeals panel reinstated the suit on appeal."

Rudberg leafed through the printed record. "Bernie Frazier," Rudberg said.

"He was convicted of murdering a black woman, Simone Simmons. This juror said all blacks could be divided into two groups. Simmons, he said, was the first type, 'a nice black lady,' while Frazier was the latter, the n-word. He said this out loud in the jury room. Three jurors attested to it."

Rudberg rifled through his own stack of paper while listening. "Bernie Frazier, right? That was Searcy's case. His office tried it in 1996. He wasn't the prosecutor; one of his assistants handled it. But it was his office."

They summoned Lucius Martin. He looked at the two records and swore under his breath. "Unbelievable. Searcy may not have tried the case himself, but no assistant state attorney requests the death penalty without running it by the boss—not here in Duval County, certainly not in a small jurisdiction like Hampton."

He shook his head. "He should have recused himself. Let me have these. I want to read the appellate court's ruling. Someone should have caught this."

―――――

The Judiciary Committee was wrapping up its hearings today without calling Searcy to account. The only person answerable for his sins today was Rudberg, and he was not looking forward to it.

He had spent the evening in the conference room, adding to his narrative of everything they knew. He organized every element of Searcy's career in a separate file—racial decisions, favorable decisions made on behalf of Coupland Industries, his frequent reversals. As the group unearthed a new piece of evidence, he added a new section, annotating it with footnotes.

It was less a book he was assembling than an indictment. He didn't know if it would ever become public, but the mere act of documenting it vindicated his decision to pursue what his father had started.

It also kept his mind off what troubled him most, but when he returned to his room after midnight, Sonja's betrayal and his stupidity kept him awake for hours. What a sap he was! What made him think an independent, attractive woman like Sonja would be attracted to an unemployed married man clinging to his last handhold on middle age? Would she have bedded him to extract more information? He didn't doubt it, but she hadn't had to. He'd given her every scrap of information he possessed.

Why had she done it? Did Coupland have something on her— something so damaging that she was willing to prostitute herself? That thought sent his mind spinning in another direction. He lay there thinking about it until he turned on the light and wrote it down. *Is Searcy beholden to Coupland or Coupland to Searcy? Why pick Searcy?*

With that, he cobbled together a few hours of restless sleep.

"I'm sorry to call so early," Barry Wheadon said.

"That's all right. I wasn't sleeping." The FDLE sergeant had called him at 7:00 A.M. and asked him to come downtown as soon as possible.

Rudberg stuffed his pocket with tissue paper and rushed downtown. "I read the story in yesterday's paper," he said when he'd seated Rudberg in his office. "You need to tell me everything you've learned. We're close to making an arrest, but there's a piece missing. This is what your father was working on, so you may know something useful."

Rudberg wasn't looking forward to entering the confessional with Aisha and Lucius and was glad for the diversion. He opened his computer and took Wheadon step-by-step through what they'd discovered. "I have all this down," he said. "Let me print it out for you." They sat together for two hours as Wheadon read the document, asking questions.

It was lunchtime before Rudberg arrived at Lucius's office. The hearings were over, Aisha explained, and the committee would vote on Searcy's nomination the following Wednesday. "They have the votes," she said, shaking her head.

"They always have had. I need to speak with you and Lucius."

"Is something wrong?"

"Yes, very. I need to discuss it with both of you."

"He's at lunch right now. Want to tell me?"

"No, I only want to do this once."

"Okay." She spoke it in a glissando, turning the word into a question mark.

He toyed with calling Sonja to confront her but dismissed the idea. What more was there to say?

"Who is this woman? What do you know about her?" Aisha, fire in her eyes, almost screamed at him across the conference table.

"She's a former reporter who knew Dad. She approached me at the memorial service to offer her condolences. I got to know her after that."

"How well did you get to know her?" she said.

"I took her to St. Augustine the night I interviewed Purty. The idea was to convince whoever was following me that we were spending the night together."

"Did you?" she said.

"No, not that night. Not ever."

"Wait a minute," Lucius broke in, "you thought you were being followed even then?"

"I knew it. The rental company found a tracking device, remember?"

"Could she have had someone place it there?"

"I visited her once at her home and had dinner with her after I returned. She was never out of my sight, but she could have had someone else plant it while we were together."

"Let's add this up. She may have had you followed, may have alerted Searcy before you interviewed him, may have led him to raise the matter of the Taylor investigation with *The Floridian* preemptively. What else?"

"There's a personal matter." He told them the person who had called Wendy Fisher to tell her about Mark and Stephanie's affair was a woman.

"How did she know?" Aisha said. "A little pillow talk?"

"No, I promise. We never—a shoulder to lean on. That's all."

"And then there's the leak to *The Floridian* about FNU's involvement," Martin said. "You told her that." Rudberg nodded.

"We were supposed to be a team," Aisha said.

"We are."

"I've introduced you to every student who's walked in here. No one joined this group without your permission. Lucius asked us before releasing the Coupland documents to Senator Hooker. We've checked with you every step of the way, yet you've never mentioned this woman."

Rudberg stared at the ceiling for help, sick from more than just a cold. "She predated your involvement to some extent...and, I have to admit, there was a personal attraction that lulled me into thinking this was only my business. She offered to help," he said in frustration.

"And did she?"

"No," he admitted.

"All right," Lucius said. "Let's calm down. Has she affected anything we've done here? Would Searcy have told a different story if you'd blindsided him? I don't think so. Would *The Floridian* have run your story if you'd gotten to them first? No."

A secretary tapped at the door. "A package for you, Mr. Rudberg." He shoved it aside. Probably divorce papers.

"As for FNU Law, Stansell's withdrawal hasn't slowed us one bit. Whatever her motivation, this friend of yours isn't our problem. Our enemy is time. We're trying to reconstruct thirty years of history in less than two weeks. I'm not happy with you, Alan, but we wouldn't be here now if you hadn't followed the trail your father blazed. Let's learn from our mistakes and get over it. Okay, Aisha?"

She kept her arms folded. "Okay?" he repeated. "We're not through yet. We need each other."

"All right," she said, "but no more surprises."

Rudberg nodded agreement and opened the package as they plotted next steps. "Wait a minute," he said. "Look at this." A package of clippings spilled onto the table along with several pages of copy. He read one sheet and passed it to Lucius, who scanned it and passed it to Aisha.

"A history of Coupland Industries," Rudberg said, "details of dozens of lawsuits, some of which never made it to trial, company principals and board members going back years."

"Who sent it?"

"Sonja. She couldn't have pulled this together in a day. She's been working on it for a while."

"But she didn't deliver it to us until the hearing ended, when it was too late," Aisha said.

"It's not too late," Martin said. "Yogi was right. It ain't over 'til it's over."

# AN UNHOLY ALLIANCE

Martin urged them to keep working. "The Judiciary Committee meets Wednesday, but the full Senate won't take up his nomination until the following week. That may be our best shot." Armed with Sonja's dossier, Rudberg, Aisha, and two of the students assembled Saturday morning at the law office.

Among the clippings was a story of a tax evasion case brought in federal court against a member of the Coupland board. Searcy had heard the case and dismissed it. Aisha looked up the case on the database. "The government appealed, and Searcy was overturned," she said. "We identified that reversal last week, but we didn't have the Coupland connection."

During the next few hours, they found several other instances in which officers or board members at Coupland received favorable treatment from Searcy. Rudberg doubted any one example would deny Searcy the nomination, but the cumulative effect might be significant.

At noon, Martin joined them bearing a message for Rudberg. "A woman called our answering service asking to speak with you," he said. "She left no name, but says it's urgent."

Rudberg moved to a small office and dialed the number. The

voice on the other end sounded tentative, frightened. Rudberg tried to get a name from her, but she was reluctant. "You called us," he said. "You have something important to tell me."

"I've never told anyone this," she said. "Not even my husband. I left all that behind me, but he's such an awful man. I saw your name in the paper and had to tell you."

"Would you feel more comfortable speaking with a woman?" he asked.

"Yes," she said, relief in her voice. "Yes, please."

Rudberg summoned Aisha, who introduced herself and asked if she could place the call on the speaker so "my brother can hear you." The woman agreed, though not without reluctance.

She identified herself as Sarah Overmeyer but said that was not her maiden name. Aisha asked for that, but she declined, and Rudberg waved her off to keep her from pressing.

"I made mistakes when I was younger. I drank a lot, did a bit of pot, and ran with some bad people."

She paused, and Aisha prompted her, saying, "Most of us made mistakes in our youth—things we'd rather not talk about."

"I was sixteen. We were looking for beer. An older guy bought it for us, and he joined us. There were four of us—my boyfriend and I, another couple, and this guy. We were in that park in downtown Palatine. You know where I mean?"

Rudberg nodded his head, and Aisha said she did. "I had too much to drink. At some point, my boyfriend passed out. This guy came on to me, and I tried to talk my way out of it—jolly him, you know what I mean?"

Aisha said she did. "It didn't work. He—he—" She choked back sobs.

Aisha comforted her as best she could, then said, "He attacked you, is that it?"

"Yes."

"And then what happened?"

"I was so ashamed. I shouldn't have been there, shouldn't have been drinking, shouldn't have been with those people—my friends. I thought it was my fault."

"But it wasn't," Aisha said. "This man did something to you without your permission. You told him no, and he did it anyway. It's not your fault."

"That's what the officer said."

"So you reported this? What happened then?"

"He was a really kind man. My mother—I never could talk to her. She was always drinking. This officer had me talk to his wife. Clara, I think her name was."

Rudberg pumped his fist, nodded his head, scrawled J. S. Barstow's name on a notepad. Aisha prompted her to continue.

"They had me file charges. We went to court. There was no jury. Just me and the state attorney and this guy and his attorney. And the judge—Searcy. He kept calling me 'the accused.' My attorney kept correcting him, saying I was the victim."

"The accused?" Aisha repeated.

"That's what he called me. Like it was a mistake, but I think he meant it. It was then I knew this would not end well."

Again Aisha prompted her. "So he said the most awful thing. I remember it word-for-word. As God is my witness. He said, 'Pain and sex sometimes go together.' Like he was a doctor instructing me. And then he said, 'Why didn't you just keep your knees together?'"

"What?" Both Aisha and Rudberg reacted.

"That's what he said. If I'd kept my knees together, I'd have been fine. And then he dismissed the case. This guy walked free, and I was —" She broke down, sobbing.

"You were pregnant."

"Yes," she choked about between sobs, "and I had to get rid of it. My mother—I had no one to help me."

"This young man, the person who attacked you, do you recall his name?"

"Oh, yes," she said. "Everyone in town knew him. Jeremy," she said.

"Jeremy—?"

"Coupland. You know. The people who own the paper mill."

"Mrs. Overmeyer, this is important," Rudberg said. "I can't tell you how critical this is. Would you be willing to share this with someone from the Judiciary Committee before—"

"No? You mustn't tell anyone. My husband doesn't know. He's a minister. He wouldn't—if he knew that I had—you mustn't tell anyone. I just wanted you to know what a bad man Searcy is."

Rudberg mouthed a silent expletive. "If we could keep that part out," Aisha said, "have you tell your story just to a woman senator—"

"No, please, no. Don't make me do that."

They promised, thanked her, and let her go. Aisha ran Jeremy Coupland's name through the database. "Nothing," she said. "There's no record of such a case ever being filed, let alone coming before Judge Searcy."

"And you're surprised?" Rudberg said.

———

"There's nothing we can do about it," Rudberg said. He and Aisha huddled together after Sunday dinner at Grace's house. "She doesn't want to go public, and we'll ruin her life if we force her."

"I wouldn't even try," Aisha said. "All these years, and she's still traumatized. You can't comprehend what it's like unless you've lived it."

Rudberg didn't pursue it. She'd tell him her story when and if she was ready. "She may not be alone. We need to learn more about this Jeremy Coupland character and see if there are similar cases in Searcy's background. We won't find them in the public record. I'll check the local newspaper."

"You think they'd publish anything like that? In Palatine?"

"Probably not, but it's the only chance we have. There's nothing for me to do here. You have things well in hand."

"Do you think so?" she said.

"I know it. You're a jewel. Without your organizational skills, we'd be adrift."

Monday morning Rudberg drove to Palatine. A private detective who did occasional work for Lucius Martin sat alongside him, riding shotgun. No one would mess with Rudberg on this day.

---

The precaution was unnecessary, for at that moment Wade Trickett, the man who'd followed Rudberg during his first attempt to interview William Purty and tried to intimidate him in Shay's Diner, the man who'd twice planted tracking devices on his rental cars, who'd slashed his tires and broken into his car ten days before, was sitting in an interview room at the FDLE offices in Jacksonville.

"Fencing Rudberg's computer was not a smart move," Sergeant Wheadon told him.

"I told you, I bought it from another guy."

"We have you on surveillance video from the antique store across the street."

"I need to see that," his attorney said. Wheadon ignored him.

"We're charging you with grand theft, breaking and entering, and that's just for starters. But that's not why you're here."

When Trickett expressed no curiosity, Wheadon said, "We want to discuss the murder of Mathew Rudberg on the afternoon of November 12."

Wheadon got the reaction he loved to see in suspects, an almost imperceptive start, a rapid movement of the eyelids. "I don't know nothin' about that. I had nothing to do with it."

"But you did," he said and reeled off the chain of evidence he had assembled.

---

"In April 1992," Charise Thornton said, "they tried a black man,

Artemis Walker, for armed robbery. Walker maintained his innocence and claimed he was miles away when the robbery occurred.
The jury convicted him, and the judge sentenced him to thirty years
at Raiford."

Aisha stood over the law student, looking at the screen as she
scrolled down it. "In 1999, his attorney moved for a new trial based
on the testimony of a witness who said Walker was with him at the
time of the robbery. He swore that he'd told that to investigators.
During discovery, the lawyer discovered the witness's statement in
the file. Searcy had it in his possession during the trial and withheld it
from the defense."

"That slime," she said.

"The Florida Supreme Court overturned the conviction and
ordered a new trial. The state attorney declined to prosecute, and the
court ordered Walker's release."

"I wonder how many more there are," Aisha said. "We know
about this because Walker had a good attorney. What about those
who don't?"

---

The main branch of the Hampton County Library was a modern,
one-story, steel-and-glass building just off US 19 in Palatine. The
microform reader, however, was of the obsolete design that required
you to hand crank between each page. Rudberg ordered the January-
July 1989 editions of the *Hampton County Times* and looked through
the roll. The paper had been a weekday daily until 2008 when it cut
back to a biweekly publication until it closed in 2015. There was no
index, requiring him to scan through every single page to find
anything related to their investigation.

He feared the search would take days until he got onto its layout.
All the news stories began in the first three pages, the second of
which contained national and world news. Wednesday's edition had
a business section, and Thursday's had a society column, replete with

photos. Nothing else was likely to be of interest. He soon cleared two weeks' of issues in less than five minutes.

The April 11 issue contained the news of Searcy's appointment as state attorney. Apart from details on three high-profile cases he had argued in his private practice, there was nothing new in the report, but he charged a print copy to his credit card and moved on.

He found nothing on the closing of the investigation into the murder of Alonzo Taylor, an omission that did not surprise him.

In the July-December roll, he found a front-page story on Searcy's candidacy, a brief story on Bradley Henderson's filing to oppose him, buried at the bottom of page 3, and a longer story on Henderson's subsequent withdrawal. He printed several accounts of criminal cases Searcy had prosecuted, scanning the rolls of microform through 1995. The *Times* had treated him as a crime-fighting hero. Reading the stories sequentially, Rudberg detected the same pattern of unequal treatment of black and white defendants he and Aisha had found in the official records.

He printed stories on Coupland Industries he found in the news pages and in the weekly business section. The *Times* devoted considerable space to any story of plant expansion or major new customers but avoided accounts of Coupland fighting regulators or paying fines for environmental offenses. Rudberg knew paying the fine often cost less than fixing the problem, but it was also clear why Coupland Industries needed a judge in its corner.

In March 1996, the firm announced that it had promoted Thomas Coupland Jr., son of the founder, to chief operating officer and vice chairman of the board, positions he held until his father's death a decade later. The younger Coupland and his wife appeared frequently in the society column. *Palatine society*, Rudberg thought, *an oxymoron*.

Rudberg continued to scroll through the rolls of microform, through the rest of 1996, all of 1997, including Searcy's appointment to the Florida circuit court and subsequent election, and into 1998.

And then he paused, emitting an involuntary whistle so loud that two nearby readers looked up in annoyance.

He reread the story to make certain he wasn't misinterpreting it. He printed it and scanned editorials and letters for the following month to see if there'd been any public reaction. There were no further references to what, for him, was the most explosive aspect of Searcy's career they had uncovered. If it were true.

He rewound the film, closed the reader, and drove the detective back to Jacksonville, saying not a word during the trip north.

———————

"The reporter who wrote this article, Glen Hanscomb, left the paper when they downsized ten years ago," Rudberg told Aisha and Lucius the following morning. "He now lives in St. Augustine and says he wouldn't be talking with me if he were still in Palatine. Not only does he stand by every word he wrote, he has a tape of the conversation."

He handed copies of the article across the table, sat back with his arms folded, and waited. The reaction was almost immediate.

Circuit Judge J. Morris Searcy, in office for less than a year, said yesterday that the county's black citizens "represent the greatest threat to law and order I have seen in a decade of law enforcement. They represent half of the county," he said, "but account for most of the crime."

The reason, he says, is that "we've been too good to them. It started when we let them into our schools. They couldn't keep up with the whites because of their attitudes and their poor home environment.

"Most of them don't have both parents at home," he said. "They have drugs in the house, the father is often in jail, and the kids come to school carrying all this anger and don't have the will to study."

Hampton County, according to Searcy, was "not yet ready to have a black on the bench, but we need a Jew or two so we can hold court over the Christmas holiday."

The pair sat stunned as Rudberg had been when he'd found it eighteen hours before. "We know what he is," Aisha said, "but here he is laying it out for us."

"Why would he say things like that to a reporter, of all people?" Martin said.

"I wondered the same thing until I talked with him. Hanscomb is from Mississippi, and his accent is so thick I can barely understand him. I'm sure Searcy thought he was talking to a good old boy who either wouldn't print it or would tone it down. But he didn't. As you can see, the whole article is just a series of quotes."

"Why did the paper print it?" Lucius asked.

"This may surprise you." Rudberg looked at them, then corrected himself. "I don't think it will. According to Hanscomb, the editor saw nothing wrong with it. He even said something like, 'About time someone said this.'"

Rudberg looked from one to the other. Neither registered any emotion. "The paper received some angry letters but didn't print them. Hanscomb urged that they run an editorial disavowing the remarks, but the editor refused."

"Why didn't this come out during his previous confirmation hearings?" Aisha said.

"The reporter supplied a copy to one of Senator Blankenship's aides when Searcy was nominated to the appeals court, but nothing came of it. He's as surprised as you are it's never surfaced."

"Casual racism in action," she said.

They debated what to do about it. The Senate Judiciary Committee's vote was less than twenty-four hours away. Late that afternoon Lucius reported back. Florida's senior senator had declined to raise the matter. "It took place nearly twenty years ago, he told me. Searcy wouldn't have made it through two hearings if he still harbored that kind of attitude. I followed up with a call to Senator Hooker. He's outraged but says there's too little time to vet the report. He suggests waiting for the debate by the full Senate."

"So what do we do now?" Rudberg said.

"We let the Judiciary Committee do its thing while we hunt for a bigger megaphone."

---

Wade Trickett sat across the table from Sergeant Wheadon and an assistant state attorney from Duval County. Despite having access to shaving cream and a razor, he was unshaven, reddish stubble tinged with gray. A public defender sat alongside him, summoned less than an hour before. Wheadon turned on the recorder, giving the date and time and the names of those present.

"You are appearing with new counsel and on your own initiative, is that correct?"

"I asked to meet with you, yeah."

"And you requested a public defender, rather than relying on the attorney who represented you yesterday, is that correct?"

"He ain't my lawyer. The company hired him."

"Please answer the question for the record. You asked for a public defender and have declined to use the counsel representing you a few days ago, is that correct?"

"Yeah, that's right."

"You told us you wish to make a statement. You may proceed."

"I want to cut a deal."

"What sort of deal?"

The public defender cut in. "Mr. Trickett has information relating to the death of Mr."—he searched his scrawled notes —"Mathew Rudberg."

"What sort of information?"

"I didn't kill him," Trickett broke in as the public defender tried to silence him. "I was there, but I didn't kill him. I know who did, and I ain't going to prison for him."

"Mr. Trickett's attorney—" the public defender began.

"He ain't my attorney. He don't have any interest in protecting me. He's out to protect Coupland."

The public defender brought a halt to the torrent of conversation. "Mr. Trickett will plead guilty to being an accessory and will want probation."

"I can ask for a reduced sentence," the assistant state attorney said. "I can't promise he will walk away free. And it depends on the strength of his information. If it's just his word against someone else's..."

"No, we have more than that. We have physical evidence."

Wheadon and the assistant state attorney exchanged glances. The prosecutor excused himself to make a call. The three of them waited, Trickett fidgeting, as the minutes ticked by. "Agreed," the prosecutor said as he returned. "Let's hear your story."

---

The Senate Judiciary Committee met at 10 A.M. on the second floor of the Dirksen Senate Office Building. The hearing room was packed. A few straggling senators drifted in and took their seats behind the three long tables, arranged in the shape of an open horseshoe.

The chairman gaveled the meeting to order and explained the procedure. He read an opening statement endorsing Searcy. The ranking minority member read a statement expressing strong reservations about his judicial record. Three members of each party followed suit.

A few minutes past noon, the committee approved the nomination of J. Morris Searcy by a vote of eleven to ten, along party lines.

---

"We just wanted to talk to him, get him to stop asking questions.

They told me, go out there, the two of you, and talk sense into him. We never meant to hurt him."

"Who's 'they?'"

"My supervisor at the plant, Mr. Clark."

The prosecutor asked a few more questions, and Trickett described how he'd served as an errand boy for Coupland Industries, doing anything they required of him. "*Anything*. Just like my dad did."

"So this Mr. Clark sent you to talk to Mr. Rudberg. What happened when you arrived?" the prosecutor said.

"When we got there, he was puttering around outside. He was banging against this downstairs door with a big rubber mallet. We interrupted him, told him we'd heard he was asking about things that didn't concern him. 'You're not from here. You need not be involved in this. It isn't your concern. No good can come from it.' That sort of thing."

"And what did Mr. Rudberg do?"

"He got mad, yelled about how he knew my father had killed this colored preacher, Taylor. Spouted off about how we couldn't keep hiding the truth, that sort of thing. He was loud—screaming—and we were afraid someone would hear us." Trickett looked at them in an appeal for understanding.

"The guy with me, he grabbed the old man and shook him. Rudberg threw a punch at him. He's weak, this guy, hasn't done a lick of work in his life, so the old man's punch stunned him. Like no one had ever taken a poke at him before, you know? He picked up the mallet the old man had been using and swung it at him. The old man turned to avoid it, and it caught him on the back of his head. He went down and didn't get up."

He'd leaned over Rudberg to help him to his feet, Trickett explained, assuming at first he was unconscious, then realized he wasn't breathing. "'He's dead,' I said. And he first says no, he can't be and then starts bawling and saying he didn't mean to do it, that it was the old man's fault. Anyway, I thought quick and decided we should dump him in the river. He was dead," he said, his voice rising in panic. "I checked for a pulse. I mean, I wouldn't have done that if he was still alive." He looked from one to the other, beseeching them to believe him. Neither man spoke, allowing him to worry.

"You said you have physical evidence," the prosecutor said.

Trickett leaned back in his chair, a cocky smile playing across his lips, in charge once more. "Yeah. After we'd dumped him, I told the guy to go sit in the car. He was still crying, shaking like a little kid. I thought he'd pee his pants, he was so scared."

Trickett looked from one to the other. "I knew what they might try, so I grabbed a pair of gloves out of the truck, picked up the mallet, wrapped it in a towel, and put it in my toolbox. It's still there."

Trickett looked from the attorney to Wheadon and back again. "They're telling me to take the fall, that they'll take care of my family and all and see I don't spend much time inside. That's all they care about, protecting themselves. You guys gotta believe me. I only went there to warn him, and I didn't kill him. He did. That's why I came to you."

"And for the record, the man who was with you?" Wheadon asked.

"Coupland. Jeremy Coupland."

---

Lucius Martin treated them to lunch at his club, reserving a private room off the main dining area that offered a view of the St. Johns as it bent eastward through the city on its way to the Atlantic Ocean. The skies had cleared after yesterday's rain, and Rudberg could see almost to the coast. He wished he were there. Anywhere. It was as if he had a loaded gun in his hand, but couldn't unlock the safety.

"You're both down at the moment," Martin said, "but the Senate doesn't vote until Tuesday. That gives us five days."

"We should take this article to the *New York Herald* and let them run with it," Rudberg said.

"We could, but even that might not work at this late date. Why did medieval fortresses have round towers and curved walls?" he asked with a grin. As they looked at him in confusion, he answered his own question. "To deflect cannon balls. If the walls were flat, the missile would tear right through them, but if it hit a round surface, it tended to skid off with minimal damage. That's what we're dealing with here. Anything you've thrown at Searcy has just banked off without penetrating. We need a frontal assault against a flat surface." He clapped his hands for emphasis.

"So give a newspaper everything we know?" Aisha said.

"Give *all* media everything we've assembled," he replied. "I'm on the board of an organization called Americans United for Justice."

"I found Carl Trickett's history with the Klan on their site," she said. "They monitor hate groups."

"They not only watch, but infiltrate hate groups, haul states with discriminatory laws into federal courts, protect migrant workers, take up cases of those unfairly convicted, and a lot more. Alan, you've kept track of everything we've discovered. How difficult would it be to pull together a report?"

"I update it every evening. I could print it now." Martin expressed mild disbelief. "I may need to polish a few edges, but you know what they say about a reporter: his first draft is the best."

That wasn't quite true. He'd been rewriting every section as he added new material, and what he had now was nearly publishable.

"Let me make a call. We may take a little trip."

———

Rudberg, Aisha, and Martin boarded the 6:05 A.M. flight to Atlanta. Rudberg had driven to St Augustine the previous afternoon and transferred the reporter's recorded interview with Searcy onto his computer. On the flight up, they took turns listening over headphones. Searcy's voice had a verbal swagger to it, an arrogant confidence that made the audio more damning than the transcript.

Atlanta's traffic was so congested that the taxi into the city took ten minutes longer than the flight. "I would never live here," Aisha said. Rudberg allowed that Portland's traffic was just as bad, but the distances were shorter.

The receptionist behind the glass partition greeted them without smiling, checked their IDs and issued passes, and called for an assistant to escort them to a conference room. "I apologize for all the security precautions," he said. "We get our share of loonies here. That glass partition is bulletproofed, but our receptionist has the most dangerous job in the city."

The assistant offered them coffee and Danish pastries, which they devoured, having had no breakfast at the airport. Five others joined them, two attorneys, two researchers, and another assistant.

Lucius summarized their project, beginning with Mathew Rudberg's effort to look into Alonzo Taylor's death. "I knew your father," one attorney said. "A remarkable man." Aisha and Rudberg nodded their agreement. With that, Lucius deferred to Rudberg.

"We have a hundred and twenty-eight page dossier for you. It deals with everything from Searcy's unequal treatment of black defendants to his consistent rulings in favor of Coupland Industries, whose owners put him in office. Together, it's a damning indictment, but the most shocking item is this."

He tapped his computer's touchpad and let Searcy speak for himself. "Coloreds just aren't up to white standards," the voice said. "They live in squalor and like it that way. They let their kids grow up in poverty and then turn them loose on society."

The voice emitted a derisive snort. "And it's our fault. We've been too good to them..."

"That's Searcy?" an attorney said. Rudberg nodded and shoved a signed affidavit across the table while the jurist's voice dragged on.

When the audio ended, a researcher let out a long whistle, as Rudberg had done in the library. They talked among themselves for a moment, sharing incredulity.

Rudberg moved on. "In April 1989," he began, "Searcy was

appointed Hampton County state attorney on the personal interven-
tion of a local industrialist and political kingmaker, Thomas Coupland Sr. Three months later, Searcy dropped a six-month-long
investigation into the slaying of a local civil rights leader..." Rudberg
spoke for an hour, paging through his dossier, answering some questions, turning others over to Aisha.

"We have sources for every allegation," he concluded, "copies of
court records, judicial decisions, and newspaper clippings. We can
substantiate everything we've told you."

"This is brilliant," a researcher said.

"But frightening," an attorney added. "What I don't get is the
source of his power. Searcy seems to have something on someone,
probably someone in this Coupland organization. What's holding
together this unholy alliance?"

"I wish I knew," Rudberg said.

---

"It was an accident." Jeremy Coupland had been sitting in the interrogation room for six hours, the overhead vent pouring cold air on his
neck and back. The chair was hard and unyielding, his legs were
cramped, and the attorney supplied him by his father seemed more
interested in procedural issues than in his welfare.

He hadn't told his attorney the whole truth. As each series of
questions caused Coupland to retreat from his previous statement,
his attorney would call for a recess and go over his new version of the
story. The attorney ran interference without knowing whether it was
a pass or a running play. They steadily lost ground.

Jeremy tried another tactic. "It just happened. He had this rubber
hammer. A door to his storage room that wouldn't close. The storm
had damaged it somehow. So he was holding this thing in his hand
and swinging it around. It almost hit me," he said, looking for
sympathy.

When neither showed the slightest reaction, he flailed on. "So I grabbed it from him, see, and he took a swing at me, and I raised my arm to ward him off, and he sort of collided with the hammer. He must have had a thin skull."

"And then what happened?"

"I checked him—actually, it was Wade. He checked the old man and said he was dead and that we had to throw him in the water to make it look like an accident. I didn't want to." He shook his head to convey his innocence.

"Why did you go there in the first place? What did you care that Rudberg was asking questions about Alonzo Taylor's death?"

Coupland thought. "It wasn't me," he said. "It was Wade. He didn't like the old guy asking questions about his father."

"But his father is long gone."

"It was pride." Coupland thought about it and nodded his head in agreement with himself. "Family pride. He didn't want people dissing his daddy. I just went along to help."

"Just along for the ride," Wheadon said.

"Yeah. It was an accident like."

"Wade says it was the other way around. He says he went along with you—his supervisor had told him to go—and that it was you who wanted Mr. Rudberg to stop looking into the Alonzo Taylor murder. He gave us the mallet. Your fingerprints and DNA are on the handle and strands of Mr. Rudberg's hair and blood still cling to the rubber head. Which means," the prosecutor said, "your story doesn't hold water. The victim didn't hit the mallet. The mallet hit him. This was no accident." Coupland thought about it.

"There's one other thing you need to know," the prosecutor said. "You may think this case will go to trial in Hampton County, where you'll get a nice friendly jury. It won't. The FDLE took this investigation from the Hampton County Sheriff's Office due to its gross incompetence, so we will move for a change of venue. Given your family's prominent role there, I don't think we'll have any trouble getting one and moving it here to Duval County, where Mr. Rudberg worked all his life."

Coupland's attorney argued the point, but the assistant state attorney was firm. "So, Mr. Coupland, witness, murder weapon, neutral venue. You're facing a long stretch."

He let that sink in. "So tell me what you were doing there."

Coupland gulped, looked to his attorney for help, and began to talk.

## PHARAOH KEPT THE SLAVES FIGHTING AMONG THEMSELVES

Reporters filled most of the two hundred seats in the AUJ lecture hall before 9:00 A.M. Rudberg paced back and forth in an anteroom muttering to himself. "Nervous?" Lucius Martin asked.

"Never more. I don't do this sort of thing. Where's Aisha?"

"In the restroom throwing up, I'm told. You'll both do fine."

"I still don't understand why the news media weren't all over this. Why was it left to us to uncover his background?"

"Three things," an AUJ attorney said. "There wasn't time. The president appointed Searcy only three weeks ago. He and the majority leader thought they had the votes, and after his Madigan debacle, they rushed this through committee. Second, the Senate has vetted him twice before, and they didn't catch these problems on either occasion. There were multiple nominations both times, and Searcy was part of a balancing act—one conservative for one moderate. He slipped through."

"And the third reason?" Rudberg said.

"Reporters were more interested in his politics than his background. What are his views on abortion? Will he stand up to the president? Not 'what did you do in the war, daddy?'"

Aisha rejoined them. "Are you okay?" he said.

"No," she answered, "are you?"

He shook his head.

"Just stick to the script," the attorney said. "You've been over it a half-dozen times, and you both did great. When the questions come, Lucius and I will be there to help."

Knowing one of the cable networks was covering their news conference live, they walked onto the stage at 9:01 A.M. Overhead lights blinded them. Rudberg removed his glasses to block out reflections, saw a row of video cameras at the back of the room, and put them back on.

AUJ's executive director, Steve Rosenkrantz, opened the news conference. "The Senate is scheduled to vote tomorrow to confirm J. Morris Searcy to a lifetime appointment on the US Supreme Court. Judge Searcy has received less scrutiny than any nominee in a half century. As we will show, that oversight could have devastating consequences for our democracy."

He introduced Rudberg and Aisha, "a journalist and a researcher who have investigated Judge Searcy under the guidance of AUJ board member Lucius Martin." Clever, Rudberg thought—we worked under the wing of AUJ, giving our work the patina of legitimacy.

Rudberg spoke first. "During his thirty-year career as a prosecutor and a jurist, J. Morris Searcy acted as an agent of a corporation in his community. Coupland Industries launched his career and promoted his rise within the judiciary. In return, Searcy prosecuted Coupland's opponents, protected its friends, and ruled in its favor at every juncture. We will cite rulings and share documents that prove this."

Aisha grasped the baton. "Judge Searcy has insulted women who appeared before him, denigrating victims of rape by suggesting it is their fault. His record on civil rights is appalling. On being appointed state attorney in 1989, he suppressed a cold case investigation into the slaying of a voting rights advocate three decades before. He prosecuted black defendants more aggressively than their white counter-parts, seeking the death penalty more often in capital cases and suppressing evidence that might have led to exoneration. On the bench, he failed to step aside when he had a clear conflict of interest, ruling for the state in criminal cases his office had prosecuted."

"There is no better evidence of Judge Searcy's racial bias than his own words," Rudberg said. "Here is an excerpt from an interview he gave to a hometown newspaper reporter in 1998." Searcy's voice filled the hall. Reporters strained to listen, then began scribbled and typing. When the clip had finished, Rudberg heard a collective gasp.

At 11:00 A.M., Judge J. Morris Searcy issued a statement denying the allegations and attacking Rudberg's credibility. The voice on the tape was not his, he maintained, Rudberg and Aisha had an agenda and had mined his court cases selectively. An hour later, he refused further comment.

The White House put out a statement supporting Judge Searcy, but the first cracks in the dam appeared minutes later when Florida's junior senator withdrew his support. At midafternoon, the majority leader announced that the Senate would delay a vote until the Judiciary Committee could meet again on the nomination. Five senators from his party withdrew their endorsements, assuring that the full Senate would reject the nomination when and if it ever came to a vote.

At 7:30 P.M., too late for the network newscasts, Judge Searcy withdrew his name from consideration, blaming a "media witch hunt" and a "rush to judgment." His week of bad news was far from over, however.

One other story competed for Rudberg's attention on the front page of *The Floridian* Tuesday morning. The Florida Department of Law Enforcement had arrested Jeremy Coupland, grandson of the founder of Coupland Industries, for the murder of Mathew Rudberg and had charged Wade Trickett as an accessory. Rudberg called Aisha, who'd already heard the news.

"Why did they kill him?" she said. "Wade was protecting his father's name. I get that. But what was Jeremy Coupland's interest in someone looking into Alonzo Taylor's death?"

Rudberg thought out loud. "Let's suppose Mathew had followed the trail we did—Taylor to Searcy to Coupland Industries. Did that cozy relationship threaten their business?"

"I don't think Dad had made that connection yet," Aisha said. "He might have in time, but J.S. Barstow told you his immediate interest was limited to Alonzo Taylor's death."

Rudberg agreed. They were missing something. He called Sergeant Wheadon to put the question to him. He was tied up and might not return the call until later in the day. It was a gutsy move, but Rudberg called Coupland Industries and asked to speak to Thomas Coupland Jr. His office transferred him to the same executive he'd spoken to weeks before.

"He's not in," she said.

"How can I reach him?"

"You can't."

"Would you give him a message for me?"

"No, I'm sure he has nothing to say to you."

"He is not the aggrieved party here. My father is dead, his son is accused of killing him, and I want to know why."

"I'm sure we all do," she said after a long pause. "I'm sorry, but Mr. Coupland cannot meet with you. He's in Jacksonville. I—I don't know when he'll return."

Rudberg spent several minutes thinking about her response—not just what she'd said, but how she'd said it. He raised his index finger, pointing to an imaginary thought bubble.

"I need to apologize." Brendan Foster stood in Lucius Martin's office door, head down, eyes averted.

"What for? Come in. What's on your mind?"

The FNU student took the offered chair and sat slumped. "I know you told us to keep what we were doing to ourselves," he began. "But I told my girlfriend. I was proud of being involved in something like this. Okay, I wanted to impress her."

"So you told her about the study, and she told someone else—"

"A friend. A reporter for *The Floridian* she'd met in a class last year. She didn't understand it was sensitive. She was excited for me and thought I should get recognition. I'm sorry."

Martin placed a hand on his shoulder. "You're not alone. Every man around here, it seems, has to impress the woman in his life. As I told another fellow several days ago, you made a mistake, but no harm was done."

After the student left, walking erect now, Martin smiled to himself. Rudberg would enjoy hearing this.

Withdrawing his name from the Supreme Court seat was one thing, but Searcy refused to step down from the appeals court, proclaiming his innocence to anyone who would listen and to those who would not. He claimed Rudberg had edited the tape, taken his remarks out of context, and were two decades old. His views had changed since then, he insisted. Just look at the record. Observers did so and found his defiance absurd.

When a fellow judge in the Eleventh Circuit said as much, Searcy doubled down, accusing him of being part of "a liberal cabal." That didn't sit well with their colleagues, all of whom signed a letter urging him to resign. He refused.

On February 1, two members of the House filed articles of

impeachment. When thirty others representing both parties signed on, Searcy caved, offering his resignation in a one-sentence letter.

———

Rudberg, who only days before had been persona non grata, was now in demand. Two newspapers contacted him and invited him for an interview. *Eyewitness Monthly*, the muckraking website, offered him a job as a roving editor. He could live anywhere and self-assign himself to topics that interested him. It was overwhelming. It was tempting.

What intrigued him, however, was a call from the executive director of Americans United for Justice, Steve Rosenkrantz. "This was terrific work," he said.

"Thanks, but more than a dozen people contributed—Lucius, Aisha, eight dedicated law students, and several informants. Plus, my father," he added.

"But you led it and tied it together in a bow. It was well organized and detailed, masterfully reported, everything we needed to make Congress and the public take notice."

Rudberg again thanked him, basking in the flattery but convinced that modesty was the more appropriate emotion. "I want you to come work for us," Rosenkrantz said. "We need experienced people on the ground who can do our work. We can't pay you what you've been making. You won't have a byline. Many won't admire you, may even vilify you. But I promise you it will be rewarding. Every day, you will feel a sense of purpose. Every evening, you'll be able to face yourself in the mirror."

Rudberg listened to more of the sales pitch, realizing why Rosenkrantz was the face and voice of the organization. He asked a few questions, then said, "I have one condition..."

———

Rudberg arrived unannounced at one of the four houses sitting atop the small hill overlooking the St. Johns, knowing that if he'd asked, he would have been refused. The gate in the front fence was open wide enough to allow a person to pass through, but not a vehicle. A maid answered the door. She wore a black dress with puffed sleeves and a white apron—straight from 1950s central casting.

"I'm here to see Judge Searcy."

"He's not taking visitors today."

"Tell him Alan Rudberg is here. I'm not here to hassle him. I have a few questions for him. I'm not leaving until he speaks to me, or until the police remove me, which I don't recommend."

"And why would that be?" Searcy stood at the top of a curved staircase looking down at him. He was still in pajamas, a robe wrapped around him, his usually immaculate hair in disarray.

"Because it would give me another soapbox," he said, "and you'll be happier if we keep this between ourselves."

Searcy stared for a moment, looking down at him, willing him to go away. "Ten minutes," he said at last. "Bessie, show him into the dining room."

*Bessie.* He wondered if Searcy had imposed this on her as a stage name. She brought him coffee. He thanked her and asked how she was. She looked at him in surprise, decided he meant it, and said, "I'm fine, sir. Thank you."

"I'm Alan," he said, extending his hand.

"I know," she said. She gave him a conspiratorial smile but did not take his hand.

"That'll be all," Searcy said as he swept into the room. He'd thrown on chinos and an open-necked polo shirt but still looked as though he hadn't slept in weeks. Which perhaps was the case. "Make this quick. You have cost me a great deal."

Rudberg leaned back in his chair and fingered his coffee cup. "I never set out to cost you a thing. I came to Florida because my father passed away. When I discovered someone had murdered him, I wanted to know why."

"Stupid thing," he said. "Those two idiots!"

"I've been asking myself why they felt the need to silence him. To protect Wade's father's name? He was long gone. Why was Jeremy's involved? To shield Coupland Industries? Dad wasn't interested in them at all. Not yet, at least.

"Then I got this idea. The more I thought about it, the more sense it made. Jeremy wanted Dad off the case to protect his father."

Searcy said nothing. "Thomas Coupland Jr. was—what?—fifteen on the night Alonzo Taylor was murdered. Carl Trickett was Coupland's muscle. He was on the plant payroll, but his real job was to take care of any dirty work the old man needed to be done. Everyone in local law enforcement understood his role, so whenever Carl came through the front door, they ushered him out the back. No harm, no foul.

"Why did Thomas Junior tag along the night Taylor was killed? For the excitement? To prove himself to his father?"

"He will never be half the man Old Tom was," Searcy said. "If it were, you wouldn't be sitting here." Rudberg looked at him to see if it was a threat, but Searcy just gave a slight shrug. He was merely stating facts.

"Young Thomas killed Taylor, didn't he? Carl Trickett drove him off the road, but Tom Junior fired the shotgun."

Searcy stared at him, two fingers held to the side of his mouth. "I'm not saying anything. You do the talking."

Rudberg considered it for a moment. "There had to be many people who knew or suspected the truth, but Coupland owned them all, so they kept silent. Then, thirty years later, a reforming state attorney resurrected this cold case. He didn't know what he was taking on, but once those two officers identified Carl Trickett, the younger Tom Coupland was in a precarious situation. Fortunately for him, Warren Justice died before they could squeeze the truth out of Trickett."

Searcy continued to stare at him. *The man is like a statue, ceding nothing.* "Or perhaps his death wasn't just luck." Again nothing. "We'll never prove that, will we?"

Searcy's impassive silence was eerie, but it convinced Rudberg he was on the right track. The rest of the story tumbled out. He spoke as much to himself as to Searcy now. "Old Senator Coupland arranged for you to become state attorney to protect his son from exposure. You played ball, so he gave you a judgeship."

Searcy remained stoic.

"Once on the bench, you protected the Coupland business interests. But you kept getting these reversals, even when you were on the federal bench. Were you more valuable as an appellate judge or did you get greedy? I keep wondering that. Was the senator using you, or were you using him? Perhaps it was a symbiotic relationship."

"No one blackmailed Senator Coupland," Searcy said, "you did as you were told."

Bradley Henderson had said as much when explaining why he dropped out of the race for state attorney years before, but Rudberg found it cynical coming from Searcy. "When young Thomas took over, roles reversed, didn't they? No longer were you their instrument, they were now yours."

Searcy leaned forward, gripping the arms of his chair, and lowered his voice. "When Old Tom died in 2006, I was free. At last, I could do the right thing." His explanation became a plea. "I'd been on the federal bench for three years, and all I wanted was to do a good job and serve my country. That's what's so unjust about all this. I am not a bad man."

Rudberg thought about all the black defendants sentenced to death, the victimized women laughed out of court, the pollution poured into the St. Johns. Was the man serious? Was this self-delusion?

"Tom Junior sat right where you're sitting the day before his father's funeral. I made some laudatory comments about the senator and then said, 'We're even now. We can start fresh.' He looked at me

—I'll never forget his gaze—and said, 'Nothing's changed. We're in this together.'"

"A poor lamb," Rudberg said, "an innocent."

Searcy clenched his teeth but didn't respond to the taunt. Three years after that conversation, Tom Junior had used his connections to boost Searcy to the appeals court. He was still Coupland's marionette.

"Here's the irony. If you hadn't gone for the Supreme Court, none of this might have come out. Yes, Dad would have grown curious as to why you killed the cold case investigation in 1989. He would have asked you to explain yourself. You would have told him the same thing you told me—what did you call it?—*a sin of omission*. That would have stymied him since there was no way to prove otherwise. You would have continued on the appellate court and lived happily ever after."

Searcy winced. Rudberg hadn't imagined it. He'd hit a nerve. He kept drilling.

"After you stonewalled me, I got discouraged. I gave up and flew home. Then you overplayed your hand. You arranged that phony job in Fort Worth. It was such a sloppy trying to silence me, it stoked my suspicions."

"That wasn't my doing," Searcy said. "It was Tom Coupland's bright idea."

"That offer came within hours of my interview with you. You must have told him you were worried." Searcy's failure to protest told Rudberg he was right. His mind went back to Searcy reaching for his phone the moment his office began to close after their meeting in December. The judge had contacted Coupland and said—what? —"We're in trouble. He knows too much."

"Every step you took belied your innocence," Rudberg said. "You had me followed. You planted Sonja in our operation—"

He paused, seeing a flicker of confusion cross Searcy's face.

"Sonja Lansberg," Rudberg said.

"Wasn't she a reporter here? What does she have to do with this?"

What, indeed? Rudberg stared at Searcy, his mouth agape. Blood rushed to his face. He sighed, shook his head. Searcy seemed to sense that he'd gained an advantage. He rose, signaling that the interview, such as it was, was over. "This is all conjecture," he said. "They've questioned Tom Coupland for two days now. He hasn't admitted a thing, and he won't. You can speculate all you want, but if you should print it..." He left the implicit threat unspoken.

He turned to leave the room, but couldn't resist one more gibe. "And he hasn't thrown Jeremy under the bus. That wimp just likes the view from there."

———

Stephanie had left two messages since Tuesday morning, but he'd avoided her. Now he returned the call, hoping he could catch her before she left for work.

After a ritual exchange of pleasantries, she said, "I saw you on the news Monday night. I've been watching you all week."

"It's not my style," he said. "It was awkward."

"I'm sure. You like to stay in the background. This is what you've been working on all this time."

She didn't state it as a question, but he took it as such. "Yes. I told you about it. Tried to, anyway. Dad was fixated on this unsolved mystery. He demanded to know who had killed an honorable human being whose only sin was to help his fellow citizens get their share of our great democracy. I picked it up and couldn't put it down."

"You did well," she said. He tried to thank her, but she rushed on.

"I've been thinking these past few weeks—we built so much during our years together. We're what passes for a power couple." She gave a self-deprecating laugh. "Are you sure you want to give it up?"

"It wasn't my first choice," he said. "Not even my second."

"So...should we drop this? I've never signed the papers. We don't need to do anything to stop it. Just not do it." Another laugh as she aped the sales pitch of a competitor.

"Let me think about it," he said. "This business isn't over. I need to clear my mental desk. Then I'll focus on where we go from here. I promise."

"Good," she said, "I love you. You know that."

"You, too," he said. Then he thought, *no, I don't know that.*

---

Sergeant Wheadon was at lunch, so Rudberg hung out in the reception area and waited. When he returned, he was with a civilian. He told Rudberg he'd have to wait. Fifteen minutes later, Wheadon invited him back to his office.

"What can you do for me?" Wheadon said.

Rudberg laughed, but Wheadon wore his poker face. "I was hoping it was the other way around. Have you arrested Thomas Coupland?"

Wheadon paused several seconds before answering. "We've questioned him, but he's well lawyered and isn't talking. I'm not sure how much you know..."

Rudberg related his conversation with Searcy. "But he confirmed nothing," he concluded. "He said you would never convict him."

Wheadon sighed. "He may be right. We have Jeremy's statement that his father murdered Alonzo Taylor, but it's hearsay. Wade Trickett says his father told him the same thing years back, but Carl's no longer around to be questioned. We have no physical evidence. The state attorney isn't willing to make a case yet."

"But we know," Rudberg said.

"Yes, we do. For all the good it does." He sighed again, leaned back in his swivel chair, and stared at the stained ceiling tiles. "And you've heard the news out of Washington?" Rudberg had not. "The president just nominated a Texas Supreme Court justice. His politics are the same as Searcy's."

And whoever it was, his nomination would sail through. The Senate was unlikely to throw two nominations back in the president's face.

———

"I'm calling to apologize." He'd played with several openings, but this was the only appropriate way to begin.

"It's taken you a while," Sonja replied.

"I had a few things to put to bed," he said.

She ignored the double entendre. "It was hurtful," she said. "It's unsettling to be distrusted by—by anyone, let alone someone you care for."

"Sonja, why did you hold on to that report for so long? By the time you sent it, we'd uncovered most of it on our own. I'm not saying it wasn't helpful. It was. But if you'd sent it earlier—"

"I wanted you to come get it, you idiot! All I cared about was seeing you. It's why I put myself out. Do you know what it's like crossing the Couplands in this town?"

"I'm sorry," he said, "truly sorry. I'd like to make it up to you. Can we get together this weekend?"

She didn't answer. He prodded her with restaurants, dates, and times.

"No, not this weekend. You hurt me. I—it's changed my impression of you. I saw your father in you, and—I need time. And space."

He stared at his cell phone after she'd disconnected. There was one question he wanted to ask, but he wouldn't do it over the phone. He needed to see her reaction. *Please be honest with me. It makes no difference now, but I need to know. You placed that call to Wendy, didn't you?*

It was a question he would never get to ask. He knew that now. *I saw your father in you.* Was that what she'd been after, chasing an ideal? *Idiot. It was never about you.*

———————

Rudberg stood on the low dune and looked out on the ocean. The day was cool for Florida, not sixty degrees. A light wind off the ocean ruffled his hair. Three hundred yards to the south, a father helped two children launch their kite.

Fathers. Wade Trickett had acted to protect his father. Jeremy had protected his father. And Rudberg had undone them both as reparation for the father he had rejected.

He had left his room the night before and driven to St. Augustine, booking a room in the same hotel where he and Sonja had not spent a night together.

Acting on Tom Coupland's orders, Wade Trickett had tracked Rudberg almost from the moment he arrived in Florida. Searcy knew all this but hadn't known Sonja. She hadn't betrayed him. He'd betrayed her.

Tomorrow he would fly home to Portland. He had booked a late flight to minimize the time he would spend with Stephanie. He would give her his verdict, spend the next day or two packing his belongings, arrange for a realtor to put the oceanfront condo up for sale once their divorce was final. Then he would fly to Atlanta to begin a new life.

"I have one condition," he had told Steve Rozenkrantz. "I want Aisha to join me at AUJ. We're one helluva team."

Rozenkrantz had agreed, but Aisha had not. "Alan," she said, "my mother is here. My husband and son return between tours. We're a Navy family. I'm not moving to some landlocked parking lot."

So here he was, walking alone on a deserted stretch of beach on Anastasia Island, facing an uncertain future. "I'm an advocate, not an observer," Lucius Martin had told him. "I can't imagine standing on the sidelines."

He had become an advocate himself. No more watching from the press box, describing the plays. Soccer was his passion. He would be down on the pitch, playing midfield, sometimes feeding the ball to the forwards, sometimes racing back to help the defense. He might score an occasional goal.

It would be challenging, but interesting. He would be lonely, but he was used to that, comfortable with it. Perhaps that's why his marriage had failed. Too often, he hadn't been in it.

He returned to his car and drove up US 1 toward Jacksonville, brooding over Palatine, Hampton County, and his country. All this fear, all the hatred, simply because a man's skin was darker than that of his neighbor.

He recalled something Lucius had said during their flight back from Atlanta. "The Couplands played an old game. They set one race against the other, convincing each that the other was their enemy. Martin often said Pharaoh kept the slaves fighting among themselves to prolong slavery. The Couplands did the same. While they kept blacks and whites fighting, they divided and conquered, keeping wages low, poisoning the water, and running the government to suit themselves."

Lucius was right, Rudberg thought. Race was a game played by the powerful against the powerless. *And if the slaves ever get together…*

He pulled to a stop outside Grace's house. Aisha met him at the door and gave him a quick hug. Grace was even more welcoming, embracing him and holding on as she said, "Thank you for all you've done for Mathew—for us."

*And for myself,* he thought, but before he could say it, Aisha tugged at his arm.

"Let him go, Mom. Let him meet the others."

She led him into the living room where a younger man and woman stood, looking awkward. "Sam, Rebecca," she said, "meet your uncle, Alan."

Rudberg shook hands with Aisha's children—"Your family," she'd said when issuing the invitation.

He took in Samuel Moser, resplendent in his Navy whites. A hand shake was insufficient. Rudberg wrapped him in his arms, unashamed of the tears that filled his eyes.

He had lost much over the past three months, but he'd gained even more—self-respect, new horizons, the father who'd been ripped from him, and his father's gift, a family he could call his own.

THE END

# ACKNOWLEDGMENTS

This is a work of fiction. Except for four historical figures discussed below, all characters are creatures of my imagination, and any resemblance to real individuals is unintended

All the organizations named are fictitious, as are the city of Palatine and Hampton County, Florida. The fictional school I call Florida Northern University is not based on the University of North Florida, and Florida Normal University, which I state is the predecessor organization to FNU, bears no relationship to Florida Normal Industrial College, today's Florida Memorial University.

The cities of Jacksonville, Florida and Portland, Oregon are real. I know them well.

But just because the story is fictional doesn't mean it's untrue. Those who know North Florida will recognize similarities to actual events that have taken place over the last seven decades.

On Christmas night, 1951, a bomb claimed the life of Harry T. Moore, the founder of the Brevard County chapter of the NAACP and an officer of the statewide organization. His wife died a few days later. The office of the Lake County sheriff did little to investigate. It often has been alleged, though never proven, that Sheriff Willis T.

McCall was involved in the slayings. Despite three investigations into these heartless murders, no one was ever brought to justice.

On May 7, 1955, a shotgun blast killed Reverend George Lee who was urging his Mississippi parishioners to register to vote. His murder remains unsolved.

In the second chapter I wrote, "Rutledge Pearson, President of the Florida Chapter of the NAACP and himself a Duval County high school teacher, called [school disaccreditation] 'the best thing that could happen' for African Americans." Rutledge Pearson was a real person whom I had the pleasure of interviewing. My quote reflects his response to the school crisis.

The history of that school system is accurate, as is the statement that the school board only recently renamed a high school honoring Nathan Bedford Forrest, a Confederate general and first Grand Wizard of the Ku Klux Klan.

Duval County and the City of Jacksonville were laced with corruption in the mid-1960s, and it took local television station WJXT, for which I worked as a young reporter, to expose it. WJXT, which was then owned by the Washington Post Company, began a series of investigative reports that chipped away at the conspiracy of silence that allowed city councilmen and county commissioners to line their pockets at public expense. These stories led to a grand jury investigation that indicted ten city and county officials. Though there were few convictions, the court of public opinion remained in session. Voters overturned not just the city and county's political leaders, but the form of government, enacting a merged city-county government that continues to serve its citizens today.

G. Harrold Carswell, the fourth historical figure named in the book, was nominated to the high court by President Nixon in 1970. He was named after a fellow southerner, Clement Haynsworth, was rejected by the Senate following revelations of conflicts of interest in cases that had come before him while a federal district judge. As discussed, Carswell was then rejected by a bipartisan majority of the Senate. Nixon's third nominee, Justice Harry

Blackmun of Minnesota, went on to write the majority opinion in Roe v. Wade, which made a woman's right to choose the law of the land.

Several individuals made valuable contributions to this book.

Rodney L. Hurst Sr., a former colleague at public television station WJCT, has spent years educating me on matters of race and injustice. He read a manuscript of this book and made valuable suggestions. Rodney is the author of two non-fiction books, It Was Never About a Hot Dog and a Coke®! and Unless WE Tell It...It Never Gets Told!, which I highly recommend to anyone interested in the history of Jacksonville's civil rights struggle. I reference Rodney in this novel as the high school student who helped organize the Woolworth's sit-ins that were the subject of the "Ax-Handle Saturday" attacks.

Vic DiGenti, another former colleague and a Florida-based writer, read a late draft and made many helpful suggestions. Vic writes the Windrusher series in which a cat is the protagonist and, under the pen name Parker Francis, the "Quint Mitchell" mysteries. They are great reads, told with Vic's typical sense of humor.

Cheryl Head, a former public media colleague who writes the "Charlie Mack" detective series and whose Long Way Home: A World War II Novel established her as a rising star, read sections of the book and made valuable suggestions about how Lucius and Aisha would have interacted with Rudberg.

Bill Sheppard, a noted Jacksonville criminal defense and civil rights attorney, to whom Rodney reintroduced me, guided me in Florida law regarding such matters as autopsies and wills. Much of the legal background in this story is accurate, but I plead contempt of court for the many departures necessary to support the narrative. That's why it's fiction, friends.

George Winterling, one of television's first true meteorologists, provided detailed information on the effects of Hurricane Irma and the nor'easter that followed.

Relatives who live along the St. Johns described the scenes of homeowners wading in the shallow water near the shoreline to clean up debris carried into the river by the flood.

A civilian in the records department of a Florida sheriff's office provided historical background on the disposal of records in criminal investigations.

Alex Ahart, a retired forensic investigator, provided guidance on the effects of river water on forensic evidence—so much so that I rewrote a major section to avoid immersing not just the evidence, but the reader in needless detail.

Aisha's angry description of what it means to be black in "Remembering Uncle Charlie" owes much to a November 10, 2016 blog post by writer Amira Rasool on the site *black girls being* entitled "The Reemergence of Black Distrust in White Americans."

My colleagues in the Pittsburgh South Writer's Group and the Mount Lebanon Writer's Group read through portions of early drafts and offered criticism and advice.

My editor, Lourdes Venard, advised me not just on grammar, but on structure. I recommend her to any writer, but particularly a first-time, independent author like myself.

I am greatly indebted to the love of my life, Julie Lewis, who allowed me the long hours necessary to breeze through the first draft and slog through three more before Lourdes performed major surgery.

I also thank my daughters, Kristen Dunder, who read an early draft, and Lisa Kalnai, who encouraged me along the way and kept my grandchildren, Caeden and Emma, from interrupting "Gwahpa" too much. (But they are welcome to do so whenever they wish.)

## ABOUT THE AUTHOR

James H. (Jim) Lewis is a former reporter, public media executive, and consultant to non-profit organizations. He has lived and worked in Washington, DC, Florida, Texas, New England, Oregon, and Sweden.

He and his wife now live in Pittsburgh where they dote on their two grandchildren. His articles on travel, fundraising, and non-profit management have been published in national newspapers and magazines.

This is his first novel.

Follow Jim on https://lewisthescrivener.com

27674915R00168

Made in the USA
Lexington, KY
06 January 2019